HIGH-POWERED, HOT BLOODED

BY
SUSAN MALLERY

Published in Great Britain 2010
Harlequin Mills & Boon Limited,
Eton House, 18-24 Paradise Road, Richmond, Surrey TW9 1SR

© Susan Macias Redmond 2009

ISBN: 978 0 263 88184 4

51-1110

Harlequin Mills & Boon policy is to use papers that are natural, renewable
and recyclable products and made from wood grown in sustainable forests.
The logging and manufacturing processes conform to the legal environmental
regulations of the country of origin.

Printed and bound in Spain
by Litografia Rosés S.A., Barcelona

Susan Mallery is a *New York Times* bestselling author of more than ninety romances. Her combination of humour, emotion and just plain sexy has made her a reader favourite. Susan makes her home in the Pacific Northwest with her handsome husband and possibly the world's cutest dog. Visit her website at www.SusanMallery.com.

Dear Reader,

There are so many things I love about this time of year. The crisp days and nights, the holiday decorations, the tempting special foods. Mostly I love curling up in front of a fire with a mug of hot chocolate and a delicious romance novel. As the craziness descends, I try to schedule a few at-home evenings to indulge myself.

For my hero Duncan Patrick, the holidays aren't the least bit special. He doesn't believe in tradition or family or even being nice to anyone. He doesn't see the point. For him, life is all about the bottom line. He's been so successful, he's completely lost what really matters.

I'll admit I love heroes like that. Guys who are totally clueless and don't see what's headed right for them. It's not the love of a good woman that changes their lives— it's *loving* a good woman. It's going to take someone special to get Duncan's attention and Annie McCoy is exactly who he needs.

Now Annie isn't looking for a powerful, determined, stubborn guy to warm her nights, but that's exactly who she's going to get. I think she'll thank me later.

I hope you love reading this story as much as I enjoyed writing it. However you celebrate at this time of year, may your days be joyous and happy and may you spend them with those you love.

Susan Mallery

Prologue

CEO knocks out the competition.

CEO Duncan Patrick has once again knocked out the competition. The shipping billionaire ends the year with two more acquisitions, including a small European trucking company and a very profitable railroad line in South America. With Patrick Industries dominating the world transportation market, one would think the wealthy billionaire could afford to be gracious, but apparently that's not the case. For the second year in a row, Duncan has been named meanest CEO in the country. Not surprisingly, the reclusive billionaire declined to be interviewed for this article.

"This is unconscionable," Lawrence Patrick said, slamming the business newspaper onto the board-room table.

Duncan leaned back in his chair and stifled a yawn. "Did you want me to do the interview?"

"That's not the point and you know it."

"What is the point?" Duncan asked, turning his attention from his uncle to the other men on the board. "Is there too much money coming in? Are the investors unhappy with all the proceeds?"

"The point is the press loves to hate you," Lawrence snapped. "You bought a mobile home park, then evicted the residents, most of whom were elderly and poor."

"The mobile home park was right next to one of the largest shipping facilities we own. I needed the land for expansion. The board approved the pur-chase."

"We didn't approve seeing old ladies on television, crying because they had nowhere to go."

Duncan rolled his eyes. "Oh, please. Part of the deal was providing the residents with a new mobile home park. Their lots are bigger and the area is residential, rather than industrial. They have bus service right outside the main gate. We paid all the costs. No one lost anything. It was the media trying to create a story."

One of the other board members glared at him. "Are you denying you bankrupt your competition?"

"Not at all. If I want to buy a company but the

person who owns it won't sell to me, I find another way." He straightened. "A legal way, gentlemen. You've all invested in my company and you've seen extraordinary profits. I don't give a damn what the press thinks about me or my company."

"Therein lies the problem," his uncle told him. "We *do*. Patrick Industries has a terrible reputation, as do you."

"Both are undeserved."

"Regardless. This isn't your company, Duncan. You brought us in when you needed money to buy out your partner. Part of the deal is you answer to us."

Duncan didn't like the sound of that. He was the one who had taken Patrick Industries from a struggling small business to a world-class empire. Not them—him.

"If you're threatening me," he began.

"Not threatening," another board member said. "Duncan, we understand that there's a difference between ruthless and mean. But the public doesn't. We're asking you to play nice for the next few months."

"Get off this list," his uncle said, waving the paper at him. "It's practically Christmas. Give money to orphans, find a cause. Rescue a puppy. Date a nice girl, for once. Hell, we don't even care if you really change. Perception is everything. You know that."

Duncan shook his head. "So you don't care if I'm the biggest bastard in the world, as long as no one knows about it?"

"Exactly."

"Easy enough," he said, rising to his feet. He could play nice for a few months, while raising enough money to buy out his board. Then he wouldn't have to care what anyone thought of him. Which was how he preferred things.

One

Annie McCoy could accept the flat tire. The car was old and the tires should have been replaced last spring. She could also understand that little Cody had eaten dirt on the playground, then thrown up on her favorite skirt. She wouldn't complain about the notice she'd gotten from the electric company pointing out, ever so politely, that she was overdue—again—and that they would be raising her rates. It was that all of it had happened on the same day. Couldn't the universe give her a sixteenth of a break?

She stood in front of her sagging front porch and flipped through the rest of the mail. No other bills, unless that official-looking letter from UCLA was actually a tuition bill. The good news was that her cousin Julie was in her first year at the prestigious college. The bad news was paying for it. Even living at home, the costs were enormous and Annie was doing her best to help.

"A problem for another time," she told herself as she walked to the front door and opened it.

Once inside, she put her purse on the small table by the door and dropped the mail into the macaroni-and-gold-spray-paint-covered in-box her kindergarten class had made for her last year. Then she went into the kitchen to check out the dry-erase bulletin board hanging from the wall.

It was Wednesday. Julie had a night class. Jenny, Julie's twin, was working her usual evening job at a restaurant in Westwood. Kami, the exchange student from Guam, had gone to the mall with friends. Annie had the house to herself…at least for the next couple of hours. Talk about heaven.

She walked to the refrigerator and got out the box of white wine. After pouring a glass, she kicked off her shoes and walked barefoot to the backyard.

The grass was cool under her feet. All around the fence, lush plants grew and flowered. It was L.A. Growing anything was pretty easy, as long as you didn't mind paying the water bill. Annie did mind, but she loved the plants more. They reminded her of her mom, who had always been an avid gardener.

She'd barely settled on the old, creaky wooden swing by the bougainvillea when she heard the doorbell ring. She thought about ignoring whoever was there, but couldn't bring herself to do it. She went back inside, opened the door and stared at the man standing on her porch.

He was tall and powerfully built. The well-tailored suit didn't disguise the muscles in his arms and chest. He looked like he could have picked up money on the side working as a bouncer. He had dark hair and the coldest gray eyes she'd ever seen. And he looked seriously annoyed.

"Who are you?" he demanded by way of greeting. "The girlfriend? Is Tim here?"

Annie started to hold up her hands in a shape of a T. Talk about needing a time-out. Fortunately she remembered she was holding a wineglass and managed to keep from spilling.

"Hi," she said, wishing she'd thought to actually take a sip before answering the door. "I'm sure that's how you meant to start."

"What?"

"By saying 'hello.'"

The man's expression darkened. "I don't have time for small talk. Is Tim McCoy here?"

The tone wasn't friendly and the words didn't make her feel any better. She set her glass on the tiny table by the door and braced herself for the worst.

"Tim is my brother. Who are you?"

"His boss."

"Oh."

That couldn't be good, she thought, stepping back to invite the man in. Tim hadn't said much about his relatively new job and Annie had been afraid to ask.

Tim was…flaky. No, that wasn't right. He could be really sweet and caring but he had a streak of the devil in him.

The man entered and looked around the living room. It was small and a little shabby, but homey, she thought. At least that's what she told herself. There were a few paper turkeys on the wall, and a pair of pilgrim candlesticks on the coffee table. They would come down this weekend when she got serious about her Christmas decorating.

"I'm Annie McCoy," she said, holding out her hand. "Tim's sister."

"Duncan Patrick."

They shook hands. Annie tried not to wince as his large fingers engulfed hers. Fortunately the man didn't squeeze. From the looks of things, he could have crushed her bones to dust.

"Or ground them for bread," she murmured.

"What?"

"Oh, sorry. Nothing. Fairy-tale flashback. The witch in Hansel and Gretel. Doesn't she want to grind their bones to make her bread? No, that's the giants. I can't remember. Now I'll have to look that up."

Duncan frowned at her and stepped back.

She couldn't help chuckling. "Don't worry. It's not contagious. I think weird things from time to time. You won't catch it by being in the room." She stopped babbling and cleared her throat. "As to my brother, he doesn't live here."

Duncan frowned. "But this is his house."

Was it just her or was Duncan not the brightest bulb? "He doesn't live here," she repeated, speaking more slowly. Maybe it was all the muscles. Too much blood in the biceps and not enough in the brain.

"I got that, Ms. McCoy. Does he own the house? He told me he did."

Annie didn't like the sound of that. She crossed to the club chair by the door and grabbed hold of the back. "No. This is *my* house." She felt more than a little panicked and slightly sick to her stomach. "Why are you asking?"

"Do you know where your brother is?"

"Not at the moment."

This was bad, she thought frantically. She could tell it was really bad. Duncan Patrick didn't look like the kind of man who dropped by on a whim. Which meant Tim had done something especially stupid this time.

"Just tell me," she said quickly. "What did he do?"

"He embezzled from my company."

The room tilted slightly. Annie's stomach lurched and she wondered if she was going to join little Cody in throwing up on her skirt.

Tim had stolen from his employer. She wanted to ask how that was possible, but she already knew the answer. Tim had a problem. He loved to gamble. Loved it way too much. Living only a five-hour drive from Las Vegas made the problem even more complicated.

"How much?" she asked in a whisper.

"Two hundred and fifty thousand dollars."

Her breath caught. It might as well be a million. Or

ten. That was too much money. An impossible amount to pay back. He was ruined forever.

"I can see by the look on your face, you didn't know about his activities."

She shook her head. "The last I heard, he loved his job."

"A little too much," Duncan said drily. "Is this the first time he's embezzled?"

She hesitated. "He's, um, had some problems before."

"With gambling?"

"You know?"

"He mentioned it when I spoke with him earlier today. He also told me that he owned a house and that the value exceeded the amount he'd stolen."

Her eyes widened. "No way. He didn't."

"I'm afraid he did, Ms. McCoy. Is this the house he meant?"

Now she really was going to be sick. Tim had offered the house? *Her* house? It was all she had.

When their mother had died, she'd left them the house and an insurance policy to split. Annie had used her half of the insurance money to buy Tim out of the house. He was supposed to use the money to pay off his college loans and put money down on a place of his own. Instead he'd gone to Vegas. That had been nearly five years ago.

"This is my house," she said firmly. "Mine is the only name on the deed."

Nothing about Duncan's cold expression changed. "Does your brother own other property?"

She shook her head.

"Thank you for your time." He turned to leave.

"Wait." She threw herself in front of the door. Tim might be a total screw-up but he was her brother. "What happens now?"

"Your brother goes to jail."

"He needs help, not prison. Doesn't your company have a medical plan? Can't you get him into a program of some kind?"

"I could have, before he took the money. If he can't pay me back, I'll turn him over to the police. Two hundred and fifty thousand dollars is a lot of money, Ms. McCoy."

"Annie," she said absently. It was more money than he knew. "Can't Tim pay you back over time?"

"No." He glanced around at her living room again. "But if you'd be willing to mortgage your house, I would consider dropping the charges."

Mortgage her... "Give up where I live? This is all I have in the world. I can't risk it."

"Not even for your brother?"

Talk about playing dirty.

"You wouldn't lose your house if you made regular payments to the bank," he said. "Or do you have a gambling problem, too?"

The contempt in his voice was really annoying, she thought as she glared at him. She took in the perfectly fitted suit, the shiny gold watch that probably cost more than she made in three months and had a feeling that if she looked out front, she would see a pretty, new, fancy, foreign car. With good tires.

It was too much. She was tired, hungry and this was the last problem she could deal with right now.

She grabbed the electric bill from the in-box and waved it in front of him.

"Do you know what this is?"

"No."

"It's a bill. One I'm late on. Do you know why?"

"Ms. McCoy…"

"Answer the question," she yelled. "Do you know why?"

He looked more amused than afraid, which really pissed her off. "No. Why?"

"Because I'm currently helping to support my two cousins. They're both in college and have partial scholarships, and their mom, my aunt, is a hairdresser and has her own issues to deal with. Have you seen what college-age girls eat? I don't know how they get it all down and stay skinny, but they do. Follow me."

She walked into the kitchen. Surprisingly Duncan came after her. She pointed at the dry-erase board. "You see that? Our family schedule. Kami is an exchange student. Well, not really. She was in high school. She's from Guam. Now she goes to college here. She's friends with my cousins and can't afford her own place. So she lives here, too. And while they all help as much as they can, it isn't much."

She drew in a breath. "I'm feeding three college-age girls, paying about half their tuition, for most of their books and keeping a roof over their heads. I also have an aging car, a house in constant need of repair and plenty of student loans from my own education. I do all of this on a kindergarten teacher's salary. So no. Taking out a loan on my house, the only asset I have in the world, is not an option."

She stared at the tall, muscled man in her kitchen and prayed she'd gotten through to him.

She hadn't.

"While this is all interesting," he said, "it doesn't get me my two hundred and fifty thousand dollars. If you know where your brother is, I suggest you tell him to turn himself in. It will go better for him that way than if he's found and arrested."

The weight of the world seemed to press down on her shoulders. "No. You can't. I'll make payments. A hundred dollars a month. Two hundred. I can do that, I swear." Maybe she could get a second job. "It's less than four weeks until Christmas. You can't throw Tim in jail now. He needs help. He needs to get this fixed. Sending him to prison won't change anything. It's not like you need the money."

The ice returned to his cool, gray eyes. "And that makes it all right to steal?"

She winced. "Of course not. It's just, please. I'll work with you. This is my family you're talking about."

"Then mortgage your house, Ms. McCoy."

There was a finality to his tone. A promise that he meant what he said about throwing Tim in jail.

How was she supposed to decide? The house or Tim's freedom. The problem was she didn't trust her brother to do any better if she mortgaged the house, but how could she let him be locked away?

"It's impossible," she said.

"Actually, it's very easy."

"For you," she snapped. "What are you? The meanest man on the planet? Give me a second here."

He stiffened slightly. If she hadn't been staring at him, she wouldn't have noticed the sudden tension in his shoulders or the narrowing of his eyes.

"What did you say?" he asked, his voice low and controlled.

"I said give me a minute. Maybe there's another choice. A compromise. I'm good at negotiating." What she really wanted to say was she was good at negotiating with unreasonable children, but doubted Duncan would appreciate the comparison.

"Are you married, Ms. McCoy?"

"What?" She glanced around warily. "No. But my neighbors all know me and if I yell, they'll come running."

The amusement returned. "I'm not here to threaten you."

"Lucky me. You're here to threaten my brother. Practically the same thing."

"You teach kindergarten you said. For how long?"

"This is my fifth year." She named the school. "Why?"

"You like children?"

"Well, duh."

"Any drug use? Alcohol problems? Other addictions?"

An unnatural love for chocolate, but that was really a girl thing. "No, but I don't…"

"Any of your ex-boyfriends in prison?"

Now it was her turn to be pissed. "Hey, that's my life you're talking about."

"You didn't answer the question."

She reminded herself she didn't have to. That it wasn't his business. Still she found herself saying, "No. Of course not."

He leaned against the chipped counter and studied her. "What if there *is* a third option? Another way to save your brother?"

"Which would be what?"

"It's four weeks until Christmas. I want to hire you for the holiday season. I'll pay you by forgiving half of Tim's debt, sending him to rehab and setting up a payment plan for the remainder of the money. To be paid by him when he gets out."

Which sounded too good to be true. "What do I have that's worth over a hundred thousand dollars?"

For the first time since entering her house, Duncan Patrick smiled. The quick movement transformed his face, making him seem boyish and handsome. It also made her very, very nervous.

She took a step back. "We're not talking sex, are we?" she asked desperately.

"No, Ms. McCoy. I don't want to have sex with you."

The blush came on hot and fast. "I know that I'm not really the sex type."

Duncan raised an eyebrow.

"I'm more the best friend," she continued, feeling the hole getting deeper and deeper. "The girl you talk to, not the girl you sleep with. The one you take home to Mom when you want to convince her you're dating a nice girl."

"Exactly," he said.

What? "You want to introduce me to your mother?"

"No. I want to introduce you to everyone else. I want you to be my date for all the social events I have going on this holiday season. You'll show the world I'm not a complete bastard."

"I don't understand." He was hiring her to be his date? "You could go out with anyone you want."

"True, but the women I want to go out with don't solve my problem. You do."

"How?"

"You teach small children, look after your family. You're a nice girl. I need nice. In return your brother doesn't go to jail." He folded his arms across his chest. "Annie, if you say yes, your brother gets the help he needs. If you say no, he goes to jail."

As if she hadn't figured that out on her own. "You don't play fair, do you?"

"I play to win. So which will it be?"

Two

While Duncan waited for his answer, Annie grabbed a kitchen chair and pulled it over to the refrigerator. She reached the overhead cupboard and pulled out a box of high-fiber cereal. After opening it, she removed a plastic bag filled with orange and brown M&M's.

"What are you doing?" he asked, wondering if the stress had pushed her over the edge.

"Getting my secret stash. I live with three other women. If you think chocolate would last more than fifteen seconds in this house, you're deluding yourself." She scooped out a handful, then put the plastic bag back in the box and slid the box onto the shelf.

"Why are they that color?"

She looked at him as if he were an idiot, then

climbed down from the chair. "They're from Hallow-
een. I bought them November first, when they're half
off. It's a great time to buy seasonal candy. They taste
just as good. M&M's are my weakness." She popped
two in her mouth and sighed. "Better."

Okay, this was strange, he thought. "You had a glass
of wine before," he said. "Don't you want that?"

"Instead of chocolate? No."

She stood there in a shapeless blue sweater that
matched her eyes and a patterned skirt that went to her
knees. Her feet were bare and he could see she'd
painted little daisies on her toes. Aside from that, Annie
McCoy was strictly utilitarian. No makeup, no jewelry
to speak of. Just a plain, inexpensive watch around her
left wrist. Her hair was an appealing color. Shades of
gold in a riot of curls that tumbled past her shoulders.
She wasn't a woman who spent a lot of time on her
appearance.

Which was fine by him. The outside could easily be
fixed. He was far more concerned about her character.
From what he'd seen in the past ten minutes, she was
compassionate, caring and led with her heart. In other
words, a sucker. Happy news for him. Right now he
needed a bleeding-heart do-gooder to get his board off
his back long enough for him to wrestle control from
them.

"You haven't answered my question," he reminded
her.

Annie sighed. "I know. Mostly because I still don't
know what you want from me."

He pointed to the rickety chairs pushed up against the table. "Why don't we sit down."

It was her house—she should be doing the inviting. Still Annie found herself dragging her chair over to the table and plopping down. Politeness dictated that she offer him some of her precious store of M&M's, but she had a feeling she was going to need them later.

He took a seat across from her and rested his large arms on the table. "I run a company," he began. "Patrick Industries."

"Tell me it's a family business," she said, without thinking. "You inherited it, right? You're not such a total egomaniac that you named it after yourself."

The corner of his mouth twitched. "I see the chocolate gives you courage."

"A little."

"I inherited the company while I was in college. I took it from nothing to a billion-dollar empire in fifteen years."

Lucky him, she thought, thinking she had nothing to bond with. Scoring in the top two percent of the country on her SATs was hardly impressive when compared with billions.

"To get that far, that fast, I was ruthless," he continued. "I bought companies, merged them into mine and streamlined them to make them very profitable."

She counted out the last M&M's. Eight round bits of heaven. "Is that a polite way of saying you fired people?"

He nodded. "The business world loves a success

story, but only to a point. They consider me too ruthless. I'm getting some bad press. I need to counteract that."

"Why do you care what people say about you?"

"I don't, but my board of directors does. I need to fool people into thinking I have a heart. I need to appear…" He hesitated. "Nice."

Now it was her turn to smile. "Not your best quality?"

"No."

He had unusual eyes, she thought absently. The gray was a little scary, but not unattractive. If only they weren't so cold.

"You are exactly what you seem," he said. "A pretty, young teacher with more compassion than sense. People like that. The press will like that."

She'd been with him, right up until that last bit. "Press? As in press?"

"Not television media or gossip reporters. I'm talking about business reporters. Between now and Christmas I have about a dozen social events I need to attend. I want you to go with me. As far as the world is concerned, we're dating and you're crazy about me. They'll think you're nice and by association, change their opinion of me."

Which all sounded easy enough, she thought. "Wouldn't it just be easier to actually act nice? This reminds me of high school when a few people worked really hard to cheat. They could have spent the same amount of time studying and gotten a better grade without any risk. But they would rather cheat."

His dark eyebrows drew together. "My reasons are not up for debate."

She picked up another M&M. "I'm just saying."

"If you agree, then I'll arrange for your brother to enter rehab immediately, under the conditions we discussed. He'll get the second chance you seem to think he deserves. However, if you let on to anyone that our relationship isn't real, if you say anything bad about me, then Tim goes directly to jail."

"Without collecting two hundred dollars."

"Exactly."

A deal with the devil, she thought, wondering how a nice girl like her got into a situation like this. Of course, her being a nice girl was apparently the point. She sighed.

The sense of being trapped was very real. As was the knowledge that while she was expected to take care of her cousins, Tim and apparently even Duncan Patrick, no one ever bothered to take care of her. Or worry about her.

"I'm not lying to my family," she said. "My cousins and Kami have to know."

Duncan seemed to consider that. "Just them. And if they tell anyone—"

She nodded. "I know. Off with their heads. Have you been through any seminars on teamwork or communications? If you worked on your people skills, you might…"

The gray eyes turned to ice. She pressed her lips together and stopped talking.

"You agree?" he asked.

Did she have a choice? Tim needed help. She'd tried to talk him into getting it before, but he always blew her off. Maybe being forced to spend some time in a safe place would make a difference. As the alternative was him being charged with a felony, she didn't see that she had a choice.

"I will," she began, "act as your adoring girlfriend between now and Christmas. I will tell anyone who will listen that you are kind and sweet and have the heart of a marshmallow." She frowned at him. "I don't know anything about you. How am I supposed to fake being in a relationship?"

"I'll get you material."

"Won't that be happy reading."

He ignored her comment. "In return, Tim will get the help he needs, fifty percent of the debt will be forgiven and he'll have a reasonable payment plan for the rest. Do you have an appropriate wardrobe?"

She nibbled on the last M&M. "Define appropriate."

He looked at her with a thoroughness that left her breathless. Before she could react, he'd scanned her battered kitchen, his gaze lingering on the warped vinyl flooring.

"Someone will be in touch to arrange a session with a stylist," he said. "When the month is over, you can keep the clothes." He rose.

She stood and trailed after him. "What kind of clothes?"

"Cocktail dresses and evening gowns." He paused by the front door and faced her.

"I have the dress from my prom."

"I'm sure you wouldn't be comfortable wearing it at one of these events."

"Is this really happening?" she asked. "Are we having this conversation?"

"It is and we are. The first party is on Saturday night. My assistant will call you with the information. Please be ready on time."

He dwarfed her small living room, looking too masculine for the floral-print sofa and lacy curtains. She would never have imagined a man like him in her life, even temporarily.

"I'm sorry my brother stole from you," she said.

"He's not your responsibility."

"Of course he is. He's family."

For a second Duncan looked like he was going to say something, but instead he left. Annie closed the door behind him and wondered how she was going to tell her cousins and Kami what she'd gotten herself into now.

Saturday morning both Jenny and Julie stared at Annie with identical expressions of shock, their green eyes wide, their mouths hanging partially open. Kami looked just as surprised.

"What?" Julie asked. "You did what?"

Annie had put off telling them as long as she could. She'd hidden the binder that had been delivered on Thursday, sliding it under her bed, then pretending it didn't really exist. Her first "date" with Duncan was that night, so she was going to have to read it sooner rather than later.

"I agreed to go out with Tim's boss for a month. We're not really dating each other," she added hastily. "We're pretending until Christmas. I'm supposed to help his image."

But she still wasn't clear on how *that* was supposed to happen. Did Duncan expect her to give interviews? She wouldn't be very good at it. She could easily stand up in front of a room of five-year-olds, but a crowd of adults would make her nervous.

"I don't understand," Kami said, blinking at her. "Why?"

Jenny and Julie exchanged a look. "This is all about Tim, isn't it?" Jenny asked. "He's in trouble."

"Some," Annie admitted. "He, ah, embezzled some money. But Duncan is going to get him into rehab and that will help."

"Him, not you." Julie tucked her light brown hair behind her ears. "Let me guess. Tim somehow threw you under the bus on this one. What did he tell his boss about you?"

"It wasn't me, specifically. It was…" She cleared her throat. While she didn't want to tell her cousins what had happened, she believed in speaking the truth. Well, except when it came to her secret M&M stash.

She quickly explained about the two hundred and fifty thousand dollars, how Duncan would forgive half the debt and allow Tim to make payments on the other half when he got out of rehab and was working again.

Julie sprang to her feet. "I swear, Annie, you're impossible."

"Me? What did I do?"

"Gave in. Let Tim do this to you again. You're always getting him out of trouble. When he was seven and stole from the mini market by the house, you took the fall and paid them back for the candy bars. When he was in high school and cutting class, you convinced the principal not to suspend him. He needs to face the consequences of what he's done."

"He doesn't need to go to jail. How will that help?"

"If the pain's big enough, then maybe he'll learn his lesson."

Jenny nodded, while Kami only looked uncomfortable.

"He needs help," Annie said stubbornly. "And he's my brother."

"All the more reason to want him to grow up and be responsible," Julie said.

Annie sighed. "I promised."

When her mother had been dying, she'd made Annie swear she would look after Tim, no matter what.

The twins exchanged another look.

"There's no getting around that," Kami told them. "You know how Annie gets. She always sees the best in people."

Annie stood and touched Julie's arm. "It's not that bad. I'm dating a really rich guy for a month, going to fancy parties. Nothing more."

All three girls looked at her. Annie felt herself starting to blush.

"Nothing," she repeated. "No sex, so don't even go there." She smiled. "I wouldn't have told you except I'll be gone a lot and eventually you'd notice. In the meantime, I kind of need your help. Duncan is sending a stylist to take me shopping for cocktail dresses and a couple of formal gowns. I won't need them after this month, but I get to keep them. So I thought you three might want to come along and give me your opinions. What with you being able to borrow them when I'm done."

As she expected, there was a general shrieking as all three of them jumped up and down, yelling.

"Seriously?" Jenny asked.

"Uh-huh. The stylist is due here any second and we're going shopping. So you want to come with me?"

They'd barely had time to agree when the doorbell rang. Jenny and Julie ran to open the door.

"Dear God," a man said. "Tell me Duncan isn't dating twins. Although you two are gorgeous. Have you thought about going into modeling?"

The twins giggled in response.

Annie went out into the living room where a tall, thin blond man stood looking over her cousins.

"Love the hair," he said, fluffing Julie's ends. "Maybe a few more layers to open up your face and give your hair volume. Try a smoky eye. You'll be delish." He looked past them to Annie and raised his eyebrows. "Now you look exactly like a stereotypical kindergarten teacher, so you must be Annie. What were you thinking, agreeing to help someone like Duncan? The man is a total ruthless bastard. Sexy, of course, not that he would ever notice me." He smiled. "I'm

Cameron, by the way. And yes, I know it's a girl's name. I tell my mother it's the reason I'm gay."

He glanced over her shoulder as Kami came in the room and he sighed. "I don't know who you are, honey, but you're giving these beauties a run for their money. Yummy."

Kami laughed. "Get real."

"I am real. The realest."

Annie introduced the girls. Cameron sat on the worn sofa in the living room and pulled out a couple of folders.

"Come on, little teacher," he said, patting the cushion next to him. "We have to go over the schedule. Duncan has fifteen social events between now and Christmas. You'll be with him at all of them."

He passed her one of the slim folders. "You got the background information, didn't you?"

She nodded, although she'd only read the basic bio. "Impressive. He put himself through college on a boxing scholarship."

Cameron's hazel eyes widened slightly. "You sound surprised."

"I was. It's not traditional."

"His uncle is Lawrence Patrick. The boxer."

"I've heard of him," Julie said. "He's, like, old, but he was really famous."

Annie had heard of him, as well. "Interesting family," she said.

"Duncan was raised by his uncle. It's a fascinating story, one I'll let him tell you himself. You're going to be spending a lot of time together."

Not something Annie wanted to think about as she took the second folder Cameron offered. This one contained a questionnaire she was to fill out so Duncan could pretend to know all about her.

What had she been thinking, agreeing to this craziness? But before she could even consider backing out of the deal—not that she would—Cameron had ushered them all to the stretch limo waiting to take them shopping.

Five hours later, Annie was exhausted. She'd tried on dozens and dozens of dresses, blouses, pants and jackets. She'd stepped in and out of shoes, shrugged at small, shiny evening bags and endured a bra fitting from a very stern-looking older woman.

Now she sat with foil in her hair, watching pink polish dry on her nails. When they'd moved from shopping to a day spa, she'd been relieved to know she could finally sit down.

Cameron appeared with a glass of lemon water and a fruit-and-cheese plate.

"Tired?" he asked sympathetically.

"Beyond tired. I've never shopped so much in my life."

"People underestimate the energy required to power shop." Cameron settled in the empty salon chair next to her. "Getting it right takes effort."

"Apparently." While she'd thought all the outfits had fit okay, he'd insisted the store seamstress tuck and pin until they were perfect.

Cameron handed her a sheet of paper. On it was a list of the outfits, followed by the shoes and bags that went with each. She laughed.

"You must think I'm totally inept, although I'll admit I'm not sure I could remember this myself."

"I couldn't stand for you to clash. Putting a look together requires a lot of skills. It's why the good stylists make the big bucks."

"So you're famous?" she asked.

He smiled modestly. "In my world. I have a few celebrity clients I keep happy. Several corporate types like Duncan, who want me to keep their wardrobes current without being trendy. Not that Duncan actually cares what he wears. He's such a typical guy."

"How did you meet?"

Cameron raised his eyebrows. "We were college roommates."

If Annie had been drinking her lemon water, she would have choked. "Seriously?"

"I know. Hard to imagine. At least we never wanted to hook up with the same person. I was an art history major back then. I lasted a year before I realized fashion was my one true love. I moved to New York and tried to make it as a designer." He sighed. "I don't have the patience for creating. All that sewing. So not my thing. I took a job as a buyer at an upscale department store. Then I started working with the store's really exclusive customers. The rest, as they say, is history."

Annie tried to imagine Duncan and Cameron sharing a college dorm room, but she couldn't get her mind around the idea.

"What about you?" he asked. "How did you get involved with the big bad?"

"Is that what you call him?"

"Not to his face. He might hit me." But Cameron was smiling as he spoke and there was affection in his tone. "So what happened?"

She told him about Tim and the money. "I couldn't let my brother go to jail," she said. "Not when there was a chance to save him."

"Honey, you are too nice by far. Be careful Duncan doesn't chew you up and spit you out."

"You don't have to worry. This is business. I'm not interested in him personally."

"Uh-huh. You say that now, but Duncan is very charismatic. A friendly word of advice. Don't be fooled by the polite exterior. Duncan's a fighter. You're not. If there's a battle, he's going to win."

"You're sweet to worry, but don't. Even if I did fall for him—" something she couldn't begin to imagine "—he wouldn't respond. Seriously. I can't imagine that I'm his type."

"You're no Valentina."

"Who?"

"Valentina. His ex-wife. Stunning, in a scary girl-snake kind of way. Cold. Remember that line from *Pretty Woman*? About being able to freeze ice on someone's ass? That's Valentina."

She was surprised to hear that Duncan had been married, although she probably shouldn't be. He was successful and in his thirties. It made sense that he'd found someone.

"How long have they been divorced?"

"A couple of years. She scared me." He shivered. "So enough about Duncan. What about you? Why isn't a nice girl like you happily married?"

She reached for a strawberry. A question for the ages, she thought glumly. "I've had two serious relationships. Both times the guy left, each claiming he saw me more as a friend than as the love of his life."

She spoke lightly, as if the words didn't matter, as if she wasn't still hurt. Not that she missed either one of them. Not anymore. But she was beginning to wonder if there was something wrong with her. Something missing. The two relationships had lasted a total of four and a half years. *She'd* been in love, or so she'd thought. She'd been able to imagine a future, marriage, children. Those men were the only two she'd slept with and for her, the sex had been fine. Maybe not as magical as she'd heard it described by friends or in books, but still very nice.

But it hadn't been enough. Not the sex or her heart or any of it. Both of them had left. And that they'd said practically the same thing had her wondering.

"I don't want to be the best friend," she whispered fiercely.

Cameron patted her hand. "Tell me about it."

Annie was grateful beyond words that Hector, the genius at the salon, had styled her hair for the evening. He'd blown out her usually curly hair into a sleek cascade of waves that fell past her shoulders. Hector's assistant had done her makeup as well, so all she had to do was pull on the dress and step into the right shoes. Cameron had suggested a cocktail dress for the event. Now Annie stared at it and wondered if she had the nerve.

The dress was simple enough—sleeveless with a sweetheart neckline. Fitted, although not tight, and falling midthigh. It was the latter that made her want to squirm as she stared at herself in the mirror above her dresser. If she kept the mirror straight, she looked fine. Of course she could only see herself from the waist up. If she tilted the mirror down, she could see to her ankles and there was way too much leg showing.

Telling herself that by many standards, the dress wasn't even that short didn't help. She was used to skirts that fell closer to her ankles than her thighs. Of course, that was in the classroom where she was constantly bending over small desks or sitting on the floor. This was different.

Unfortunately the girls weren't around to ask. They'd gone out to the movies, leaving her to decide on her own. She could always change her clothes, but she didn't know what else would be appropriate for the party.

Before she could decide what to do, the doorbell rang. She glanced at the clock radio on her nightstand. Duncan was about ten minutes early. She would be wearing the dress she had on.

She stepped into her high heels, teetered for a second, then walked into the living room. Not sure what Duncan was going to have to say or what to expect from the evening, she drew in a deep breath and pulled open the door.

But the man standing there wasn't her date and he didn't look happy.

"What the hell did you do?" Tim demanded as he pushed past her into the house. "Dammit, Annie, you don't have the right to force me to go to one of those places."

"I see you finally decided to talk to me," she said coolly. "I've been leaving messages for three days." Ever since she and Duncan had made their deal.

Her brother faced her, his blue eyes flashing with anger. "You had no right."

"To do what?" she asked, feeling her own temper rise. "Help? You got into this, Tim. You stole money from your boss. How could you?"

He shifted slightly and dropped his gaze to the floor. "You wouldn't understand."

"I'm sure that's true. You have a problem. It's either rehab or jail."

"Thanks to you," he said bitterly.

She put her hands on her hips. "This is not my fault. I'm not the one who gambled and I'm not the one who told Duncan Patrick this house was yours. You stole and lied, Tim. You were willing to risk everything on a roll of the dice."

"I play cards."

"Whatever."

He glared at her. "You're my sister, Annie. You're supposed to help me, not throw me into some institution. What would Mom say?"

A low blow, she thought, more resigned than angry.

"She would think you're a big disappointment. She would tell you that it was time to grow up and take responsibility."

Tim didn't even flinch. "It doesn't have to be like this," he said. "You could mortgage the house. It's half mine, anyway."

"It *was* half yours. I bought you out, remember? I'm tired of this, Tim. Tired of you expecting me to bail you out. I've always taken care of you and you've never been grateful or tried to change."

"You owe me." Tim moved closer. He was a lot bigger and taller. "You're going to mortgage the house, Annie. One way or the other. Do you hear me?"

She was too surprised to be afraid. Before she could figure out what to do next, Duncan walked through the half-open door.

"McCoy," he said.

Tim spun to face his boss. "What are you doing here?"

"I have an appointment with your sister."

Tim swung back to Annie, then looked her up and down. "You're going out with him?"

She nodded.

Tim's mouth twisted into a bitter smile. "Figures. I'm getting screwed and you're going on a date. Nice. Talk about ignoring your family."

The accusation burned down to her belly. "You don't know what you're talking about," she whispered. "This is about saving our family, something you don't care about."

Duncan grabbed Tim's arm. "She's right. As we

discussed, you'll report to the treatment facility by nine tomorrow morning or there will be a warrant for your arrest."

Tim looked between them. "You're in this together. You're selling me out with this bastard? Dammit, Annie."

Duncan stepped between them. "Enough, McCoy. It's time for you to leave. Remember, by nine in the morning."

"Why wait?" Tim asked bitterly. "I'll go now."

"That's probably for the best."

Tim shook off Duncan's hand, then walked to the door. He paused and glanced back at her. "Do you even care?"

Annie pressed her lips together and refused to answer. Tim would manipulate her if she gave him the chance. She'd never been able to stand up to him, but maybe it was time to start learning how.

She squared her shoulders. "Good luck, Tim. I hope this works."

He glared at her. "It doesn't matter if it does, Annie. Either way, I'm never going to forgive you."

Three

Duncan drove toward the hotel. Annie was silent, but he was aware of her next to him. He could inhale the scent of her subtle and feminine perfume. When he turned his head to the right, he caught a glimpse of her sleek thighs. Every now and then he heard a soft sigh.

"Are you mad at me or Tim?" he asked.

"What? Neither of you." She shifted toward him. "Mr. Patrick, I really appreciate your help with Tim. And he will, too. Eventually."

Unlikely, Duncan thought. But he'd been wrong before. Maybe rehab was what Tim needed. If it didn't work, he would screw up again and find himself in jail.

"I've been calling him all week," she admitted. "Trying to explain. Today is the first time I've seen him since we made our deal. He was so angry."

"You know he's lashing out at you because it's safe, right?" he asked. "He can't admit he has a problem, so it has to be everyone else's fault."

"I know, but it was still hard to hear."

Tim was damn lucky to have Annie for his sister, Duncan thought. Unlikely he would recognize that, either.

"You going to be all right?" he asked.

"You mean can I still do my job?" she asked with a smile. "Yes. As well as I could have before Tim showed up." She bit her lower lip. "I'm not very good at this sort of thing."

Hell of a time to admit that, he thought, amused by her honesty. "Going to parties? There's not much of an expectation. Look pretty and smile adoringly at me. You got through college. This should be easy by comparison."

"There's a little more to it than that," she said. "Or aren't I expected to hold a conversation?"

"You're talking just fine."

"You're less scary than a room full of people I don't know."

"Then maybe you should call me Duncan instead of Mr. Patrick."

Her breath caught. He liked the sound. It was unexpected and sexy as hell. The kind of sound a woman made when…

He stopped himself in midthought. Hold on there, he

told himself. Annie McCoy was many things, but sexy? He slid his gaze across her bare thighs. Okay, yeah, maybe sexy applied, but it was beside the point. He'd hired her to do a job—nothing more. Besides, she wasn't his type.

"Duncan," she said softly.

He looked at her and their eyes met. Hers were a deep blue, wide, with dark lashes. Her hair was different, he thought, remembering the curls. Tonight it was smooth, with waves. Sleek, he thought, although he preferred the curls. The dress was appropriate. He appreciated the way it emphasized her curves, not to mention the flash of thigh.

"You look good," he said.

She tugged at the hem of her dress. "It's Cameron's doing. He was great. Funny and really knowledgeable about fashion. He made a list of what shoes and evening bags go with each dress."

"Cameron knows his stuff."

"He mentioned you were college roommates."

Duncan chuckled. "That was a long time ago. I'll admit he was the first openly gay guy I'd ever met and that I wasn't happy to have him as my roommate."

"Too macho to understand?" she asked.

"Partially. I also had the idea that he would attack me in my sleep, which was pretty stupid of me. It took a while, but we became friends. When he moved back to L.A. a few years ago and opened his own business, he looked me up. I signed on as a client."

"He was nice," she said. "My cousins and Kami had a great time shopping, too."

"They went with you?"

"Uh-huh. You said I can keep the clothes, which is very nice of you, but honestly, can you see me wearing anything like this ever again? It's not exactly suitable for the classroom." She smiled. "So everyone came with me and offered opinions. As long as Cameron agreed with the choices, I got outfits they can wear later. We're all about the same size."

"You're going to give your cousins and their friend your clothes when this is done?"

"Isn't that okay? You said you didn't want them back."

"I don't have a lot of use for them. They're yours."

"Thank you."

He turned the idea over in his mind. He couldn't picture any other woman giving up an expensive wardrobe without a whole lot of motivation. Her comment about wearing them, or not wearing them, in the classroom made sense. But didn't she date? Didn't she want to hold on to them just because she could? The situation didn't make sense, which meant Duncan was going to have to figure it out. Success meant winning and winning meant understanding his opponent and exploiting his or her weakness. He might have bought Annie's time, but he didn't trust her. Not a big deal as he didn't trust anyone. Ever.

Annie ran her hands over the smooth leather of the seats. The car, an expensive German sedan, still smelled new. The engine was quiet, the dashboard filled with complex-looking displays. She had a feeling that an engineering degree would make working the stereo easier.

"Your car is really nice," she said. "Mine has this weird rattle in the dash. My mechanic says there's nothing wrong with how it drives, so I live with it. But it makes it tough to sing along with the radio."

"You can't get it fixed?"

She looked at him out of the corner of her eye. "I could," she said slowly. "And I will. Right after I win the lottery. But first I need new tires. It's always something, right? But that's okay. My car is really dependable. We have a deal—it starts for me every morning and I don't replace it."

His mouth twitched. "You talk to your car?"

"Sure. You probably don't."

"Your car and I have never met."

She laughed. "I can introduce you, if you'd like."

"No thanks." He turned left at the light.

"I've been thinking, we're going to have to tell people how we met. That's always the question right after 'How long have you been dating?'"

"Three months."

"Okay." She made a mental note. "How about saying it was Labor Day weekend. You were on your way to the beach when you saw me on the side of the road with a flat tire. You stopped to help."

"No one will believe that."

"You wouldn't stop?" She did her best not to sound disapproving. "You have to help people. It's good karma."

"Maybe I don't believe in karma."

"You don't have to—it still happens. I think the universe keeps the score pretty even."

"Doubtful. If that were true, I wouldn't be a success."

"Why not?"

"Haven't you read anything about me? I'm a total bastard. I hired you to prove otherwise."

"If you were a total bastard, you would have had Tim arrested the second you found out what he'd done. You were willing to let him pay back the money."

"Only because I didn't want the negative press." He glanced at her. "Be careful, Annie. Don't make the mistake of thinking I'm nicer than I am. You'll only get hurt."

Maybe. But didn't his warning her prove her point?

The hotel ballroom was large, elegant and extremely well-lit. Music from a suit-wearing combo drifted under the hum of conversation. Annie held on to her glass of club soda and lime and did her best not to look panicked. Well-dressed people chatted and laughed with each other. There were enough diamonds glittering to stretch from here to Montana. She had a feeling the cost of all the designer shoes would easily settle the national debt.

Duncan's world was an interesting place and about as far from her classroom as it was possible to get while staying on this planet. Still, she was here to do a job, so she remained by his side, smiling at him adoringly, endlessly shaking hands with people whose names she would never remember.

"How long have you and Duncan been dating?" a well-dressed woman in her forties asked.

"Three months," Annie said. "We met on Labor Day weekend."

"That's an eternity for our Duncan. You must be special."

"He's the special one," Annie said.

"You're not exactly his type."

Duncan must have heard. He put his arm around Annie and pulled her against him. "My type has changed."

"So I see."

Annie leaned into him, finding the closeness less awkward than she would have expected. Duncan was tall and well muscled. She could feel the power of him, but instead of making her nervous, his strength made her feel protected and safe. As if nothing bad could happen while he was around.

An illusion, she reminded herself. But a nice one.

When the woman moved away, Duncan led Annie over to another group of people and performed more introductions. One of the men there worked for a business magazine.

"Mind if I ask you a few questions?" he asked.

"No," she said. "As long as you don't mind me being nervous."

"Not into the press?"

"Not really."

"You can't date a guy like Duncan Patrick and expect to go unnoticed."

"So I've been told."

The man, slight and pale, in his mid-thirties asked, "How did you meet?"

She gave him the story about the Labor Day tire trouble. He didn't look convinced.

"Someone said you teach?"

"Kindergarten. I love working with kids. They're so excited about school. I know that it's up to me to keep that excitement alive, to prepare them to be successful in the education system. If we can show young children the thrill of learning, we can keep them in school through graduation and make sure they get to college."

The reporter blinked at her. "Okay. So why Duncan Patrick?"

She smiled. "Because he's a terrific guy. Although I have to tell you, the first thing I noticed was his laugh. He has a great laugh."

The reporter blinked again. "I've never heard him laugh."

"Then I guess you're going to have to be more funny."

Duncan moved toward them. "Charles," he said, shaking the other man's hand. "Good to see you."

"You, too."

Duncan turned his attention to her. "Let's dance," he said, taking the glass from her and putting it on a tray by the wall. He grabbed her hand and led her from the reporter.

Annie waved at Charles, then tapped Duncan on the arm. "I don't really dance."

"It's not hard. I'll lead."

She didn't know if that would help. "Do you think we could convince everyone to play Duck, Duck, Goose instead? Because I'm really good at that."

Duncan stopped, turned to her and started to laugh. She was pleased to realize she hadn't lied about his laugh—it was great.

"You'll be fine," he said, pulling her into his arms.

"Okay, but I apologize in advance for stepping on your toes."

Despite the fact that he was taller, she fit easily against him. He moved with a sureness that made him easy to follow, guiding her with his body and the hand on her waist. After a few steps, she managed to relax a little.

He smelled good, she thought absently. Clean but masculine. His suit was soft under her fingers as she rested her hand on his shoulder. Heat enveloped her. Heat and something else. The whisper of a tingle low in her belly.

Annie kept moving on the outside, but on the inside, everything went still. Tingles? There weren't supposed to be any tingles. This was a job. She couldn't have *feelings* for Duncan Patrick. She shouldn't like him or be attracted to him. He was her boss and their time together was just for show.

Maybe it was just because she hadn't been on a date in so long, she told herself. It was like being really hungry. Any kind of food would make her stomach growl, even something she didn't really want. Duncan was a good-looking guy. Of course she would respond. But she was smart enough to be careful. This was kind of like a fairy tale. She was Cinderella and the ball would end at midnight. Or in her case, Christmas. Only, there wouldn't be a shoe to leave behind and in the end, no handsome prince would come after her.

Annie held up better than he'd expected, Duncan thought two hours later. She'd managed to tell the story of his stopping to help her with her flat tire a dozen times. She was so enthused and sincere, even he was starting to believe her. The guests at the party seemed equally charmed and confused by Annie. He'd caught more than one questioning look, as if they were wondering what he was doing with someone so…nice.

Even Charles Patterson, a business reporter, had liked Annie. All Duncan needed was a couple of favorable articles to balance the negative ones.

He collected the drinks from the bartender and returned to Annie's side. He handed her the club soda with lime she'd requested—so far she hadn't had any alcohol—and bent toward her as she touched his arm.

"I was telling Charles that his information is wrong," she said to Duncan. "You're not closing a shipping facility in Indiana, are you?" Her eyes widened. "It's practically Christmas. Not only wouldn't you put people out of work for the holidays, but it's your busiest season. You need all the workers you can get."

She was half-right, Duncan thought grimly. This was his busy time, but he'd had every intention of closing the facility. The rural routes it served weren't profitable.

Annie stared at him, waiting for his response. He had a feeling she wasn't playing—that she actually believed he wouldn't want to put people out of work at Christmas. Charles looked smug, no doubt assuming the worst, which had always worked for him in the past.

Duncan swore silently and reminded himself that currently his reputation was more important than the bottom line.

"Annie's right," he said easily. "The facility is staying open at least through the first."

Charles raised his eyebrows. "Can I quote you on that?"

Duncan nodded.

"Interesting." The reporter moved away.

"Why would he think that about you?" she asked when they were alone. "No one would be that mean. It's Christmas." She took a sip of her drink. "It's my favorite time of year. In my family, we're big believers in more-is-more at the holidays." She laughed. "We always buy a really huge tree and then can't get it home, let alone in the house. Last year we had to cut off the top two feet, which is kind of sad. But they don't look that big on the lot. Then there's the decorating, the baking. I love Christmas carols. Jenny and Julie start to complain after a couple of days, but I keep playing them. Then we have Christmas movie-fest weekends when we watch all our favorites. What are some of your traditions?"

"I don't have any."

Her eyes widened. "Why not?"

"It's just a day, Annie."

"But it's Christmas. That makes it more than a day. It's about family and love and giving and imagining the best in the world."

"You're too naive. You need toughening up."

"And you need to spend some quality time listening to Christmas carols. Don't you decorate your house?"

He thought of his expensive condo and the look on his housekeeper's face if he dragged in a live tree to shed on the bamboo flooring.

"I usually travel for Christmas. Skiing or maybe somewhere warm."

"What about your family?"

"There's only my uncle and he does just fine without me."

She looked confused, as if he'd started speaking a foreign language. "Next you're going to tell me you don't exchange gifts."

"We don't."

She winced. "Tradition is important. Being together. It's special."

"Have you been a hopeless romantic your whole life?"

"Apparently. How long have you been a complete cynic?"

"Decades."

She surprised him by laughing. "At least you'll admit it. They say that's the first step in starting the healing process."

"There's nothing wrong with me."

"Want to take a survey of ten random people? I'll put

my Christmas traditions up against your noncelebration and we'll see who falls on the side of normal."

"I don't need anyone else's opinion to tell me I'm right."

She grinned. "You don't have to go to the gym, do you? Carrying around that ego is enough of a workout."

"It keeps me in shape."

She laughed again. The sound made him smile. She was prettier than he'd first thought. Opinionated when she forgot to be shy. Loyal to the point of stupidity, at least when it came to her brother, but everyone had flaws. The answers she'd e-mailed earlier had given him facts about her life but hadn't told him much about who Annie really was. In a practical sense, she was what he'd needed—a nice girl. But she was also appealing in a lot of ways.

Without thinking, he leaned forward and pressed his mouth against hers. She stiffened slightly before relaxing into the kiss. Her mouth was soft and yielding. Aware of the people around them, he drew back. As he straightened, he heard the sound of her breath catch and caught the flash of surprise in her eyes. Then she blinked and it was gone.

"You didn't say anything about kissing," she whispered, her voice a little husky. "I think we're going to need a special clause to cover that."

"The kissing clause?"

She nodded. "Set limits early and reinforce them."

He chuckled. "I'm not one of your students."

"That doesn't mean you won't be getting a time-out."

Four

Duncan arrived on time for his weekly lunch with his uncle. A tradition, he thought as he walked into the restaurant. Annie would be proud.

Lawrence was already there, sitting at their usual table, a Scotch in front of him. The older man waved him over.

"I didn't order you one," Lawrence said as he stood and the two men shook hands. "I know you don't drink during business hours."

They sat down. Duncan didn't bother with the menu. He had the same thing every week. The server brought him coffee, then left.

"Good job," Lawrence said, tapping the folded newspaper next to his place setting. "The article is positive. You said you wouldn't be closing the

Indiana facility before Christmas. You can't change your mind now."

"I won't."

"The girl sounds interesting. What's her name?"

"Annie McCoy."

"Is she really a kindergarten teacher?"

"Yes. She's exactly who you told me to find. Nice, connected to her family, pretty and articulate."

"The reporter is smitten," Lawrence said and picked up his glass. "How long are you going to see her?"

"Until Christmas."

His uncle's gray eyes sharpened. "It's strictly business?"

Duncan thought about the brief kiss he and Annie had shared, then did his best to convince himself he'd only done it for show. "We're not dating, if that's what you're asking. I've hired her to do a job, nothing more."

"I'd like to meet her."

"You're too old for her."

His uncle grinned. "We'll let her be the judge of that."

They ordered lunch and talked business through the meal. On the way to his car, his cell phone rang. He looked at the screen—the number was unfamiliar.

"Yes?"

"Hi. It's Annie."

They had a business dinner to attend tomorrow night. "Is there a scheduling problem?"

"No. We're going to get our Christmas tree this afternoon and I thought you might want to come with us."

He stared at the phone a second before putting it back against his ear. "Why?"

He heard the smile in her voice as she spoke. "Because it's fun and you need a little Christmas in your life. No pressure. You don't have to if you don't want to."

Which he didn't. But instead of telling her that, he found himself asking, "What time?"

"Four. My house. I don't suppose you have a truck we could borrow? The tree never fits well on the top of my car."

"I have a fleet of trucks, Annie. That's what I do."

"Oh. Right. Could we borrow a little one? Nothing with more than four wheels."

He shifted the phone to the other ear. "This isn't about me at all, is it? You just wanted to borrow a truck."

"No. Well, the truck is a part of it, but I would have wanted you to come even if you'd said no to the truck."

"I'm not sure I believe that."

The humor fled her voice. "I won't lie to you, Duncan."

"I'll see you at four."

He hung up.

Women had lied to him before. A lot of them. They lied to get what they wanted. He would swear sometimes they lied for sport. Valentina had been the biggest liar of them all. She had told him she loved him and then she had left.

Annie changed out of her dress and low heels. She usually put on jeans after she got home from school, so there wasn't anything unusual about that. The difference was this time she wasn't just going to be hanging out at home. She would be seeing Duncan again and as much as she told herself it wasn't a big deal, she'd yet to be totally convinced.

To be honest, the man confused her. He'd bought her services as a pretend girlfriend to improve his reputation. Not exactly something that happened every day. She'd gone online and read several articles about him, which had proven he really was considered something of a bastard in the business world. But he'd also paid for an impressive party wardrobe, given Tim a second chance and he'd kissed her.

The kiss was actually the most startling event, but she didn't like to think about it too much. It had probably been for show, so everyone would think they really were together. A meaningless, practically sexless gesture. Well, for him. For her…there had been tingles.

Not like the tingles when they'd danced. Those had been in her chest, more about feeling safe and content than anything else. But the kissing tingles were completely different. They'd zipped and zinged all the way through her body, pausing in her breasts and between her legs. Those tingles had made her think about kissing him again and what Duncan would be like in bed.

Focus, she thought as she pulled on jeans. All the articles she'd read had talked about how he always got the details right. It was an excellent quality for a man to have in bed.

She didn't usually daydream about making love with

a guy after a single date. Especially not a date that wasn't real. But something had happened when his mouth had briefly claimed hers. Something wonderful.

Now she reached for a red sweatshirt with Christmas geese marching across the front. Before putting it on, she wondered if she should wear something less boxy and more flattering. Something that would cause Duncan to see her as a…

What? A woman? He already did. An actual girlfriend? Not likely. They were only pretend dating. She couldn't let herself forget that. Besides, two guys had already broken her heart. Was she going for a personal best by making it three?

She grabbed the sweatshirt and pulled it firmly over her head. She knew better, she reminded herself. The trick was going to be remembering that.

"We won't be decorating the tree tonight," Annie said as she sat next to Duncan in the cab of the truck he'd driven to her house. "The girls all have something they have to get to. A class or work. Besides, you're supposed to let the tree sit out in the garage for a couple of days before bringing it in."

"Why? It's not a puppy. It doesn't need to get used to being away from its mother."

She laughed. "I think it's about the branches settling. I have the tree stand set up in the garage, so we can put it in water as soon as we get it home."

Duncan had arrived right on time. Based on the suit he wore, he'd come from work.

"Did I take you away from something important?" she asked.

"Nothing that can't wait." He smiled. "My assistant was surprised when I said I was leaving."

"Imagine what she'd think if she knew where you were actually going."

He chuckled.

She studied his profile. She liked the strength of his face, the chiseled jawline, the shape of his mouth. Her gaze lingered on the latter as she thought about him kissing her. Would he do it again? If he kissed her in a nonbusiness setting, then she would know for sure that he'd liked it as much as she had. Craziness, she told herself. She couldn't think about Duncan as anything but her boss. The hard part was that she wanted a husband and a family to love, but all she had was a bruised heart and a fear that no man was going to think of her as more than a friend.

They pulled into the Christmas-tree lot. Jenny, Julie and Kami were already there. Duncan parked next to Jenny's car.

"Brace yourself," Annie told him. "You're about to meet your match."

He raised his eyebrows. "I can handle it."

She grinned. "That's what every man thinks, right before he runs into trouble. You've been warned."

Annie watched Duncan get out of the truck and introduce himself to her cousins and Kami. By the time she reached them, the easy stuff was done.

"That article about you in last March's issue of

Time was interesting," Julie said. "The press really hates you, huh?"

"A hazard of my occupation," Duncan said calmly.

"Except there are a lot of CEOs out there," Jenny pointed out. "They're not all hated. Although I'll give you the coverage of the purchase of the mobile home park wasn't fair. You offered the residents a fair deal and made sure they were taken care of."

"The thing is," Julie added, "If one person thinks you aren't nice, it's probably them. But if all the press people feel that way…"

"I'm misunderstood," Duncan said.

"Uh-huh." Jenny and Julie moved between him and Annie. Kami seemed more comfortable keeping out of the conversation.

"What is this, the Inquisition?" Annie joked, warmed by her cousins' protective questions but trying to lighten the mood. She might not have a husband and a baby, but she still had a family. She had to remember that.

"They have bright futures in the law."

"I'm not going to be a lawyer," Jenny said. "But I am watching out for Annie. We all are."

Duncan did his best to look attentive rather than incredulous. Were these two college girls going to threaten him? They had neither the money nor the resources, and if it came to a battle of wills, he would leave them coughing in the dust.

None of which he said to them.

"I don't need that much defending," Annie said,

looking uncomfortable. "Duncan, I'm sorry. I didn't know the twins were going to gang up on you this much."

"But a little would have been okay?"

"Sure."

He turned to the cousins. "Annie and I have a business arrangement. She'll be fine."

"You have to promise," one of the twins said. Duncan couldn't tell them apart.

"You have my word on it." Even if he and Annie didn't have an agreement, she wouldn't be at much risk. He didn't get involved enough for anyone to get their feelings hurt. Life was easier that way.

They went into the lot. The girls fanned out to look at trees, but Annie stayed by him.

"I'm sorry if they offended you," she began.

"Don't be. I respect them for thinking they can take me."

She tilted her head. Blond curls tumbled to her shoulder. "No, you don't," she said slowly. "You think they're foolish."

"That, too."

"It's a family thing. We're a team. Like you and your uncle."

He and Lawrence were many things, but a team wasn't one of them. Duncan nodded because it was easier than having to explain. He watched Annie turn her attention to the rows of cut trees.

The air was thick with the smell of pine. There were a few shoppers talking over the sound of Christmas carols.

As Annie moved from tree to tree, he scanned the lot until he found the girls checking the price tag on a tree. Kami shook her head. The twins looked frustrated before moving to another tree. He turned back to Annie, who was gazing longingly at a tree that had to be fifteen feet, easy.

"You have eight-foot ceilings," he said, coming up behind her. "Learn from your past mistakes."

"Meaning we shouldn't buy something that won't fit." She sighed. "But it's beautiful." She glanced at the price tag. It was eighty-five dollars. "Maybe not."

"How much did you want to spend?" he asked.

"Under forty dollars. Less would be better. This is a family lot. They bring in the trees themselves. They cost a little more, but they're really fresh and it's kind of a tradition to come here."

"You're big on tradition, aren't you?"

"Uh-huh. The rhythm of life, year after year. It's fun."

He felt like Scrooge. The only thing he did year after year was count his money.

She stopped in front of another tree, then glanced at him. "Not too tall?"

"It looks like a great height."

She fingered the tag. It was sixty-five dollars. When she hesitated, he wanted to ask if twenty-five dollars really made that much difference. But he knew it did or Annie—the spokesperson for the wonders of Christmas—would cough up the money.

Duncan excused himself and found the owner of the

lot. After a quiet conversation and the exchange of money, Duncan returned to Annie's side.

"Let's ask the guy if they have anything on sale," he said.

She looked at him pityingly. "Trees don't go on sale until a couple of days before Christmas."

"How can you be sure? Maybe there's a return or something."

"No one returns a Christmas tree."

He smiled. "And if you're wrong?"

She sighed. "Fine. I'll ask. But I'm telling you, there aren't any returns or seconds in the Christmas-tree business."

She looked around for the owner, then walked over to him. As Duncan watched, the man in the Santa T-shirt pointed to three different trees clustered together. Annie glanced at Duncan, then back at Santa guy.

"Seriously?" she was saying. "You have returns?"

"All the time. How high is your ceiling?"

"Eight feet." She turned to the girls, who had joined her. "Did you hear that? These are only thirty dollars."

They had a lengthy conversation about the merits of each tree. Finally one was chosen and put in the back of Duncan's truck. Annie watched anxiously as he tied it down, then she took her seat in the cab.

She waited until he climbed in next to her before touching his arm. "Thank you," she said quietly. "I don't know how much you paid him, and normally I wouldn't have accepted the gift. But it's Christmas and the girls love the tree. So thank you."

He started to say it wasn't him, then shrugged. "I need to get back to the office. You were taking too long, looking for a discount tree."

Her blue gaze never wavered. "You're not a bad guy. Why do you want people to think you are?"

"It's not about nice, it's about tough. Staying strong. That means making the hard decisions."

It also meant depending only on himself—the one person he could trust to be there for him. She might think connecting was everything, but he knew better.

"You don't have to be mean to be strong," she said.

"Sometimes you do," he told her and started the engine.

Annie had never paid attention to magazine articles on relaxation. Her life was busy—she didn't have time to become one with the moment. On her best day, she was only slightly behind. One her worst day, her to-do list stretched for miles. But now, as she sat in the elegant beachfront restaurant with Duncan's business associates and stared at the nine pieces of flatware around her place setting—most of which were totally foreign to her—she wished she'd at least read the paragraphs on how to breathe through panic.

She knew enough to start from outside and work her way in. There was also a fairly good chance that the horizontal three pieces above the decorative plate were for dessert. Or maybe dessert and cheese, and possibly coffee. The weird little fork could be for shrimp or even fish and the steak knife was clear, but what were the other three for?

Even more intimidating was the menu. While it was in English, there weren't any prices. Did that mean everything was priced à la carte? Or was there some jumbo total given out at the end of the meal? It wasn't that she was so worried about the price. Even the cost of a bowl of soup would probably make her faint. But she didn't want to order the most expensive thing on the menu by mistake.

She scanned the offerings again. There was a lobster tail, a market-price fish and Kobe beef. She was pretty sure if she avoided those, she would be fine. Her gaze lingered over the pasta dishes. Two of them were homemade ravioli. The twins would love that, she thought.

"You all right?" Duncan asked, leaning close. "You're looking tense about something."

"We couldn't have gone to a diner? Maybe ordered a burger?" she whispered, making him laugh.

The low chuckle seemed to move through her, making her aware of how close they sat and how great he looked in his dark suit. Duncan might be the meanest CEO two years running, but he sure could wear clothes.

"It's business," he told her. "This place is quiet."

"So is my McDonald's, anytime after eight."

One of the three waiters serving the table appeared at her elbow. "May I get you a cocktail?" he asked.

She hesitated, not sure what the best—make that appropriate—drink would be. Or should she wait for wine?

"Ever had a cosmopolitan?" Duncan asked.

"Like in *Sex in the City*? No, but I'd love to try one. Are they really pink?"

"Unfortunately," Duncan told her, then ordered Scotch for himself.

An older man sat down on the other side of Annie. She smiled at him as Duncan introduced him with the fact that Will Preston was the largest plumbing supply distributor on the West Coast.

"Nice to meet you," the man said as he sat down. "Do you work?"

"I'm a kindergarten teacher."

Will leaned toward her. "Then maybe you can answer a question for me. My wife loves to have the grandkids stay the night with us and they always want me to read them a story. It's not that I mind doing that, but they want the same story over and over again. I read it to them and they want to hear it again. Why is that?"

"Their brains aren't as developed as yours," she said. "They don't have the lifetime of experiences to draw on. So everything is new, all the time. A bedtime story offers the comfort of the familiar and they like that. They feel connected by the repetition, plus they probably hear something new every time. I would guess they also like having you read it to them, as well. Your voice, the way you pronounce the words, all become associated with time with you. You're making memories."

He frowned. "I hadn't thought about it like that." The frowned cleared. "Thank you, Annie. That makes me want to read to them more."

"I hope you will. Because thirty years from now, when they're reading to their children, they'll remember this time. It will always be something you've shared."

"Do you know what you want?" Duncan asked, reclaiming her attention.

She glanced at the menu. "I was thinking the twins would have enjoyed doggie bags from here."

She was about to say more when she caught Duncan's startled expression. Maybe talking about taking food home to her family wasn't a good thing, she thought, suddenly uncomfortable. She closed her menu and pressed her lips together.

"Annie here has some real insights into my grandkids," Will was telling the man across from him.

The man looked bored, although he nodded. Annie shifted in her seat.

Although she was dressed in one of the pretty cocktail dresses Cameron had picked out for her, she felt out of place. Everyone at the table was older and seemed to know each other. The women were laughing and talking with a casual ease that made her want to slowly back out of the room. Anywhere but here, she thought. What if she failed? What if Duncan decided she wasn't doing a good job? Would he change his mind about their deal? Would Tim be pulled out of rehab and sent to jail?

Stop it, she told herself. So what if everyone in this room had some impressive job and knew what all the forks were for? She was smart. She had a career she loved and she knew she made a difference. Duncan Patrick needed her to make himself look good. If anyone should be worried about the deal being changed, it was him, not her. He was lucky to have her.

"Do I want to know why you're smiling?" Duncan asked, leaning close and putting his arm on the back of her chair. "Are you drunk?"

"I've taken one sip."

"You don't seem like much of a drinker."

"Maybe not, but even I can handle a cocktail."

"Are you putting me in my place?"

"Do you need me to do that? I'm tougher than I look, Duncan."

He laughed. "I'm sure you are."

While it hadn't been her best time ever, Annie managed to get through the dinner without spilling, saying anything she regretted or withdrawing completely. She'd managed to hold her own on a debate about charter schools and had offered an opinion on the latest movie sensation. When everyone was standing up to leave, the waiter appeared with two large brown bags.

"For those hungry college girls you have at home," Duncan said. "Three entrées and dessert for all. It'll keep them out of your secret stash."

She was both surprised and touched. Talk about thoughtful. As they moved toward the exit, she walked slowly, waiting until everyone else had left. Then she put the bags on the nearby table, rested her hand on Duncan's shoulder, reached up and kissed him on the cheek.

"You're a total fraud," she whispered. "You're not mean at all."

He dropped his arm around her waist and drew her

closer. When he kissed her back, it wasn't on the cheek and it wasn't meaningless. Duncan pressed his lips to hers with a force that took her breath away. He claimed, his mouth moving against hers. There was no doubt of what he wanted, or of the fact that his intensity hinted he might just take it without asking.

She was pressed against him, his arm like a band around her, holding her in place. There was no escape, but there also wasn't any fear, either. Instead of wanting to struggle with him, she found herself yielding, instinctively realizing that he expected a fight. Surrender was the only way to win.

As soon as she relaxed, so did his hold. His mouth gentled, still taking but with a teasing quality. She was aware of silence around them, the air of expectation. He lightly brushed her bottom lip with his tongue.

Fire shot through her. She parted for him and he claimed her with a passion that left her weak. The second his tongue touched hers she was lost. Wanting poured through her, making her surge closer. Unfamiliar desperation swamped her. She wrapped her other arm around his neck and pressed harder against the thick muscles of his chest. He could snap her like a twig, if he wanted, and that was very much a part of his appeal. The strength of him. If Duncan ever fully committed to someone, that woman would be cared for and protected forever.

He stroked the inside of her mouth, exploring, arousing. She answered each touch with a brush of her own. His hands moved against her back, before dropping lower to her hips.

Heat invaded. Wanting grew. The need was unexpectedly powerful. She'd dated before, had made love before, had even thought she'd been in love before. But none of those experiences had prepared her for a passionate kiss in Duncan's arms.

Slowly, almost reluctantly, he drew back.

"Annie," he began, his tone warning.

She didn't know if he was going to remind her that their deal didn't include sex or that she was playing with fire. She met his dark, smoldering gaze and shook her head, then collected the doggie bags and turned to leave.

She didn't want to hear that she wasn't anyone he could be interested in. Not tonight. As to the danger of playing with fire…it was simply something she was going to have to risk.

Five

"I'm sorry I can't make it tonight," Annie said, both frustrated and worried. She was starting to enjoy her evenings with Duncan at the various functions he took her to. But she was also worried about their deal. "I hope you understand. It's a holiday emergency."

"A contingency we seem to have missed in our agreement."

Annie couldn't tell if he was pissed or not and found herself a little nervous about asking.

"It's just we had a lot of no-shows last weekend when the parents were supposed to help with the set decorations."

"For the Christmas play?" he asked.

"It's a winter festival, Duncan. We don't promote any one holiday celebration."

"And calling it a winter festival fools people?"

She heard the humor in his voice. "It's inclusive. So there are a bunch of sets to be built and painted. I have to stay and help."

"What is your class doing?"

"Singing 'Catch a Falling Star' while using American Sign Language at the same time."

"Multitasking at five. Impressive. All right, Ms. McCoy. Call me when the sets are decorated. If there's time, I'll take you to the cocktail party with me."

"I'm sorry to miss it," she said, sincere in her regret.

"You don't know that you will yet, do you?"

"We're not exactly a talented group when it comes to woodworking, Duncan. We're going to be here all night."

"Just call me."

She hung up and walked back into the main auditorium building. The other teachers and a couple of volunteers were dividing up the work. As the closest Annie had come to construction was the knitting class she'd taken the previous summer, she was given paint detail.

Thirty minutes later everyone was hard at work, building, sanding and painting. Fifteen minutes after that, four big guys in T-shirts, jeans and work boots walked in. Each man had an impressively large toolbox with him. The principal turned off the saw and removed her safety goggles.

"Can I help you?" she asked.

"We're here to help with the sets," one of the guys said. "Duncan Patrick sent us."

The teachers looked around in confusion. Annie cleared her throat. "He's, ah, a friend of mine. I mentioned we hadn't had our usual parent volunteers." She was trying to look perfectly normal, which probably wasn't working, seeing as she couldn't stop smiling. A light, happy feeling made her think she just might be able to float home instead of drive.

The principal sighed gratefully. "We are desperate. Have you ever worked on sets for a school play before?"

The men exchanged glances. "Two of us are cabinet makers, and two of us are house painters, ma'am. We can handle it. If you'll just tell us what needs to be done, leave us to finish it and we're good."

Annie pulled her cell phone out of her pocket and dialed Duncan's number. "Thank you," she whispered when he picked up. "This is amazing."

"This is me making sure you don't back out of our deal. I'll pick you up at five. It won't be a late evening."

She wanted to say more, to have him admit he'd gone way out of his way to help her. But something inside her told her he didn't want to take credit for what he'd done. The question was why. What in Duncan's past made him believe that being nice and kind and honorable was a bad thing? Had someone hurt him? Maybe it was time to find out.

"I don't understand," Annie said as she put the key in the front door lock and turned it. "He's a banker. He has lots of money. So why does he care about yours?"

"Banks get money from other people and make profit off it," Duncan told her. "Loaning it out, investing it. The bigger the accounts, the more income for the bank."

"Okay," she said slowly, obviously not convinced.

They'd spent the past two hours at a boring cocktail party. In theory the evening had been about networking, but it had become clear that Duncan had been invited so a prominent banker could solicit his business. Normally he didn't mind being courted—it could make for an excellent deal. But tonight he hadn't been in the mood.

Instead he'd been watching the clock and checking his cell phone.

Annie shrugged out of her black wrap and dropped it on the sofa. She bent over to remove her high heels, wincing as she pulled them off.

"They weren't kidding," she murmured, curling her toes into the carpet. "Beauty *is* pain."

Normally Duncan would have responded to the comment, but he was too busy watching her dress gape open, exposing her full, pale breasts. The curves looked big enough to fill his hands. Staring at them, he wondered how the soft skin would taste. He imagined his tongue circling her tight nipples, flicking them quickly as she writhed beneath him.

The image was vivid enough to cause blood to pool in his groin. He shifted uncomfortably.

Annie straightened, took a step and winced again. "I think the injury is permanent. How do women wear those shoes every day? I couldn't stand it." She pointed to the corner. "Isn't it beautiful?"

He glanced in that direction and saw the decorated Christmas tree by the window. It filled the space and spilled into the room. Hundreds of ornaments seemed to cover every inch of branch. Annie flipped on the lights, which flicked on and off at a dizzying speed. It wasn't something he would have liked and yet there was something special about the tree.

"Very nice."

"Did you get one yet for your place?" she asked.

Of course not, but he didn't want to hurt her feelings. Instead he pointed to the coffee table where an instruction manual lay inside a clear plastic sleeve. "What's that?"

She looked down, then picked up the package. "I don't know. It's for a freezer. We don't have a…"

Slowly she raised her head until she stared at him. "You didn't."

He pointed to the kitchen. Beyond that was a utility room with a washer, dryer and as of an hour ago, a brand-new freezer. She ran through the kitchen. He followed. When he'd caught up with her, she was running her hands lovingly down the door before opening it and gazing at the full shelves.

There were packages of meat, chicken and fish, a stack of frozen pizzas, bags of vegetables, containers of juice and ice cream. Annie stared for nearly a minute, her eyes wide, her mouth open. Then she closed the door and turned to face him.

He'd known a lot of beautiful women in his life. He'd slept with them, dated some, left more than a few. He'd been seduced by the best, even been married, but no one had looked at him the way she did now—tears in her blue eyes, a expression of pure happiness on her face.

"You didn't have to do that," she told him.

"I know. I wanted to. You can buy in bulk. It's cheaper. I know how you love a bargain."

"It's the best gift ever. Thank you." She reached for his hand and squeezed it. "Seriously, Duncan. This is life-changing."

He pulled back his hand, not wanting to be sucked into the moment. He'd seen a need and filled it. Big deal. "It's just a freezer."

"To you. To me it's something I don't have to worry about for a while. It's a chance to catch my breath."

He'd given gifts before. Jewelry. Cars. Vacations. Now, standing in Annie's shabby little house, he realized he'd never given anything that mattered. No one had been touched by something he'd done before. Maybe because Annie was one of the few women he'd ever liked.

Wanting and liking were completely different. He'd gone into this arrangement to improve his reputation and get his board of directors off his ass. But somewhere along the way, he'd started to like Annie. He couldn't tell if that was good or bad.

"This is my good deed for the holiday season," he said. "Don't read too much into it."

"Right." Her smile was knowing. "Because you're not a nice guy."

"I'm not."

"So I've heard." She pulled open the freezer again and removed a pizza. "This has everything on it. Does that work?"

"You're cooking a pizza?"

"They served only sushi at that cocktail party." She wrinkled her nose. "Raw fish isn't my favorite."

"Pizza it is."

She went back into the kitchen and started the oven. "Want to watch a Christmas movie while we wait?"

"No."

She laughed. "I'd let you pick which one."

"I'd still say no."

The tears were gone and now her eyes sparkled with laughter. "You're not overly domesticated, are you?"

"I never had a reason."

"But you were married. Didn't the former Mrs. Patrick tame you?"

He moved closer. "Do I look tamed?"

"Hmm." She squinted. "I think I can see little marks on your cheeks where the reins went."

He reached for her and she ducked away. But she slipped on the vinyl floor. He caught her in his arms, her body yielding against his. The need to pull her close was strong, the desire instant. But the reminder of his ex killed the moment. He let her go.

"Valentina wasn't interested in domesticating me," he said, deliberately stepping back.

Annie leaned against the counter. "What was she like? Cameron said she was interesting."

"I doubt that. Cameron would have said she was a bitch."

"That, too."

Duncan didn't think about his ex-wife any more than he had to. "It was a long time ago," he said. "She was a journalism major in college. I'd just bought my first billion-dollar company. She came out to interview me for a paper she was writing. Or so she said. I think it was a way to meet me."

Valentina was four years younger than him, but she'd been cool, sophisticated and confident. He'd been a former boxer, over-muscled and accustomed to using his size to get his way. She was all about the subtle win.

"Is she beautiful?" Annie asked, not quite meeting his gaze.

"Yes. Blond hair, blue eyes." He studied the woman in front of him. Technically the description fit Annie as well, but the two women had nothing in common. Annie was soft and approachable. She trusted the world and thought the best of people. Valentina played to win and didn't care who got hurt in the process.

She'd smoothed his rough edges, had taught him what it meant to be a gentleman. Through her he'd learned about wine and the right clothes and which topics of conversation were safe for polite conversation. She was all about doing the right thing—until the bedroom door closed. There she preferred him as uncivilized as possible.

"How long were you married?"

"Three years."

"Did you…" Annie cleared her throat. "I assume you were in love with her. It wasn't a business arrangement."

"I loved her," he said curtly. As much as anyone could love a woman who kept her heart firmly protected in a case of ice. "Until I walked in on her screwing one of my business partners."

Not even in their bed, Duncan thought, still more angry than hurt at the memory. On his desk.

"I threw her out and borrowed enough money to buy off all my partners," he said, looking past her but not seeing anything around them. Instead he saw a naked Valentina tossing her long hair over her shoulder.

"You weren't foolish enough to think I really loved you," she'd said in answer to his unspoken question.

He *had* been that foolish. All the time he'd been growing up he'd known he had to be strong to stay safe. With Valentina, he'd allowed himself to forget the painful lessons he learned in his youth. He never would again.

Annie touched his arm. "I'm sorry. I don't know why she would do something like that."

"Why, because in your world marriage is forever?"

"Of course." She looked shocked that he would even ask. "My dad died when I was really young. My mom talked about him all the time. She made him so real to me and Tim. It was like he wasn't dead—he'd just gone on a long trip. When she died, she told me not to be sad because when she was gone, she got to be with him again. That's what I want."

"It doesn't exist."

"Not every woman is like Valentina."

"You find anyone worthy of those dreams of yours?"

"No." She shrugged. "I keep falling for the wrong guy. I'm not sure why, but I'll figure it out."

She was optimistic beyond reason. "How many times have you had your heart broken?"

"Twice."

"What makes you think the next time will be different?"

"What makes you think it won't be?"

Because being in love meant being vulnerable. "You would give a guy *everything*. Only for him to use you for what he can get, then walk away? Life is a fight—better to win than lose."

"Are those the only two options?" she asked. "What happened to a win-win scenario? Don't they teach that in business school?"

"Maybe. But not in the school of hard knocks."

She reached for his hands and curled his fingers into fists. "It must have been frustrating to learn you couldn't use these to battle your way out of every situation."

"It was."

Annie hadn't known much about Duncan's ex-wife beyond what Cameron had told her. Now she had a clearer understanding of what had happened. Valentina had hurt Duncan more than he would admit. She'd broken his trust and battered his feelings. For a man who was used to using physical strength when backed into a corner, the situation had to have been devastating. He'd allowed himself to lead with his heart, only to have it beaten up and returned to him.

"There hasn't been anyone important since Valentina?" she asked, even though she already knew the answer.

"There have been those who tried," he said lightly.

"You're going to have to trust one of them. Don't you want a family?"

"I haven't decided."

She shook her head. "You have to admire the irony of life," she said. "I would love to find someone and settle down, have a houseful of kids and live happily ever after. The challenge is that I can't find anyone who sees me as the least bit interesting in the romantic department. You, on the other hand, have women throwing themselves at you, begging to be taken, but you're not interested." She stared into his gray eyes. "You shouldn't give up on love."

"I don't need your advice."

"I owe you something for the freezer."

"The pizza is enough."

"Okay. Want to go find something violent on television while I put this in the oven?"

"Sure."

She watched him walk out of the kitchen.

Knowing about his past explained a lot. What Duncan didn't realize was that under that tough exterior was a really nice guy, which he wouldn't want to hear anyway. Guys hated to be called nice. But he was. She couldn't turn around without tripping over the proof.

What had he been like before he'd met Valentina? A strong man, willing to trust and give his heart. Did it get any better than that? The oven beeped. She opened the pizza box, then slid the contents onto a cookie sheet and put it in the oven.

Did Duncan's ex have any regrets? Had she figured out everything she'd lost and wished for a second chance? Annie didn't know her, so she couldn't say. She only knew that if she were ever given a shot at a man like Duncan, she would hold on with both hands and never let go.

The office Christmas party was a complete disaster. Annie hated to be critical, but there was no escaping the uncomfortable silence, the uneasy glances being exchanged and the unnaturally loud bursts of laughter from nervous attendees. She could feel the fear of those around her. No one was eating or drinking, and nearly everyone kept checking the time as if desperate to make an escape.

"Interesting party," she murmured to Duncan as they stood by the main entrance to the hotel ballroom. While she thought it was nice Duncan wanted to greet everyone who attended, his presence wasn't helping the situation. He was big and powerful, which made relaxing even more difficult.

"These things are always tedious."

"Maybe if there'd been some music."

"Maybe." He looked over her head. "There's Jim in accounting. I need to go speak with him. I'll be right back."

She retreated to a private spot by a fake potted plant and called home. Jenny picked up on the first ring.

"Can you and Kami bring the karaoke machine?" she asked in a low voice. "I have a dead party that needs help." She gave the name of the hotel and which ballroom.

"Fancy," Jenny said.

"Disaster. Please hurry."

"We'll be there, Annie. Just keep sipping the wine."

"I'm not sure it will help." She pushed the end button, then put her cell back in her purse.

Across the ballroom, Duncan talked to several men. Probably his executives, she thought, noticing how everyone else also kept their eyes on the group.

Three nights ago, he'd ended up leaving before the pizza was cooked, claiming he was going back to work. It was probably true, she told herself. Work was an escape. Not that she was anyone to complain. While she didn't work the crazy hours he did, she spent plenty of time avoiding what was wrong with her life. Her cousins and Kami kept her busy, not to mention all the projects through school and the various classes she'd signed up for. If she was constantly running, she didn't have to think about the fact that she hadn't been on a date in nearly six months. Not counting Duncan, of course.

After the holidays, she promised herself. She would get back out there and start dating. She would look for someone who saw her as more than a sister or a friend. Tim had offered to set her up with a couple of guys he knew. Although that had been before he'd gone into rehab. She wondered if her brother was still angry with her. Because he wasn't able to get calls or have visitors for a couple more weeks, there was no way to know.

For the next twenty minutes, she sipped her wine and tried to talk to people at the party. They were all too tense to do more than say they were fine and yes, this was a great party. Just as nice as last year. Finally Jenny and Kami appeared with the karaoke machine and microphone.

"I put in songs from the eighties," Jenny said as she helped Kami set up the machine on a table by a plug. "I figured everyone here would be really old."

"Nice," Annie told her. "You're kidding, right?"

Jenny grinned. "You're so serious about everything. Yes, I'm kidding. There's mostly Christmas music loaded." She looked around at the dying party. "How are you going to get this started?"

Annie took another sip of wine. "I plan to sacrifice myself."

Kami winced. "Tim doesn't deserve you looking out for him the way you do."

"Tell me about it."

Annie nodded and Jenny flipped the switch. An electronic hum filled the room. Everyone turned to look. Annie waved weakly, then scrolled through the songs until she found "Jingle Bell Rock." Maybe that would put people in the holiday spirit.

The music came on. Kami turned it up, then mouthed, "Good luck."

Annie picked up the microphone and began to sing.

She had a modest voice, at best. Soft, without a lot of range. But someone had to save the party and everyone else was too afraid. So she did her best and ignored the waver in her voice and the heat burning her cheeks.

At the chorus, Jenny and Kami joined in. Then a couple of people in the crowd sang along. A few more sang the second chorus and by the third time around, most of the people in the room were nodding along.

A couple of women came up and said they wanted to sing. By the time they were done, there was a line of people waiting. She gratefully handed off the microphone.

She grabbed her wine and finished it in a single gulp. She was still shaking. The good news was people were actually talking to each other and she saw a couple filling plates with food.

Duncan joined her. "You were singing."

"I know."

His expression was hard to read. "Why?"

"Was it that bad?"

"No, but you were uncomfortable."

"The party was dying. Something had to be done."

Duncan looked around at his employees, then back at her. "This wasn't your responsibility."

"People should have a good time at an office party. Isn't that the point of giving it? So they can hang out together, talk and learn about each other in a way that isn't about work?"

He stared at her blankly.

She pointed at the people in the room. "Go talk to them. Ask questions about their lives. Pretend interest."

"Then what?"

"Smile. It will confuse them."

He looked at her quizzically, then did as she said. She watched him approach a group of guys who were drinking beer and tugging at their ties.

The employees weren't the only ones who were confused, she thought, staring at Duncan. She was, as well. She was with him for a reason that had nothing to do with caring or being involved. He'd basically blackmailed her into pretend dating him so he could fool the world into thinking he was a nice guy. So why did she want to be next to him now, helping him? Why did the sight of his smile make her want to smile in return?

Complications she couldn't afford, she reminded herself. She wanted forever and Duncan wanted to be left alone. She was staff, he was the boss. There were a thousand reasons why nothing would ever work out between them.

And not one of them could stop her from wishing for the very thing she could never have.

Six

Duncan kept his hand firmly around Annie's elbow as he guided her toward his car in the parking lot. One of the first rules of boxing was not to fight mad. It gave your opponent an advantage. He'd learned the lesson also applied to all areas of life, so he wasn't going to say anything until he was sure he was under control. A state hard to imagine as anger pulsed in time with his heartbeat.

He was beyond pissed. He could feel the emotions boiling up inside him. The need to lash out, to yell—something he never did—nearly overwhelmed him.

"Just say it," Annie said calmly, when they reached the car.

He pushed the button to unlock the doors, then opened hers. "I have nothing to say."

She rolled her eyes. "You're practically frothing at the mouth. You need to just say it."

"I'm fine," he growled, waiting until she got into the car, then closing her door.

He walked around and got in on the driver's side. She put her hand on his arm.

"Duncan, you'll feel better."

He angled toward her, staring into her wide blue eyes, nearly vibrating with rage. "You had no right."

"So you *are* mad."

"What the hell were you thinking."

She sighed. "So much for the warm fuzzies."

He narrowed his gaze. "Excuse me?"

"Before, at the party, when I brought in the karaoke machine and humiliated myself by singing and saved the day, there were warm fuzzies. But now, all because I make a simple little suggestion, you're upset."

"A simple suggestion? Is that what you call it? You have no right. This isn't your business. Our bargain in no way gives you any kind of authority over me or my decisions. You don't know what you're talking about and because of that, I have to deal with your mess."

She nodded slowly. "Feel better?"

"I'm not a child to be placated."

"I'll take that as a no."

She wasn't afraid of him. In the back of his mind, he appreciated that she was sitting calmly while he ranted. Most people couldn't do that. They were too aware of his size, his background, his ability to physically rip them in two if the mood struck.

She shifted toward him. "It's not a bad idea."

"You're not the one who has to pay for it."

"You're paying for it already," she said reasonably. "Parents have to miss work because their day care isn't available. Or they can't stay late because of the hours. It's out of their control and that makes people worry. Worried people don't do as good a job."

"I'm not offering in-office day care. It's ridiculous."

"Why?"

"It's expensive and unnecessary."

"Do you know that for sure?" she asked.

"Do you know that it really helps?"

"No, but I'm willing to find out if it does. Are you?"

"I don't come into your classroom and tell you how to teach. I would appreciate it if you didn't come into my business and tell me how to run it." The anger bubbled again.

"I'm not doing that. I was talking to a group of your employees and they spoke pretty passionately about it. I said it was an interesting idea and something you'd look into."

"You do not speak for me."

"What was I supposed to do?" she asked, a slight edge to her voice. "As far as they're all concerned, I'm your girlfriend. The entire point of this exercise is to make the world think you're a nice guy. Nice guys listen to good ideas."

He couldn't take much more of this. "It's not a good idea. I listen when the person talking has something worthwhile to say."

"Oh, and I don't?" Now she was glaring. "Do I need an MBA to be worthy of a meeting? No wonder everyone was afraid to speak at that party. You don't allow them to communicate without your permission. Do they have to get it in writing in advance? Not listening to anyone else must make for short meetings. But why have a meeting at all? You're so damned all-knowing. That must make their jobs easier. You issue proclamations and they go forth and produce. What a concept."

She was seriously pissed. Her eyes flashed and color stained her cheeks. She actually leaned forward and poked him in his shoulder.

"Don't be a jerk," she said loudly. "You know this idea has merit. Other companies have put day care in place successfully. Maybe you're right—maybe it won't work, but the current system is causing problems. So fix it. Contract with a couple of day care places so they'll stay open later. Offer a program that allows employees to pay for day care with pretax dollars. I'm saying that if people who work for you think there's a problem, then there's a problem, whether you like it or not."

He leaned back against the door. "You about done?"

"No. The people at that party tonight were scared of you, Duncan. That's not a good thing."

He knew she was right about that. A frightened workforce put more energy into protecting themselves than into the company.

"I don't want them to be afraid," he admitted. "I want them to work hard."

"Most people can be motivated by a common goal a whole lot better than by intimidation."

"What intimidation? You're not scared of me."

"I don't work for you. Well, I guess I kind of do, but I know you. They don't. You can be a scary guy and you use that to your advantage. Maybe that was a successful strategy at one time, but now it's getting in your way."

"I'm not going to get all touchy-feely. I don't care about their feelings."

"Maybe not, but you don't have to be so obvious about it. You know I'm right about the day care problem. You should look into it."

She was right, dammit. Even more frustrating, he wasn't pissed anymore. How had she done that?

"You're a strange woman, Annie McCoy."

She smiled. "Part of my charm."

It was more than charm, he thought, reaching for her hand. He laced his fingers with hers, then pulled her close. She came willingly, leaning across the console. He stretched toward her, then pressed his mouth to hers.

Annie had never experienced makeup sex, but she'd heard it was terrific. If the fire shooting through her the second Duncan's lips touched hers was any indication of what it could be like, it was something she was going to have to look into.

Her body was energized from their argument. She'd enjoyed battling with him, knowing she could stand up for herself. While he could easily overpower her physically, emotionally they were on equal ground. And they would stay that way. A feeling in her gut told her Duncan fought fair.

She tilted her head, wanting more from the kiss. He tangled his free hand in her hair and parted his lips. She did the same, welcoming his tongue. He tasted of Scotch and mint. Heat from his body warmed her. She leaned closer and wrapped her arm around his neck.

They kissed deeply, straining toward each other. She ached inside—her breasts were swollen and there was a distinct pressure between her legs. If the car console hadn't been between them, she would have had a tough time keeping herself from pulling off his jacket and tearing off his shirt.

But instead of suggesting they take this somewhere else, he straightened, putting distance between them.

In the dark, she couldn't see his eyes and wasn't sure what he was thinking.

"You're a complication," he said at last.

Was that good or bad? "I'm also a Pisces who enjoys long walks on the beach and travel."

He laughed. As always, the sound made her stomach tighten.

"Dammit, Annie," he muttered before kissing her again. When he pulled back, he said, "I'm taking you home before we do something we'll both regret."

Regret? She had no plans for regrets. But not being sure of his response, she stayed silent. Wanting Duncan was one thing. Wanting Duncan and having him flat-out say he didn't want her back was more than she was willing to take on.

Courage was a tricky thing, she thought as she fastened her seat belt. Apparently she needed to work on hers.

Annie survived the next two parties fairly easily. She was getting the hang of meeting businesspeople and explaining that yes, she really did teach kindergarten and loved what she did. She'd made friends with a couple of the wives, which was nice, and had met several more business reporters. The world of the rich and successful was less intimidating than it had been at the beginning, as was Duncan himself. The only regret she felt was that he hadn't kissed her again.

She told herself it was probably for the best and in her best moments, she actually believed it. Duncan had made it more than clear that theirs was a business relationship. Anyone who didn't listen only had herself to blame if it all ended badly. She had been warned.

"What's in the box?" Duncan asked, after they'd left the marina hotel and were driving back toward her place.

She'd brought it out with her on the date and had told him she wouldn't discuss it until after the party.

"Christmas decorations," she said. "For your place. A small thank-you for all you've done."

He glanced at her. "What kind of decorations?" he asked, sounding suspicious.

"Nothing that will eat you in your sleep. They're pretty. You'll like them."

"Is that an opinion or a command?"

She grinned. "Maybe both."

"Fine," he said with a sigh. "Come on. I'll even let you put them where you think they should go."

Before she realized what he was doing, he'd gone north instead of south on the freeway. Fifteen minutes later, they pulled into underground parking at a high-rise condo building.

Annie told herself to stay calm. That his bringing her home didn't mean they'd gone from a fake couple to a real one. They were friends, nothing more. Friends who pretend dated. It happened all the time.

She followed him into the elevator where he pushed the button for the top floor. A penthouse, she thought, feeling her stomach flip over. She shouldn't be surprised.

The elevator opened onto a square landing. There were four condo doors. Duncan walked to the one on the left. He opened it and flipped on a light, then motioned for her to step inside.

The space was large and open, like the lofts she'd seen on the Home and Garden channel shows she liked. There were hardwood floors, a seating area in the middle, a flat-screen TV the size of a jumbo jet, windows with a view of Los Angeles and a kitchen off to the right. Her entire house, including the backyard, would easily fit just in what she could see. No doubt his place had more than one bathroom. Maybe she could send the twins over here to get ready on Friday nights. There would be a whole lot less screaming for the mirror at her place if she did.

Duncan closed the door, then glanced at her.

"It's nice," she said, taking in the neutral beige walls and taupe sofa. "Not a lot of color contrast."

"I like to keep things simple."

"Beige is the universal male color. Or so I've heard."

She followed him into the sitting area. Or great room. She wasn't sure what it was called. The leather furniture looked comfortable enough and there were plenty of small tables. She put her purse on a chair and set the box on the table next to it. Duncan walked into the open kitchen.

"Want some wine?" he asked.

"Sure."

He looked back at her, his eyes bright with humor. "It's not in a box."

She laughed. "Lucky me."

While he poured, she brought out her decorations. There were three musical snow globes with different holiday settings. Two flameless candles that sat on painted bases. Some garland, a snowman liquid soap dispenser and a nativity scene. The last was still in the box, the small porcelain figures protected.

She glanced around the room. The candles and the garland could go on the dining table. The snow globes fit on the windowsill. Duncan didn't seem to have any blinds to get in the way. She spotted a hall bathroom and put the soap there, then set up the nativity display on the table under the massive TV. When she was done, Duncan handed her a glass of wine.

"Very nice," he said. "Homey."

"Are you lying?"

"No."

She couldn't tell if he meant it or not. "I wanted to bring a tree, but wasn't sure you were the type."

"My housekeeper would be unamused."

She wasn't surprised.

"Want to see the rest of the place?" he asked.

She looked around at the open room, the tall ceilings, and resisted the need to say "There's more?" Instead she nodded.

Next to the half bath she'd noticed was a guest room. It was bigger than any two bedrooms at her house, but that no longer surprised her. On the other side of the bath was a study. The walls were paneled, a big wood desk stood in the middle, but what caught her attention were the trophies on the built-in bookcases. There were dozens of them, some small, some large. A few were of boxing gloves, but most were figures of a man boxing.

"You won these," she said, not really asking a question.

He nodded and sipped his wine.

She crossed the carpeted floor to read a few of the engravings. Each trophy had his name. There were dates and locations. She also saw medals in glass cases.

"I don't get it," she said, facing him. "Why do people want to hit each other?"

The corners of his mouth turned up. "It's not all about hitting. There's an art to it. A talent. You need power but also smarts. When to hit and where. You have to out-think your opponent. It's not all about size. Determination and experience play a part."

"Like in business," she said.

"The skill set translates."

She wrinkled her nose. "Doesn't it hurt when you get hit?"

"Some. But my uncle raised me. Boxing is what I knew. Without it, I would have just been some kid on the streets."

"You're saying hitting people kept you from being bad?"

"Something like that. Put down your glass."

She set it on the desk. He did the same, then stepped in front of her.

"Hit me," he said.

She tucked both hands behind her back. "I couldn't."

The amusement was back. "Do you actually think you can hurt me?"

She eyed his broad chest. "Probably not. And I might hurt myself."

He shrugged out of his suit jacket, then unfastened his tie. In one of those easy, sexy gestures, he pulled it free of his collar and tossed it over a chair.

"Raise your hands and make a fist," he said. "Thumbs out."

Feeling a little foolish, she did as he requested. He stood in front of her again, this time angled, his left side toward her.

"Hit me," he said. "Put your weight behind it. You can't hurt me."

"Are you challenging me?"

He grinned. "Think you can take me?"

Not on her best day, but she was willing to make the effort. She punched him in the arm. Not hard, but not lightly.

He frowned. "Anytime now."

"Funny."

"Try again. This time hit me like you mean it or I'll call you a girl."

"I *am* a girl."

She punched harder this time and felt the impact back to her shoulder. Duncan didn't even blink.

"Maybe I'd do better at tennis," she murmured.

"It's all about knowing what to do." He moved behind her and put his hands on her shoulders. "You want to bend your knees and keep your chin down. As you start the punch, think about a corkscrew." He demonstrated in slow motion.

"That will give you power," he said. "It's a jab. A good jab can make a boxer's career. Lean into the punch."

She was sure his words were making sense, but it was difficult for her to think with him standing so close. She was aware of his body just inches from hers, of the strength and heat he radiated. There were so many responsibilities in her life, so many people depending on her. The need to simply relax into his arms was powerful.

Still, she did her best to pay attention, and when he stepped in front of her again so she could demonstrate, she did her best to remember what he'd said.

This time, she felt the impact all the way up her arm. There was a jarring sensation, but also the knowledge that she'd hit a lot harder.

"Did I bruise you?" she asked, almost hoping he would say yes, or at least rub his arm.

"No, but that was better. Did you feel the difference?"

"Yes, but I still wouldn't want to be a boxer."

"Probably for the best. You'd get your nose broken."

She dropped her arms to her sides. "I wouldn't want that." She leaned closer. "Have you had your nose broken?"

"A couple of times."

She peered at his handsome face. "I can't tell."

"I was lucky."

She put her hand on his chin to turn his head. He looked away, giving her a view of his profile. There was a small bump on his nose. Nothing she would have noticed.

"You couldn't just play tennis?" she asked.

He laughed, then captured her hand in his and faced her. They were standing close together, his fingers rubbing hers. She was aware of every part of him, of the way jolts of need moved up her arm to settle in other parts of her body.

The knees he'd told her to bend went a little weak. Her mouth went dry. She shivered slightly, but from cold. His eyes darkened slightly as he seemed to loom over her. For the first time in her life, she understood the statement "getting lost in his eyes."

His gaze dropped to her mouth. He swallowed.

"Annie."

The word was more breath than sound. She heard the wanting in his voice and felt an answering hunger burning inside her. There were a thousand reasons she should run and not a single reason to stay. She knew that she was the one at risk, knew that he wasn't looking for anything permanent. But the temptation was too great. Being around Duncan was the best part of her day.

He reached for her and she went willingly into his arms. He kissed her deeply, claiming her. She responded by parting her lips, wanting all that he offered. He slipped his tongue inside. She met him stroke for stroke, feeling the waves of shivers washing through her. Even as his mouth claimed hers, his hands were everywhere. Tracing the length of her spine, squeezing the curve of her butt, sliding up her hips to her waist.

There was a confidence to Duncan, a sureness that allowed her to relax. His strength made her want to surrender, because being around him was inherently safe.

She raised her hands to his shoulders, feeling the smoothness of his shirt against her palms. She brushed the back of his neck, then slid her fingers through his short dark hair. When he moved his hands up her sides, toward her breasts, she tensed in anticipation.

There was no fumbling, no hesitation. He cupped her curves in his palms, then used his thumb and forefinger to gently tease her tight nipples.

Sensations shot through her. As he brushed her nipples again and again, she found it difficult to breathe. She sucked on his tongue, then plunged into his mouth, taking as well as giving. She moved her hands up and down his back, feeling his strength. There were muscles everywhere. She supposed she could have been afraid, but she wasn't. Not of him.

He found the zipper to her dress and drew it down. She pulled back enough to shrug out of the short sleeves. The dress pooled at her feet. Wearing nothing but bikini panties and a low-cut bra, she gazed into his eyes. The fire there, the raw wanting, gave her courage. She looked lower and saw his erection.

Annie had always been a shy lover. She preferred the lights off and not a lot of talking. She hoped for the best and was understanding when the man in question seemed confused about what to do for her. She'd never found the act of making love anything other than…nice.

Watching Duncan's face tighten with need gave her a courage she hadn't realized she had. Holding his gaze with her own, she reached behind her and unfastened her bra. When it fell, a muscle in his cheek twitched. She reached for his hands, took them in hers, then brought them to her bare breasts.

The sensation of skin on skin made her gasp. Even as he caressed the sensitive skin, he bent down and took one of her nipples in his mouth. He sucked deeply, pulling until she felt the answering tug between her thighs. He moved to the other breast.

Back and forth, licking and sucking, arousing her until every inch of her skin was on fire. She was ready to be taken, right there in the living room, on the sofa, the kitchen counter. At this point, she wasn't picky. Anything that would relieve the building pressure inside her.

As if reading her mind, Duncan moved a hand across

her belly, then to the edge of her panties. He tugged at the elastic. The scrap of fabric fell and she stepped out of it.

Naked except for her shoes, she stood before him. She expected him to lead her to the bedroom. Instead he stunned her by dropping to his knees in front of her. He reached between her legs and gently parted her, then bent toward her and kissed her intimately.

It was a kiss unlike any other, she thought, her eyelids sinking closed as perfect pleasure swept through her. The hot, warm friction of his tongue on that one sensitive spot made her tremble. She had to hold on to his shoulder to keep from falling. Over and over he stroked her, licking that single place again and again.

The steady pace caused her to tense. He seemed to know exactly where and how often and just the right pressure. She had trouble breathing. She wanted to part her legs and press against him, but told herself to stay in control. Only, control seemed impossible.

Back and forth, back and forth, he moved his tongue against her. Her muscles tightened, she strained toward a heat, a force she couldn't understand and didn't want to stop. Her heart pounded in her chest. Then he slid one finger between her legs, pushing into her and rubbing her from the inside in perfect rhythm with his tongue.

Her climax exploded without warning. She opened her legs wider, wanting to feel all of it. The pleasure flooded her, making it difficult to stay standing. Her body shook and trembled, her legs threatened to give way. She called out his name and hung on as the pleasure slowly faded.

She'd barely found her way back to normal when he stood and swept her up in his arms. No one had carried her before, but she was too boneless to do anything but hang on.

He took her to the other side of the condo, into a large master suite. Light spilled in from the hallway. She had a brief impression of a large bed, a fireplace and more tall windows, although these were covered. He lowered her to the bed.

Somewhere along the way, she'd lost her shoes. Naked, she sat up to watch him quickly undress. When he pulled off his shirt, she saw the muscles she'd only felt before. He was as big and powerful as she'd imagined. He kicked off his shoes, pulled off his socks, then removed his pants and briefs in one quick movement.

His erection was impressive and a little scary. He pulled a box of condoms out of the dresser drawer, then slid next to her on the bed. But instead of going into his arms, she sat up so she could look at him. She put a hand on his chest and felt the sculpted muscles there. She traced the length of his thigh, smiling as his arousal jumped slightly as she moved by without touching. She explored the hair angling down his belly and ran her fingers along the outline of his six-pack.

Once again she was aware of his physical power. That he could crush her without breaking a sweat. She looked into his eyes, then reached for his erection and stroked the length of him. His mouth curved in a satisfied male smile.

"Want to be on top?" he asked.

"Next time."

What she really wanted was to feel him over her, moving in her. She wanted to run her fingers across his shoulders and arms, reveling in the force and power of him.

Without warning, he shifted. Suddenly he was kneeling over her and she was on her back. He put on the condom, then eased open her thighs.

She reached down to guide him in. He pushed into her, moving slowly, steadily, stretching her, filling her until the pressure was beyond exquisite. He braced himself and thrust in her again.

She lost herself in the sensation of him inside her. She gave herself over to their lovemaking, wrapping her legs around his hips and hanging on for the ride. Happy nerve endings came to life again. She'd wanted to watch his face as he got closer, but found her eyes slipping closed as the pleasure filled her, taking her beyond where she'd ever been before.

Seven

Duncan stood by the coffeemaker. He'd already showered and dressed. On a normal morning, he would have left for work by now. But nothing about this morning was normal.

Annie had spent the night.

There were several problems with that statement. Usually he preferred to be at the woman's place so he could control when he left. But between the twins, Kami and what he would guess was a small, girly bedroom, his place made more sense. There was also the fact that last night hadn't exactly been planned. When he and Annie had set up their deal, he'd promised her he wasn't interested in sex. Apparently he'd been lying.

While making love with her had been pretty damned great, he was concerned about what happened next. Annie wasn't like his usual women, nor was she the affair type. Would she read too much into what had happened between them? Would she expect things? He also didn't want her to get hurt.

He heard footsteps in the hall. She walked into the kitchen, wearing the same cocktail dress she'd had on the night before. Her hair was still damp from the shower, her face free of makeup. She looked pretty and innocent and not at all the woman who had surrendered so passionately just a few hours before.

"You're looking tense," she said as she picked up one of the mugs he'd left on the counter and poured coffee. "Afraid I'm expecting a proposal?"

Shocked, he quickly said, "No." Proposal? As in…

She smiled. "I was thinking that a simple ceremony would be best, under the circumstances. The twins and Kami will want to be bridesmaids, of course."

He'd thought she might be confused or upset or even embarrassed. He'd been wrong on all three counts. It had been a long time since a woman had surprised him in a good way.

He crossed to her and took her free hand in his. "Will you wear white, my darling?"

She sighed. "I was trying to make you nervous."

"I was playing along."

"You were supposed to be scared."

He kissed her. "Maybe next time." He released her hand.

"You're too in control of every situation," she complained, then sipped her coffee. "While you were snoring away, I had to stumble through a conversation with Jenny, trying to explain why I wasn't coming home without mentioning the fact that we'd had sex."

He looked at her. "Why would she have to know anything?"

"Because everyone would have noticed my empty bed and been worried."

"Life is easier without family."

"You're too cynical. One phone call is a small price to pay for having the girls in my life and don't pretend you don't understand that."

He did understand but didn't agree the price was worth it.

She smiled. "Now you have the thrill of them knowing about your sex life."

Something he could have lived without. Not that he didn't like the girls, but didn't this fall under the category of too much information? "Tell me they didn't ask any questions," he muttered.

"Only if you'd used a condom."

Annie kept her chin high as she spoke, but he saw the flush on her cheeks. She was an interesting combination of shy and determined, bossy and yielding.

"What did you say?"

She cleared her throat. "I said you had…. All three times."

He held in a grin. "And?"

"Jenny hung up."

They laughed together.

Annie looked good in the morning light. The riot of still-damp curls seemed to glow, like a halo. Her mouth was full, her cheeks still pink. Hers was a quiet beauty, he thought. One that would age well. She would be even more striking in her fifties. If he'd met her before he'd met Valentina, he would have been intrigued by the possibilities. Or maybe not. Maybe the appeal of the bad girl would have been too strong. Maybe he'd needed to be burned to learn his lesson.

And learn it he had. Trust no one. Don't give away anything for free and never, under any circumstances, risk his heart.

"You know this can't be more than it is," he said flatly.

Annie sipped her coffee, then drew in a breath. "Is that your way of saying not to get my hopes up? That this is simply a business arrangement with benefits?"

"Something like that." Too late he remembered he'd promised that sex had no part in their bargain. "When the holiday season ends, so do we."

"I've never had a relationship with an expiration date," she said, staring into his eyes, a faint smile on her lips. "It's okay, Duncan. I know the rules and I won't try to change them."

"I'm not sure I believe you. You're a happy-ending kind of woman."

"It's what I want," she admitted. "I want to find someone I can love and respect. A man who wants desperately to be with me. I want kids and a dog and some hamsters. But that's not you, is it?"

"No."

Years ago, maybe. Now, the price was too high. Getting involved meant putting too much on the line. He only played to win and in marriage, there was no guarantee. Valentina had taught him that, as well.

"You weren't supposed to sleep with me," she said.

"I know." He couldn't figure out her mood. Was she teasing or pissed? "Do you want me to apologize?"

She drew in a breath. "No. I want you to promise that when this is over, you won't tell me you want to be friends. It will just be over. You have to promise."

"We won't be friends," he said, and then felt an odd sense of loss at the words. Annie was one of the few people he liked. He would miss her. But he *would* let her go.

Annie spent the day trying not to grin like an idiot. She wasn't worried her students would notice, but her fellow teachers certainly would. Then they would start to ask questions and she wasn't that good a liar. Probably a good quality, she told herself as she drove into her driveway and got out of the car. Under normal circumstances.

As she walked to the mailbox, she felt the lingering soreness in her legs and hips. Muscles not used to being stretched and used complained a little. Not that she minded. It was a good kind of ache—one that reminded her what had happened the night before. In Duncan's bed.

No regrets, she'd promised herself and that was how

she felt. No regrets. Being with him had been spectacu-
lar. Her body had done things she hadn't known were
possible. The time in his arms had shown her what she
wanted in her life. Not just a great love, but also great
passion. With the two other men, she'd been settling.
She hadn't realized it at the time, but it was true. She
would never settle again.

"Big words for someone who isn't even dating," she
murmured, picking up the envelopes and flipping
through them. "Well, not real dating." No matter how
much she wanted him to, Duncan didn't count.

She reached the last envelope and winced. It was
from the college, probably reminding her that tuition
had to be paid. As she opened the envelope, she
thought about her sad little bank account and
wondered where she was going to find the money.
Everything was so expensive. Maybe after the holidays she should get serious about finding a second job.
One that…

Annie stared at the single sheet of paper. The one that
said the tuition had been paid for for the rest of the year.
Not just the quarter but the year. Paid in full.

. Just looking at the total made her feel queasy. But
the big "Paid" next to it wasn't possible. She hadn't
and it wasn't as if Jenny had suddenly come into a
bunch of money.

Annie walked into the house and looked through the
mail again. There was also an envelope from Julie's
college. The letter said the same thing. Tuition was
paid for for the rest of the year. In full.

The shock made sense. The information, not to mention the action required, was unexpected. Before last night she might have been a little upset but more grateful. Now she felt all twisted up inside. Confused and slightly tarnished.

Dropping the rest of the mail, she returned to her car. The drive to Duncan's office wasn't far. His shipping empire was run out of a huge complex of buildings close to the Port of Los Angeles. She gave her name to the guard at the gate and had to wait while a series of calls were made. Finally she was given a visitor's parking permit and directions to where she should park.

She passed large warehouses and eighteen-wheelers waiting to be loaded. There were dozens of people walking and driving in every direction. Following the signs that pointed to the corporate offices, she managed to find the visitors' parking spaces and make her way into the six-story building.

It was an empire and a half, she thought as she stood in the lobby of Patrick Industries. A huge lit board showed a world map. Thousands of lights indicated the location of various company vehicles. Little icons indicated trucks, railcars and ships.

Annie had always known Duncan was a rich, powerful man. But those were just words. They hadn't been real. An intellectual understanding wasn't the same as looking at that map and seeing how incredibly successful he was.

She tugged at the sleeve of her oversize sweater,

aware that the Christmas elves dancing across the front and back of it were great for a kindergarten classroom but a little out of place in corporate America. There was a big paint stain on her skirt and the back was wrinkled from the time she'd spent sitting on the floor while reading to her students.

"Ms. McCoy?"

Annie turned toward the speaker. A well-dressed woman in her thirties smiled.

"Mr. Patrick is expecting you. If you'll follow me, please."

Annie nodded.

They took the elevator to the sixth floor and stepped out onto a quiet floor of conference rooms and offices. People in suits moved purposefully, barely glancing at her. She followed the woman to an open double door. Inside, a middle-aged woman nodded.

"You can go right in."

Annie stared at the tall, wood door in front of her. It looked heavy and impressive. Unexpected nerves danced in her stomach.

Still clutching the letters from the colleges, she opened the door and walked into Duncan's office.

The space was even larger than his condo. Big windows overlooked the shipping yard on one side and the lobby on the other. Apparently this particular king enjoyed looking at his empire.

His desk was practically big enough for a plane to land on. There was a grouping of sofas in one corner and a conference table in another.

The man himself sat looking at a computer screen. He tapped a few keys, then glanced at her and raised his eyebrows.

"An unexpected pleasure," he said as he stood and walked around the desk.

He looked good. Too good. She'd seen him in his tailored suits before, so that wasn't anything she couldn't handle. Maybe the problem was less than twelve hours ago, she'd been in his bed and they'd both been naked. They'd slept in a tangle of legs and arms, only to awaken and make love again.

He stopped in front of her. "Everything all right?" he asked. "You look pale. Don't you feel well?"

Apparently unable to speak, she thrust the letters at him, then managed to find her voice. "You did this, didn't you? I won't even ask how you got the information to make the payments. It was the twins, wasn't it? You talked to them."

One corner of his mouth curved up. "I thought you weren't going to ask."

She shook the papers. "This isn't funny. You can't go around doing this."

"Helping people? I would have thought you would approve. Aren't you the one who told me it would be easier to actually *be* nice than to hire you and pretend?"

"What?" She dropped her arm to her side. "Duncan, why did you do this?"

"Because I could. Are you the only one who gets to be nice?"

"Don't be reasonable." She was tired from lack of

sleep and felt the beginnings of a headache. "It makes me uncomfortable."

His smile faded. "That's not what I wanted. It's just a check, Annie. Don't make it into anything else."

"A big check. Two big checks." She glanced around to make sure they were alone, then lowered her voice. "We had sex. You can't buy me stuff."

The humor returned. "Most women would tell you the opposite. That after sex is when the buying begins."

"Maybe. If we were dating. But we're not. We have an arrangement. A deal. This isn't part of the deal."

"You're complaining because I'm giving you more?"

No. She was worried that if he was nice, if he was approachable and kind, she wouldn't have a chance of getting out of this with her heart in one piece.

The truth slammed into her and it was all she could do to stay standing. Of course. Why hadn't she realized it before? Duncan was a force of nature and she was just a regular person. He was rich and strong and powerful and unlike anyone she'd ever known. She'd been in trouble from the second they'd met.

"I…" She swallowed. "You didn't have to do this."

"I wanted to."

"It will make things a lot easier. Thank you."

He moved close and cupped her face in his large hands. "Was that so hard?"

"No."

He was going to kiss her and she was going to let him. It was already too late to try to protect herself. The best she could do was see this to the end and pray she wasn't totally devastated when it was over. A test of strength, she thought. A trial by fire.

His mouth moved against hers in a way that had become familiar. There was always the taking, but it was tempered somehow. Maybe by her own hunger, her need for him.

She released the papers and let them fall to the floor so she could wrap her arms around his neck. He drew her against him and she went willingly. The kiss deepened. Passion swept through her. Now, she thought, burning with hunger. She wanted him now.

She squirmed to get closer and felt his arousal, thick and hard against her belly. It would be so easy, right here on his big desk. The one in the room with all the windows. Where anyone could see or walk in.

He drew back and looked into her eyes. "Reality check."

She nodded. "There are a lot of people all around."

"At the time, the windows seemed like a good idea."

Now it was her turn to smile. "And today?"

"Not so good."

He kissed her again, more lightly this time. Then he released her.

She stepped away reluctantly. He picked up the papers she'd dropped and handed them to her.

She folded them and put them in her purse. "Thank you for doing this. It really helps."

"You're welcome." He put his arm around her and guided her to the door. "My uncle Lawrence wants to meet you."

"I'd like to meet him, too." she said. Maybe find a moment to ask what Duncan had been like when he'd been younger.

"How about Sunday for dinner? My place?"

"I'd like that."

She'd like a lot more, she thought as she made her way back to her car. A chance to make this all real. A foolish wish, she reminded herself. Duncan had been clear about what he wanted from the beginning. From all that she knew, he wasn't the kind of man who changed his mind about anything.

After Annie left, Duncan found it difficult to refocus on work. The report on his computer was a lot less interesting than it had been before she'd stopped by. He found himself wanting to go after her. Maybe take her to his place for the rest of the afternoon...and the evening. But he had meetings and something inside him warned him that he would have to be careful. He didn't want her reading too much into their relationship. He appreciated all that Annie had done and didn't want her getting hurt.

At four, his assistant buzzed to tell him a Ms. Morgan had arrived for their meeting. Duncan glanced at his calendar, then frowned as he couldn't place the name. Someone from accounting, the note said.

"Send her in."

Seconds later a short, fifty-something woman walked in and smiled shyly. She wore her hair short and had on a drab suit and sensible shoes.

"Ms. Morgan," he said, pointing to the chair on the other side of his desk.

"Thank you for seeing me, Mr. Patrick."

The woman had a folder in her hands. She looked both determined and nervous.

When she was seated, he offered her coffee, which she refused. She cleared her throat.

"I talked to Annie at the Christmas party," she began. "She's very nice and when I mentioned I had some ideas about making a few changes, she encouraged me to come talk to you."

Typical, he thought, both annoyed and unsurprised. "Annie is a big believer in communication," he said shortly.

Ms. Morgan swallowed. "Yes, well, I thought about what she said and decided to make the appointment. I'm a CPA, Mr. Patrick. I wasn't sure if you knew that. I'm required to take continuing education every year. I recently attended a class on depreciation."

"Rather you than me," he murmured.

She flashed him a smile. "It was more interesting than it sounds. There have been several changes in the tax code that could have a big impact on the bottom line. If I could just show you."

She opened the folder and passed over several pages. They went over them, line by line, as she explained how they weren't taking advantage of new classifications and schedules. The small changes were significant when applied to his large fleet of trucks.

"The tax savings alone is well into the high six figures," she said twenty minutes later.

"Impressive. Thank you, Ms. Morgan. I appreciate you bringing this to my attention. I'll speak to the vice president of finance and make sure these changes are implemented."

His employee beamed. "I'm happy to help."

She was. He could see it in her pleased expression. He'd always been one to manage through fear and intimidation. He'd never nurtured anyone, preferring to do it himself rather than be part of a team. Growing the company had required him to change his style. Entrepreneurs either learned how to work in a large organization or their companies stayed small.

But while Duncan had learned the lesson, he'd never liked it. Now, watching Ms. Morgan gather up her papers, he saw the benefit of encouragement. Maybe Annie was right. Maybe he should talk to his employees more. Trust them to do the right thing. Reward good behavior. What was it she'd told him? Set limits and reinforce them often.

"You'll be getting a check for ten percent of the savings," he said.

Ms. Morgan blinked at him. "Excuse me?"

"You're saving the company a lot of money. I appreciate that. You'll share in the benefit. It's a new policy. I want to encourage people to offer suggestions that either grow the business or save us money. If we implement the idea, that employee gets ten percent of the increase in sales or the savings."

The color drained from her face. "But ten percent of that amount is nearly my year's salary."

He shrugged. "That makes it a good day."

She opened her mouth, then closed it. "You're sure?"

He nodded.

"Thank you, Mr. Patrick. I'm— I don't know what to say. Thank you. Thank you."

She rose and hurried out. By the time she got to the door, he was pretty sure she was crying.

When he was alone, Duncan leaned back in his chair. He felt good—like he'd done the right thing. Maybe it was possible to find the occasional win–win scenario, he thought as he turned back to his computer. He began to type an e-mail to his chief operating officer, explaining the new policy of giving employees ten percent of saving or sales increases. Maybe someone in PR could leak the memo to the press. That should go a long way to getting him off the meanest CEO list.

After that, he would move forward with his plan to buy out his board and run the company himself. The way he liked—answering to no one. Although he would keep the new policy. Not for Annie, he told himself. He'd keep it because it made business sense.

Eight

Annie knocked on Duncan's front door. She was more nervous than she had been before their first date, but this anxiety had nothing to do with Duncan. Instead she was about to meet his only living family member—Lawrence Patrick—and she desperately wanted the older man to like her.

She'd brought a Bundt cake and two DVDs, but wasn't sure about either. Maybe she should have brought her cousins or Kami to be a distraction.

The door opened and she saw a tall, handsome, older man with graying hair and eyes that were exactly like Duncan's.

"You must be Annie," the gentleman said. "Come in, come in. I've been waiting to meet you, but Duncan has insisted on keeping you all to himself. Probably because he knows I have a way with the ladies." Lawrence winked at her, then gave her a warm smile that melted away her nervousness.

He took the cake container from her and sniffed. "Do I smell chocolate? My favorite."

"I'm glad. It's lovely to finally meet you," she said, closing the door behind her.

"And you, young lady. I'm hearing very good things about you. My nephew isn't one to speak well of others, so you must be something special."

Duncan strolled toward them. "Come on, Lawrence," he said with a resigned sigh. "Let's wait at least ten minutes before you go telling Annie all of my flaws."

His uncle chuckled. "All right, but no longer." He turned to Annie. "Duncan has a teleconference with China in a few minutes. We'll have plenty of time to get to know each other while he's tied up."

"I look forward to it," she said.

"Great," Duncan muttered, but there was humor lurking in his gray eyes and he pulled her close for a brief kiss. "Don't fall for the old guy's charm. He's had decades of practice with the ladies."

She laughed. "Maybe I like a man who knows what he's doing."

"Sassy," Lawrence said. "I like that."

They went into the great room. Annie pulled out one of the DVDs she'd brought. "I saw this and couldn't resist."

Lawrence stared at the cover, then started laughing.

Duncan shook his head. "You're encouraging him."

Annie set the copy of the movie *Rocky* on the coffee table and settled on the sofa across from Lawrence. The older man took a comfortable chair, while Duncan sat next to her.

"Rocky was a southpaw," Lawrence told her. "Left handed. They're a special breed. A lot of fighters don't want anything to do with them. They can't adjust. A great boxer knows how to think, how to anticipate."

Duncan stood. "I'm going to get ready for my call. Feel free to doze off, Annie. Lawrence loves to talk."

"I'll be telling her your secrets," Lawrence said.

"I have no doubt."

Duncan went into his study. Lawrence barely waited for the door to close before saying, "I know about the deal you have with Duncan. Why you're helping him."

"Oh." She hadn't been expecting him to say that. "My brother has some problems. This seemed the only way to get him help."

"I'm not saying it's a bad thing. But you're not acting like someone doing a job. Are you that good an actress?"

She looked down at her lap, then back at him. "No. I'm not. I like Duncan. He can seem really hard and distant, but I don't think that's who he is. There's kindness in him. He's a good man."

Lawrence nodded slowly. "Not too many people see that side of him. They believe the press. It takes strength to take a failing business and grow it into an empire.

He did that. He fought his way out of his circumstances."

Circumstances Annie didn't know much about. "I know you helped raise him," she said.

"The blind leading the blind," Lawrence told her. "My sister was a flake. She was a lot younger than me—a surprise baby. Our parents were so happy to have another child. They adored her. She was spoiled, always getting her way. After they died, she took her half of the money and disappeared. A couple years later, she came back pregnant. Wouldn't say who the father was. I'm not sure she knew. She had Duncan, then took off again. That's how it was, the first dozen or so years of his life. She would come and go. It broke his heart."

Annie looked at the closed study door and wondered about the little boy who had been abandoned over and over by his mother.

"When Duncan was eleven or twelve, he told his mother to either stay or go. She had to pick. I think he was hoping she would choose to be a part of his life. Instead she disappeared. He never mentioned her again. I got word a few years later that she'd died. I told him. He said it didn't matter."

Hiding the pain, she thought sadly. Because it had to have mattered. First his mother had betrayed him, then Valentina had. Duncan had learned difficult lessons from the women who were supposed to love him. No wonder he didn't let anyone inside.

"I was hard on him," Lawrence admitted. "I didn't

know anything about raising a kid. I took him to the gym with me, taught him to box. He was set on college, which confused the hell out of me, but he made it. Got a scholarship and everything." There was pride in his voice.

"He's a good man, and a lot of that is because of you," she said.

"I hope so. You know about his ex-wife?"

She nodded.

"There was a disaster. I never liked her and I'm glad she's gone, but now I worry Duncan won't ever settle down. He needs a family. Someone to come home to."

Not a very subtle message, Annie thought, wishing it were a possibility. "Duncan was very clear," she said. "This is a business relationship, nothing more."

"Is that what you want?"

A simple question with an easy answer. "I'm not the only one who gets to decide."

"Maybe not, but you can influence him."

"You're giving me too much credit."

"You'd be surprised."

If only, she thought. After all he'd been through, she wasn't sure Duncan would ever be willing to give his heart and she couldn't settle for anything less.

"I hope he finds someone," she said.

"Even if that means someone other than you?"

"Of course."

Lawrence stared at her for a long time. "You know what? I believe you. Which makes me hope things work out. Don't give up on my nephew, Annie. He's not easy, but he's worth it."

Before she could say anything in response, the study door opened and Duncan came out.

"You about done telling her all my secrets?" he asked his uncle."

"No, but we made a good start at it."

Duncan chuckled. "Glad I could help. Ready to watch the movie?"

"Sure." Lawrence winked at her. "While he's playing with his electronics, let me tell you about the time I beat a southpaw. It was back in '72. Miami. Talk about a hot day."

Duncan groaned, putting the DVD into the player.

"I don't mind," Annie said honestly. "Were you the favorite?"

Lawrence grinned. "Honey, I was practically a god."

Annie shelved her heart-to-heart with Lawrence as her commitments with Duncan took center stage. The following Monday, she attended a party at an art gallery that featured stark modern paintings that were beyond confusing. The single tiny red dot on the snow-white canvas was the least of the strangeness. There was a collection of black paintings. Just black. Apparently they were supposed to represent bleakness, and as far as she was concerned, the artist had done a fine job.

Wednesday night was a charity fund-raiser with an auction of ornaments painted by celebrities. Duncan bought a beautiful tree done by Dolly Parton. For Lawrence, he claimed, but Annie wondered if he might have a little crush on the singer himself. Tonight was a dinner at the Getty Museum in Malibu. Duncan was picking her up at five, which meant she had to be home no later than four so she could get ready. She was nearly on time, a positive sign. Then she felt the telltale uneven thudding that signaled another flat tire.

"No!" Annie yelled, slapping her steering wheel. "Not tonight. It's not a good time." Although she couldn't think when a better time might be. She was always running somewhere.

She pulled into a mini-mart parking lot and got out of her car. The sun blazed down on her. It might be December everywhere else, but in L.A. it felt like August.

She walked around her car. Sure enough, the right front tire was flat. She had a spare and a jack. She even knew how to change the tire. Assuming she could get the lug nuts unfastened.

She glanced at her watch, groaned at the time, then reached for her cell phone. No way she was going to be ready by five.

Seconds later the call was picked up. "Mr. Patrick's line."

"Annie McCoy for Duncan."

"Of course, Ms. McCoy. I'll put you right through."

"Another crisis?" Duncan asked when he took the call.

"Yes. I have a flat tire. I'll be a little late. Do you want me to meet you there?"

"You need new tires."

She stared at the worn treads and rolled her eyes.

"Obviously. I'll get them. I've been saving. In another two months I'll have enough."

"It's nearly the rainy season. You need them before then."

Probably, but no amount of needing brought in more money each month. She rubbed her temple, feeling the exhaustion creep into her bones. She'd been out late every night this week and still had to get up early for school. Fifteen five-year-olds kept her running all day. The last thing she needed was Duncan stating the obvious.

"I appreciate the heads-up," she said, trying not to sound as annoyed as she felt. "Look, it's hot, I'm tired. Just tell me what you want me to do."

"Let me buy you the tires."

"No." She drew in a breath. "No, thank you."

"You're supposed to be where I say, when I say. If new tires are required to get you there, then you'll get new tires."

"That is not a part of our deal," she told him, angry and sad at the same time. "You're not buying me tires. You're not buying me anything else. The freezer was too much, and I've already accepted that."

"Why are you mad?"

"I just am." She wanted to get out of the sun and heat. She wanted to curl up somewhere and sleep for two days. But mostly she didn't want to be Duncan Patrick's charity case.

"Annie? Talk to me."

"I don't have anything to say. I'll meet you there. I know how to change a tire. It won't take long."

He was silent. Worry replaced annoyance.

"Duncan, I'm sorry I snapped. I know this is part of our deal. I'm not backing out of it."

"Is that what you think? That after all this time, I would pull your brother out of rehab and toss him in jail?"

"No, but…"

"Which means yes."

"It means I owe you. I'm just crabby. It's hot, I'm tired. Let me get home and dressed and I'll be better."

"No," he said. "Just go home. You've got the Christmas play at school tomorrow night. You have to be rested for that."

"Winter festival," she corrected.

"Right. Because everyone is fooled."

"Exactly." Her bad mood faded a little. "I want to come to the party."

"No, you don't. Go home. Rest. It's okay."

She could take a bath, she thought wistfully. Sip some wine from the box. "Really?"

"Yes. About the tires…"

She groaned. "Don't make me have to hit you the next time I see you. I have a great jab."

"You have a sad excuse for a jab. It would be like being attacked by a butterfly."

Probably true, she thought. "You're not buying me tires."

"What if I set up an employee discount? I buy a lot of tires for my trucks. I have a service bay here. If it was available to everyone who worked here, would you use it?"

She would guess a lot of Patrick Industries employees would appreciate the discount as much as she would. For the greater good, she told herself. "After I see the announcement in writing."

"You're a tough negotiator."

"I spend my day dealing with five-year-olds. I have skills."

"I can see that. Are you okay changing the tire? I could send someone."

"By the time he got here, I'd be finished. I've done this before."

"Call me when you get home so I know you're okay."

The request stunned her. "Um, sure. I will."

"Okay. Bye."

"Bye."

She pressed the end button to disconnect the call, then walked around to the trunk where the jack and spare waited.

Suddenly it wasn't nearly as hot as it had been and she wasn't tired anymore. Duncan wanted her to let him know she was all right. He worried about her. Maybe it wasn't much, but as it was all she had, she was going to hang on to it with both hands.

Friday evening, Annie checked to make sure all her students were in their white men's T-shirts, with the fabric wings sewn on the back. Glitter-covered cardboard halos bounced over the five-year-olds' small heads. Once everyone was accounted for, she took a second to glance through the edge of the thick drapes to see if Duncan had arrived. Something she'd been doing every half minute or so since she'd arrived.

He still wasn't there. Which was fine, she told herself. He'd said he would *try* to get there, which was probably a polite way of saying he wasn't interested. It wasn't as if they were really dating. What gorgeous single guy wanted to spend Friday night with a bunch of other people's kids?

She held in a sigh as she backed away from the drapes. Only to bump into something warm and solid.

She turned and saw Duncan standing behind her.

"What are you doing here?" she blurted.

"You asked me to come."

She laughed, hoping she wasn't blushing. "No, I mean backstage."

"I wanted to say hi before the program started. One of the moms is saving me a seat."

Annie took in the broad shoulders, the strong features and the way he filled out his suit. "I'll just bet she is."

"What?"

"Nothing. Thanks for coming. You didn't have to."

"I wanted to see if you were still pissed."

"I was never pissed."

Humor brightened his gray eyes. "Now you're lying about it."

"I'm not. I was annoyed. There's a difference."

"You were pissed. You were practically screaming about the tires. Talk about shrill."

He was teasing, which she liked a lot. Back when they'd first met, she would never have imagined it possible.

"I was calm and rational," she told him.

"You were a girl. Admit it."

"I could hit you right now."

"You could and no one would notice. Especially not me." He took her arm and led her into a shadowy alcove. "Here." He handed her a piece of paper.

She looked at it. The sheet was a printout of a memo, detailing the new policy on discounted tires.

"Now will you get your damn car fixed?"

She stared at him, knowing that while he'd been helping her, he was also helping a lot of other people. "I will," she said, raising herself onto tiptoes and lightly kissing him. "I promise."

He put his arms around her and pulled her close. "Good. You're a pain in the ass. You know that, right?"

She giggled. "Yes. You're dictatorial. And annoying."

They hung on to each other for several seconds. Annie loved the feel of him, the strength and heat of his body. As always, being close to him made her feel safe.

"I have to get back to my class," she said reluctantly. "They're wearing cardboard halos that won't really survive very long."

"Okay. I'll see you after the Christmas thing."

"Winter festival."

"Whatever. I'll see you."

"Yes," she said and watched him walk away.

She knew then that despite the fact that she'd only

known him a few weeks, she was well on her way to being in love with him. He was unlike anyone she'd ever met. He was better in every way possible.

He'd promised not to ask her to be friends and she trusted him to keep his word. But he'd also promised when the holiday season was over, so was their relationship. And she knew he would keep his word on that, as well. Wishing for more wouldn't change the outcome. Duncan had told her once that, in his life, somebody always won and somebody always lost. This time, she had a bad feeling the loser would be her.

Monday morning Duncan walked into his office to find a plate of cookies on his desk. They were covered in holiday plastic wrap and there was a handwritten note attached.

Dear Mr. Patrick,

Thank you so much for the new tire discount you announced on Friday. I'm a single mom with three kids and money is always tight. I've needed new tires for a while now and simply couldn't afford them. The discount means safer driving for my family.

I've always enjoyed working for Patrick Industries. Thank you for giving me another reason to be proud of my place of employment.

Have a wonderful holiday season.

Sincerely,

Natalie Jones

Accounts Payable

* * *

Duncan had no idea who the woman was or how long she'd worked for the company. He unwrapped the cookies and bit into one. Chocolate chip. His favorite.

Still chewing, he crossed to the windows overlooking the six-story atrium in the center of the building. He could see people coming in to start their week. People he'd never bothered to get to know.

Ten years ago, he would have been able to name every employee. He'd worked twenty-hour days, struggling to make the company profitable, then to grow it as quickly as possible. For the past few years, he'd had contact with his senior management team, his assistant and no one else. He didn't have time.

Who were these people who worked for him? Why had they chosen this company and not another? Did they like their jobs? Should that even matter to him?

He looked back at the note and the plate of cookies. Annie would be a disaster as a boss, giving away more than the company made. But maybe it was time for him to leave the confines of his office and remember what it was like to know his employees. To listen instead of command. To ask instead of demand. Maybe it was time to stop being the meanest CEO in the country.

Nine

Duncan had never really enjoyed his board of director meetings, but this was worse than usual. Not because they were complaining—that he could handle. It was the way they were all *smiling* at him. Beaming, really, as if with pride. What the hell was up with that?

"The last two articles on you have been excellent," his uncle said. "Very positive."

"Just doing what we agreed."

"This reporter…" One of the board members adjusted his glasses and frowned at the business journal. "Charles Patterson seems to think you've had an awakening. Who's this Annie person?"

"Annie McCoy," Lawrence said, before Duncan could answer. "The woman Duncan's seeing."

The other board members looked at him.

"You told me to find someone nice," he reminded them. "She's a kindergarten teacher. Very pretty. Charles has a crush on her."

"Well done," the oldest board member said. "You should bring her around here so we can all meet her."

"There's no need for that," Duncan said, thinking the last thing Annie needed was a bunch of old guys trying to flirt with her.

"Annie's special," Lawrence announced. "Good for Duncan, too."

Duncan narrowed his gaze. "I'm seeing her through the holidays. It's a business arrangement, nothing more. You told me to find someone nice and clean up my act. I did. Don't make it more than it is."

"It didn't look like a business arrangement to me," Lawrence said.

"Looks can be deceiving."

There was no way he was telling his uncle or anyone on the board that he also thought Annie was special. They didn't need to know how she'd wormed her way into his life. The kicker was he didn't think she'd even been trying. But regardless of his feelings for her, when the holidays were over, so was their relationship.

The board moved on to other business. When they were finished, Lawrence lingered in the conference room until the other men had left.

"Are you serious about ending things with Annie?" his uncle asked. "I saw you two together, Duncan. You like her. You should marry her."

Duncan shook his head. "I've been married."

"To the wrong woman. I don't know what Valentina wanted, but it wasn't you or a real marriage. Annie's different. She's the kind of girl you spend forever with."

This from a man who'd been married five times? "You know this how?"

"I've lived a lot longer than you. I've seen things, made bad choices. There are few regrets more painful than knowing you let the woman of your dreams get away. You've always been smarter than me about most things. Don't be an idiot now."

"Thanks for the advice," Duncan said, standing up to leave.

"But you're not going to take it."

"I did what the board asked. That's all you're getting from me."

Lawrence stared at him for a long time. "Not everyone leaves."

Duncan didn't react to the statement, even though he knew the old man was wrong. Nearly everyone who mattered left. He'd learned that a long time ago. It was better not to care. Safer.

"Annie doesn't leave," his uncle added softly. "Look at her life."

"What do you know about it?"

"What you told me. She has her cousins and their friend living with her. She's helping to pay for their college educations. She agreed to date you to help her brother, after he tried to throw her under the bus. She's not a person who gives up easily."

True, Duncan thought uneasily. Annie took responsibility, hanging on with both hands. "That's different," he said.

"It's not and you know it. Annie scares the hell out of you because with her, everything is possible. Don't let what happened before ruin this for you. Don't live with regrets about letting her go. They'll eat you alive."

"I'll be fine."

"You can keep telling yourself that, but it won't be true. You've never been afraid of anything but risking your heart. Annie's the closest to a sure thing you're ever going to find."

Duncan found himself wanting to listen, which would only lead to trouble. "Annie got into this to save her brother. It has nothing to do with caring about me."

"Maybe it didn't, but it does now. Just pay attention. All the signs are there. She's falling for you. Maybe she's already in love with you. Chances like this don't come along very often. Trust me, you don't want to blow this one."

Lawrence walked out of the conference room. Duncan stood there, alone, wondering if the old man was telling the truth. Would he regret letting Annie go? In time he would find out. His uncle was also right about Annie scaring the crap out of him. There were possibilities with her. Great ones.

But he'd already given his heart to someone. He'd already believed in forever, and he'd learned a hard lesson. Love was an illusion, a word women used to sucker punch men. Maybe Annie was different, but he didn't know if he was willing to take the chance.

Despite three late nights at the office, getting by on minimal sleep and a workout schedule that would exhaust an elephant, Duncan still couldn't get his uncle's words out of his mind. He couldn't stop thinking about Annie.

Taking a chance violated everything he knew to be true and yet…he was tempted. It was the only possible explanation for his being in a mall less than a week before Christmas, fighting the crowds and looking for presents for her cousins and Kami.

He should have had his assistant buy something online, he told himself, as yet another shopper stepped in front of him without looking. What did he know about the wants and needs of college-age girls? He was about to leave the department store when he saw a sign that proclaimed every woman loved cashmere.

There was a display of sweaters in an array of colors. A well-dressed salesperson came up and smiled. "Are you buying something for your wife or girlfriend?"

"Her cousins," he said. "And a friend. They're in college. Does cashmere work?"

"Always. You don't happen to know sizes, do you?"

He shrugged, then pointed to a young mother walking by. "About like that?"

"Got it. Do you want to pick the colors?"

"No."

"Should I gift wrap?"

"That would be great."

"Give me fifteen minutes and it will all be done. There's a coffee bar over by shoes, if you want to get away from the crowd."

He nodded and wandered in the direction of coffee, only to be stopped by a display of Christmas trees. They were small, maybe two feet, covered with twinkling white lights and miniature ornaments. The one that caught his eye was done in white and gold and decorated with dozens of angels.

They were all blonde and innocent, with big eyes. For some reason, they reminded him of Annie. He picked up the tree and carried it to the register.

Annie glanced anxiously at the box of fudge next to her. Despite her sudden stop at the unexpected light change, the box stayed firmly on the passenger seat of her car. Normally she was a careful driver who anticipated stops, but tonight she couldn't seem to get herself together. Probably because Duncan had completely rattled her with his invitation to "drop by."

They were in a lull—a four-day stretch with no parties—right before the last-minute craziness started. On Thursday, there was a party every night through Christmas Eve. When she'd first seen the party schedule, she'd been excited about the break, but now she found herself missing being around him. The four days, and nights, had seemed endless.

And then he'd called, inviting her over.

Why? She wanted it to be because he was missing

her, too, but she couldn't be sure. There was no reason to think anything about their relationship had changed—at least not from his end. She was in serious danger of falling desperately in love with him, which, if she'd thought things through at the beginning, shouldn't be a surprise. Handsome, smart, funny, caring man suddenly in her life. What was there not to like?

If only, she thought, before shaking her said. No. She was going to be sensible. Falling in love might be inevitable, but she wasn't going to let herself be swept away by her feelings. When this was over, pride might be the only thing she had left. She needed to remember that.

She parked in the guest spot, then took the elevator to his penthouse condo. Duncan opened the door right away.

"Thanks for coming," he said, his gray eyes dark with a smoldering need that made her thighs tremble.

"Thanks for asking me." She held out the box of fudge. "I made this. I don't know if you like chocolate. If not, you could take it into the office or…"

Instead of taking the candy, he grabbed her wrist and pulled her inside. The second the door closed behind her, she was in his arms, his mouth on hers.

She hung on as the world began to spin. There was only the heat and the man and how she felt pressed up against his strength. He was already aroused, his hardness flexing against her belly. She managed to shove the fudge onto a table by the door and drop her purse, before hanging on to him with both hands.

She parted her lips and he deepened the kiss. Their

tongues danced, touching, tracing, playing an erotic game. He bent her over slightly, then straightened, pulling her up off the floor.

Instinctively, she wrapped her legs around his hips. Despite being up in the air, she felt safe. Duncan would never drop her. He carried her into the bedroom, then slowly lowered her to the carpet. When her feet touched solid ground, he drew back, put his hands on her shoulders and turned her to face the room.

On the dresser there was a tiny Christmas tree. White lights twinkled, the only source of light in the huge room. She could see little angel ornaments on every branch.

Her throat got a little tight. "I thought you didn't want a tree," she whispered.

"I saw it and thought of you."

The words, whispered in her ear, made her eyes burn. Telling herself he wouldn't appreciate a girly show of emotion, she did her best to blink them away. He hugged her, pulling her close. She turned in his embrace and stared into his gray eyes.

Emotions raced through her. Not just desire, but love. There was no escaping the truth. She loved Duncan with all her heart. Whatever might happen, however it might end, she loved him.

The feeling was different, more powerful than anything she'd ever experienced. Getting over him would take a whole lot of time and effort, because as much as she wanted to believe everything would work out, she tried to be a realist. Her and Duncan? On what planet?

But for now there was the night and the man and she was determined to have as much as possible of both. She leaned into him, claiming him with a kiss. She couldn't tell him how she felt, but she could show him, she thought as she traced the powerful muscles in his arms.

She raised the hem of his sweater and ran her fingers across his broad chest. He took the hint and pulled off the sweater, then tossed it away. She pressed her lips to his breastbone, tasting his warm skin.

For a second, he was passive, accepting her caress. Then he reached for her, cupping her face and kissing her.

Even as they held on to each other, he was moving her toward the bed. When the backs of her legs bumped the mattress, he stopped. He pulled back enough to pull off her knit shirt. She stepped out of her shoes. Then they were tumbling onto the bed, him landing next to her.

They reached for each other. Even as they kissed, she reached for the hooks on her bra. She wanted to feel her bare breasts against his chest. He pushed her hands away and unfastened the bra in one easy movement. The lace-covered garment went flying.

Her jeans followed, as did his. She barely had time to notice that his briefs were also gone, before he settled his hand on her stomach.

Up or down, she thought, rolling onto her back. Either would work for her. He could move up or down. Another moment of hesitation and his fingers moved down. When he reached the barrier of her panties, he gripped the elastic and peeled them down. His large, strong hands made the return trip slowly, massaging as he went, teasing the insides of her knees before trailing up her thighs. He moved closer and closer to the promised land, but didn't touch her most sensitive spot. She held her breath, wanting, desperate, willing to do anything to have him touch her there. While he kissed her breasts, he rubbed his fingers against her inner thigh, then up onto her belly, making her squirm in anticipation.

Finally, slowly, he shifted again and slid through her swollen flesh. He touched the tiny center of her pleasure. A shiver raced through her. Gently at first, never pressing too hard or going too fast, he began to circle. Slowly, then a little more quickly, pushing her forward. She rotated her hips in time with him. Sensations raced through her. Muscles tensed. There was nothing but the movements and how he made her feel. Closer and closer still. Until the fall was inevitable.

She hung suspended for a brief moment. Intense pleasure pulsed through her and then she was falling. She came over and over, shuddering and moaning. He continued to touch her, gently, lightly, drawing out her release.

When she opened her eyes, he was watching her. His gray eyes seemed to see down to her soul. She smiled slowly, then kissed him.

"Thank you. That was…nice."

His eyebrows shot up. "Nice?"

She laughed. "Very nice. Extremely nice."

"You're crushing my ego."

She reached between them and stroked his erection. "Your ego seems to be doing just fine. We should take advantage of that."

"If you insist."

"I do."

In a matter of seconds, he put on a condom and was nudging at her thighs. She shifted to welcome him.

He filled her with one long, steady thrust. She felt herself stretching as he pushed in again and again. The sensation was delicious. Pleasure hardened his features, pulling at the muscles. His eyes were closed.

She closed hers as well, enjoying the ride—focusing on him and what he was feeling. She was so aware of his movements that at first she didn't even notice the pressure deep inside. The sort of tingling ache, the instinct to move against him, increasing the friction. The need started slowly, then grew more frantic. She found herself clinging to him, wanting him to go faster, deeper, harder.

She opened her eyes and found Duncan watching her. She couldn't control herself. This wasn't quiet, almost-boring sex. This was messy, frenzied desire. She held on to his upper arms, pumping her hips with each thrust. She opened her mouth to gasp in a breath and found herself panting. Her body wasn't her own. There was a driving force she didn't understand and couldn't control. There were—

Her climax caught her off guard. One second she was doing her best to catch her breath and the next she was lost in a shuddering, convulsing release that caused her to arch her back and cry out in a way she never had before. Her muscles tightened over and over again, then Duncan moaned and shuddered. They came together, a tangle of need and pleasure.

When they were done, Annie knew nothing would ever be the same again. She would never be the same. *She* might not be able to win Duncan, but she would never settle for anything less than loving someone with all her heart. That's what had been missing before, she thought, blissfully exhausted. True love and passion. An explosive combination.

Later, when Annie lay next to him, her head on his shoulder, his arm around her, she closed her eyes. She had to remember everything about this moment, everything that had happened. So later she could relive each moment in detail.

"Going to sleep?" he asked, his voice teasing.

"No. Enjoying the aftermath. Making love with you is pretty amazing."

"Thank you. Amazing is much better than nice."

She smiled, opened her eyes, then shifted so her chin was on his chest and she could stare into his eyes. "That's not what I mean. The other guys I was with—all two of them—weren't like you. Or maybe it was me. But I never felt…" She sighed. "It wasn't the same thrill ride."

He frowned. "Why not? Don't take this wrong, Annie, but you're easy."

She sat up, pulling the sheet with her so she stayed

covered. Easy? She'd been thinking love and romance and he thought she was easy?

He sat up as well, then raised both hands. "I take it back. I should have said responsive. I've been with women who are difficult to get over the edge. You're not one of them." He smiled. "That's a good thing. Having you do what you do is the best kind of positive reinforcement."

"Oh. Okay."

"It wasn't like that with the other guys?"

"No. Sex was kind of…uninteresting." And she hadn't been truly in love with them. She got that now.

"No fireworks?"

"Not even a sputter. I liked it, but I never got the fuss." Now the fuss was perfectly clear. The fuss was her favorite part.

He shifted his pillow so it was behind his back, then leaned against the headboard. "Tell me about these guys."

"There's not much to say. I met Ron in college. He was studying engineering. I'm not sure he'd been with anyone before. I know I hadn't. We sort of figured it out together."

"Or not," Duncan said. "If you weren't happy."

"I was happy." She hadn't known there was more. Not physically or emotionally.

"Satisfied, then."

"I didn't know what to ask for. He was funny and smart and we had a good time. I thought everything was fine."

She and Ron had been together nearly three years. She thought she was in love with him and had assumed he felt the same way.

"At the beginning of our senior year, he ended things," she admitted. "He said he'd met someone else. That he didn't mean to hurt me, but she was the one. But that he and I should still be friends." She wrinkled her nose. "I passed on that offer."

"Smart move. And guy number two?"

Should there have been more men? Was two a small number? Duncan probably had dozens of women before and after Valentina.

"A.J.," she said with a sigh. "He was the assistant principal at my school. I met him my first day. We went out right away. Everything was so easy."

Duncan realized he'd made a huge mistake in asking about Annie's love life. While he wanted the information, he didn't like hearing about her with other men. The fact that the relationships had ended badly didn't change his sense of annoyance. He wanted to find both Ron and A.J. and beat the crap out of them. How dare either of them hurt Annie. Not that he wanted her with one of them now. He wanted her for himself.

Until the holidays were over, he reminded himself. Nothing more.

"He was also funny and smart. He loved kids." Annie shook her head. "I don't know. It was as if we were destined to be together. Everything fell into place. No complications. We were talking about getting married by our fifth date."

Something heavy seemed to fall into his stomach. He ignored the sensation. "What happened?"

"While I was dreaming about a June wedding, he got

a job offer from a school in Baltimore. He wanted me to go with him. Jenny and Julie were seniors in high school and living with me. I couldn't just leave them. So he went without me. We agreed to date long distance, seeing each other once a month."

"Did you miss him?"

"Sure." She shifted so she was sitting next to him, then leaned her head against his shoulder. "I thought everything was fine. Over Memorial Day weekend, he told me while there wasn't anyone else, he wasn't interested in dating me anymore. Time away had shown him he wasn't as interested in me as he'd thought. But he would very much like us to be friends." She drew in a breath. "I never knew what went wrong."

He had a feeling she really meant to say what *she* had done wrong. But how to make her understand that none of this was about her? She'd found two stupid guys. It happened.

"Better to find out before you moved in with him rather than after."

She looked up at him, her blue eyes wide with shock. "I wouldn't live with him before we were married."

He held in a smile. "But you'd sleep with him."

"That's different. It's private. Living arrangements usually aren't. I'm a teacher. What would it say to my students if I lived with a guy without being married to him? What would it say to my cousins or Kami? Children don't learn by what we say, they learn by what we do."

Not ten minutes ago, she'd been screaming in his

bed. Annie was nothing if not interesting. He could go his whole life and still not know everything about her.

"You're not giving up on Mr. Right, are you?" he asked.

"No. I'll find him." She leaned against his shoulder again. "I want to be married and have a family. I want to grow old with my husband, to be friends and lovers. I want to take care of him and have him take care of me. Which is all too traditional for you, huh?"

"I know how you enjoy your traditions."

"You don't believe in them."

"I got a tree. That's traditional."

"At least it's a start."

He sensed she needed more—needed him to make some kind of a promise. But he couldn't. He'd tried that once—trusting a woman with his heart.

Annie couldn't be more different than his ex. If he'd met Annie first… But he hadn't. And being what she needed, what she deserved, was impossible. He hoped she understood that. Nothing about their deal had changed. When it was over, he would walk away—and he wouldn't offer to be just friends.

"Why are you walking like that?" Duncan asked. "Relax."

"I can't," Annie whispered, trying to look casual, but barely able to breathe.

It wasn't the fitted evening gown that was constricting her breathing, or the four-inch heels that altered her walk. Instead it was the weight of the necklace and earrings. Not their physical weight so much as their value.

She fingered the large diamond pendant hanging several inches below her throat. She didn't know much about fancy jewelry, but this was the biggest stone she'd ever seen. There were smaller diamonds leading to the platinum chain that held the piece securely around her throat. Matching earrings dangled in her upswept hair.

The jewelry ensemble had been delivered by a burly guard who had made Duncan sign several official-looking documents before he'd handed over the velvet cases containing the treasures.

"You're insured, right?" she asked quietly. "If someone attacks me or a clasp breaks."

Duncan sighed. "I arranged for the jewelry because I thought you'd enjoy the pieces. I didn't mean for you to be nervous."

Probably true, she thought. A sweet gesture and one she really appreciated. Or she would, just as soon as she got over the burning need to vomit.

"Tell me they're not worth a million dollars and I'll relax."

He winked. "They're not worth a million dollars."

That was too easy. "You're lying."

"Me? How can you say that?"

Better not to know, she told herself as they walked into the elegant hotel ballroom. Fine. She would wear the borrowed jewelry and be excited that Duncan had wanted to make her happy. His actions were thoughtful and sweet. Once she got past the need to throw up, she would feel all quivery inside.

The party was large, with at least two hundred

people milling about and talking. As a rule Annie didn't drink at any of the cocktail parties, but she might give in and have a glass of wine. With a crowd this big, no one would be having anything close to a serious conversation and she wouldn't be expected to do much more than smile and nod. Which meant her chances of messing up were that much less.

Besides, a little wine would make the idea of wearing all those diamonds more fun than terrifying.

As they moved through the crowd, Duncan kept her close. He held her hand in his, guiding them through the crush at the entrance. She saw an open area to her left.

"There's dancing," she said.

"I thought dancing with me made you nervous."

"Not anymore."

Their eyes locked. She didn't know what he was thinking, but she was remembering the last time they'd made love. When he'd made her feel things she hadn't known were possible and she accepted the fact that she was in love with him. No maybe, no almost. Just totally and completely in love with Duncan.

Fire flared in his gaze. She felt an answering heat in her belly.

"We don't have to stay long," he told her.

"Are you sure?" she asked, her voice teasing. "I was thinking we'd be here at least three or four hours."

He drew her close. "Fifteen minutes, tops. Or we could get a room in the hotel. The suites have jetted tubs."

"And you know this how?"

"Duncan?"

The person speaking his name had a low, sexy voice—the kind that belonged on radio. Annie turned and saw an incredibly tall, beautiful woman in a sexy black dress standing next to them. The woman smiled warmly, her blue eyes sparkling with delight.

"I was hoping to see you here," she said in her throaty voice. "I've missed you so much."

Duncan stiffened. Annie felt the tension fill his body as he turned toward the woman. "What the hell are you doing here?"

The smile never wavered. "I came to see you, Duncan." The woman glanced at Annie. "Are you going to introduce me to your friend?"

He hesitated, then released Annie's hand. "Annie, this is Valentina. My ex-wife."

Ten

After convincing Annie to give him a few minutes, Duncan stood in the private alcove off the main ballroom, his arms folded across his chest, watching the woman he'd once wanted to spend the rest of his life with. Valentina stood completely still, gazing at him, a smile tugging at the corners of her lips.

"You look good," she said. "Time is such a bitch—always nicer to the men than the women."

"Why are you here?" he asked bluntly. "And spare me the bullshit."

The smile broadened. "There's no one quite like you, Duncan. My mistake was in thinking I could replace you."

"You mean do better? That was the point, wasn't it? Move up the food chain."

"Well, I suppose. I remarried, if that's what you're really asking. Eric was charming, easy to get along with." She wrinkled her nose. "Boring. I thought being rich was the most important thing in the world. I thought it gave me power and made me feel safe. I was wrong."

"Thanks for the update," he said. "I need to get back to the party."

"Wait, Duncan. Aren't you even a little happy to see me?"

He stared into her catlike eyes, then dropped his gaze to the full mouth that had known how to take him from zero to sixty in less than a minute.

When she'd first left, he'd been devastated. He'd retreated into anger, had vowed revenge, had understood the primal fury of a man longing to lock up the woman he loved. To keep her from the world. When the anger had ceased to burn quite as brightly, humiliation had joined rage. The knowledge that she had betrayed him, that he had been a fool, had kept him up nights.

He'd loved her. She had promised him everything he'd ever wanted and he'd believed her. That she would love him forever, that they would always be together. That he was the one.

Over time he'd accepted that he had been a means to an end. He'd looked back on their relationship and had seen her for what she was. The anger had faded, the wounds healed. A few days after she'd left, his uncle had told him that the opposite of love wasn't hate—it was indifference. Now, staring at the woman he'd once married, he knew that to be true.

"You don't matter enough for me to have any emotion on the subject," he said.

"Wow. Talk about honest. So you didn't miss me at all?"

He thought about those long nights when he'd lain awake, staring at the ceiling. He would have sold his soul for her return. Good thing the devil had been busy making deals with other people at the time.

"I loved you," he told her. "Having you leave hurt like a son of a bitch. So what? That was three years ago, Valentina. I've moved on."

"I wish I could say the same, but I haven't. I know I was wrong and I know I'll have to earn back your trust. That's why I'm here. I still love you, Duncan. I never stopped. I want us to have a second chance."

He heard the words, let them sink into his skin, then waited. Was there any part of him interested? Did a fiber or a cell long to be with her again? Were old scars still tender?

No, he thought with relief. There was nothing. Not a hint of longing or curiosity. She was nothing more than someone he used to know.

He started for the door. "Sorry. Not interested."

Annie sat next to Duncan in his car. After he'd gone off with Valentina, she'd circled the ballroom, smiling at anyone who had made contact with her. He'd returned to her side about ten minutes later and had said they should leave.

So much for the romantic night in the hotel room, she thought sadly.

Duncan hadn't spoken while they'd waited for the valet to bring around his car. Now, aware that he was driving to her place rather than his, she resigned herself to a very brief ending to their evening. If the girls weren't home, they would be shortly. Inviting him in wouldn't give them any time alone. She carefully removed the earrings, then the necklace and passed both back to him.

"Thank you for letting me wear these tonight."

He took them and dropped them into his suit-jacket pocket. "You're welcome. I'm sorry we didn't stay longer. After Valentina showed up…" He tightened his grip on the steering wheel. "She's back to make trouble."

What she really wanted to ask was "What did she say?" but lacked the courage, so instead she said, "How do you know?"

"She's breathing. I didn't know what kind of a scene she would make. Leaving seemed easier. I don't want you in the middle of anything."

"I appreciate that." She cleared her throat. "It must have been a shock, seeing her after all this time. It's been what? Three years?"

He nodded. "I could have gone a lot longer without having to deal with her again."

"You're going to be dealing with her?"

"I hope not, but my luck isn't that good. She wants something and she won't stop until she's made every attempt to get it."

Wanted something? As in money…or did Valentina

want Duncan back? Annie told herself she should be happy if that was what was going on. A marriage repaired was a good thing. Assuming Valentina was sincere.

Annie told herself she was mature enough, in love enough, to want what was best for Duncan. The ache in her chest and the need to cry were beside the fact.

Duncan pulled up in front of her small house. "The party tomorrow will be easier. It's smaller. Quieter. I'll pick you up at six-thirty."

He barely glanced at her as he spoke, making her realize he wasn't even going to kiss her good-night. Holding in the hurt, she forced herself to smile as she got out of the car.

"Good night, Duncan. I'll see you tomorrow."

"Good night."

She barely had time to close the passenger door before he gunned the engine and drove off. She stood on the sidewalk, watching his taillights disappear.

Telling herself he hadn't broken the rules didn't make breathing any less painful. And wondering if he was returning to the party to be with Valentina only made her wish she could go back in time a couple of hours and keep the other woman from ever speaking to Duncan in the first place. Not that she could change the past the two of them shared. A past that was very likely going to have a big impact on her present.

"Okay, so owning a bank is even better than I thought," Annie said the following night as Duncan pulled up behind a Rolls, in front of a large Beverly Hills estate. "Didn't bankers take a financial hit in the past year or so?"

"Not all of them."

It had been nearly twenty-four hours since Duncan had dropped her off the previous evening. She'd spent about twenty of them trying to convince herself that even if she wasn't fine, she could pretend. Acting might not be her gift, but she would work at faking it. He'd been his normal self when he'd arrived to pick her up, so maybe last night was like a bad dream—something that would fade in the light of day.

When she climbed out of the car, she stared at the glittering three-story mansion. It was huge, with lights everywhere, a long, wide walkway and a fountain roughly the size of a semi.

"This rich thing," she said as Duncan moved next to her. "Looks like fun."

"The taxes would kill you," he said with a grin, then leaned in and kissed her on the mouth.

"Just paying for the lightbulbs would make me whimper." She leaned into him and laughed. "Do you think they take in boarders? I mean, a room in this place would be bigger than my whole house."

"Want me to get an application?"

"If they have them lying around."

He put his arm around her and they walked toward the front door. A uniformed butler let them in. They were shown to a massive living room with a roaring fire. Sofas and comfy-looking chairs filled the football field–sized space. To the left was a bar. In front of them were four sets of French doors leading out to a huge patio.

"There is a light buffet outside," the butler told them. "The area is heated and very comfortable."

Duncan thanked the man. Annie waited until he left before whispering, "So they're the reason L.A. is always warm in the winter. They're heating the whole outdoors. Interesting."

Duncan laughed and pulled her close. She wrapped her arms around him, feeling the vibration of the sound. Then it stopped and he tensed. She felt every muscle, heard the sudden increase in his breathing and knew, without turning around, that someone else had walked into the party.

"Duncan," she breathed.

He touched her cheek and stared into her eyes. "It doesn't matter."

But she had a feeling that it mattered a lot. More than either of them wanted to admit.

Annie stepped back and turned around. Valentina stood in the entrance to the beautiful home. Her eyes locked with Duncan's, but she didn't do anything more than nod at him before walking into the party.

"You going to be all right?" he asked, pressing his hand to the small of her back and guiding her outside.

"I'm fine," she lied.

What else was there to say? That Valentina terrified her? That she believed Duncan was still in love with his ex-wife? That she'd always known she didn't have a chance with Tim's boss, but she'd allowed herself to hope and it was all going to end badly? All she could do was pray that he remembered not to tell her he wanted to be friends. It was what she'd asked for, and Duncan was the type of man to remember.

Maybe the problem wasn't Valentina, she thought as they stepped outside. Maybe it was her. Maybe she should learn to ask for more.

Time crawled by. Annie did her best not to glance at her watch every five minutes. The party was small enough that she and Duncan had to stay for at least a couple of hours. So far they'd been outside and Valentina had stayed inside, avoiding each other. She wondered if that would last for the entire party.

When Duncan got into a conversation about oil futures, she excused herself and went in search of the restroom. It was as lovely as the rest of the house, complete with a marble vanity and dozens of expensive soaps, hand creams and hair products. After she'd washed her hands and fluffed her curls, she opened the door and stepped into the hallway. Only to find Valentina waiting for her.

Duncan's ex was dressed in black pants and a cream-colored off-the-shoulder sweater. She was tall, thin and beautiful, with the kind of sleek, straight hair Annie had always envied.

"Hi," Valentina said, clutching a martini glass. "You're Duncan's girlfriend, right?"

Annie nodded slowly. The truth was different, but Valentina didn't need to know about their deal.

"Have you been going out long?" the other woman asked.

"We met in September," Annie said, hoping she didn't look as nervous as she felt. "I, ah, had a flat tire and Duncan stopped to help."

"That doesn't sound like him at all. You're a teacher?"

"Kindergarten."

"Let me guess. You're sweet and kind. You take in orphans and stray pets."

Annie couldn't read the other woman's voice. There was tension in it, but the source wasn't clear. Was she mocking Annie or herself?

"If you'll excuse me," Annie said, moving around her.

"Wait. Please. I…" Valentina set her drink on a small table and sucked in a breath. "I don't know how things are between you and it's really none of my business. I gave up any rights to Duncan a long time ago. I was stupid. I thought I could do better. I was wrong. It's not just that he's the best man I know, it's that I never stopped loving him."

Tears filled Valentina's blue eyes. One trickled down her cheek. She brushed it away impatiently.

"I want a second chance. I know it's practically impossible. He's not going to forgive me easily, but I have to try. Have you ever been in love? Have you ever known down to your bones that you'd finally found the only man on the planet who would complete you?"

Annie nodded slowly. She wanted to point out that

love wasn't about being completed. It was about giving, not getting, but that wasn't the point.

"I love him," Valentina said. "Before, when we were together, he held so much of himself apart. I think it had something to do with his past. I was young and impatient. Now I know better. He's worth waiting for, fighting for. I made a mistake and he paid the price. I'm back for a second chance. I'm back to convince him how much he means to me. To me, he's my husband. He'll always be my husband. I want a chance to make our marriage work. Can you understand that?"

Annie nodded because it would hurt too much to speak. Valentina had said the only words that would have convinced her to give up. She couldn't argue against a chance of Valentina and Duncan making their marriage work. If they were successful, maybe he could let go of his fear of being left. Maybe he would learn to love again. Better Valentina than no one, she told herself. In time, she would even believe that.

The mall might be closed at three in the morning, but the Internet was always open. Annie clicked on a link, then stared at the picture of the painting. It was small, maybe twelve-by-twelve, with a plain black frame. The artist, a famous sports painter, had chosen boxing as his subject.

The colors were vivid, the expressions fierce. There was something about the way the two men stared at each other that reminded her of Duncan.

"Annie, what are you doing up?"

She smiled at Kami, who looked sleepy as she stepped into Annie's room.

"It's late," Annie said. "You have classes."

"I could see your light was still on."

"Oh. Is it bothering you?"

Kami sat on the edge of the bed and shook her head. "No. I'm worried about you. You were acting weird when you got home. Are you sick? Is this about Duncan? Did he hurt you?"

"Duncan's getting back together with his ex-wife."

"Since when?"

"It hasn't actually happened yet, but it probably will. I can't stand in the way of that. Not that I would be. I mean, he's just dating me because of our deal."

Kami wore her long dark hair in a thick braid. Her oversize T-shirt and PJ bottoms made her look young, but her eyes were wise. "He's not going out with you because he has to. Not anymore. He got his good press a while ago. Besides, what about the freezer and the food and the presents under the tree?"

A few days ago, a box of presents had been delivered. Well, presents for the girls. There hadn't been anything for her. At the time she'd told herself that he would give her something later. Privately. Now she wasn't so sure.

"She's still in love with him."

"So? She left him. The bitch had her chance. Now it's yours."

"While I appreciate the support, she's really not a bitch. I wish she was. Then I could hate her." And fight for Duncan. "They deserve a second chance."

"What about you? You're in love with Duncan."

"I'll get over it." She clicked on the Buy It Now button and tried not to wince at the price. She wanted to give Duncan something special. Something that would make him happy.

"You should tell him you love him," Kami said. "He needs to make an informed decision."

Annie managed a smile. "He's not buying auto insurance. He doesn't need to comparison shop."

"Maybe he needs to be reminded about what's important. You're the best thing that ever happened to him. If he doesn't see that, he's an idiot."

"Should I tell him that, too?"

"Absolutely."

Annie arrived at Duncan's office shortly after four. She'd called and made an appointment, wanting to be sure she saw him. They were supposed to go out that night. Nearly their last event. A cocktail party. But he wouldn't need her for that or the other parties to follow. His reputation had been saved and he had more important things to do. Like get on with his life.

She'd spent the day telling herself that she had to do the right thing. That loving Duncan meant wanting what was best for him rather than for herself. That she had to be strong. Losing Ron and A.J. hadn't mattered. She'd recovered in a matter of weeks. But losing Duncan was different. She had fallen madly, hopelessly, totally in love with him.

She'd learned early that life could be a challenge.

She'd been ten when her mom had first gotten sick and barely eighteen when she'd died. Her aunt wrestled with immobilizing depression, spending more time in hospitals than out. Over the years, Annie had helped raise her brother and her cousins. She'd always done her best. They were family and that mattered more than anything.

She'd made sacrifices, but nothing she regretted. It was her nature to give—she knew that. So the fact that she'd given her heart to Duncan shouldn't be a surprise. Nor was the reality that he didn't want it.

She waited outside his office door until four and then was shown in. Duncan put down his phone and smiled when he saw her.

"Why do we have an appointment?" he asked, walking around the desk to greet her. "I'm picking you up in a couple of hours."

He looked good, she thought, taking in the shape of his mouth, the breadth of his shoulders. His eyes—how could she ever have thought them cold?—brightened with pleasure. He smiled, then kissed her.

"Let me guess," he said. "You're here to convince me to start a profit-sharing plan."

"You can profit share with your employees? You should think about it."

Typical Annie, Duncan thought, leading her over to a sofa and sitting next to her. Good thing she'd never gone into business. She would have given away her entire worth the first day.

She'd come straight from school. He could tell by

her clothes—the long plaid skirt, the cardigan covered with beaded snowmen. Her curls were mussed, her light makeup mostly faded. This wasn't the glamorous Annie he usually saw on their evenings together. This was more real, more beautiful.

She leaned toward him and covered his hands with hers. Her gaze was intense.

"Duncan, I talked to Valentina at the party last night."

His good mood vanished. Why wasn't he surprised? "Whatever she said, she's lying. You can't trust her, Annie. She'll do anything, say anything, to get what she wants."

"She wants you."

Annie paused, as if waiting for a reaction. His was to swear loudly, then punch the wall. Dammit all to hell. "You believed her."

"She loves you, Duncan. She realizes she made a mistake and wants to be with you again. You were married—you owe her the chance to try to make it work."

She believed her words. He could see the truth in her big blue eyes. There was something else there, too. Pain, maybe. Regret.

Or was he reading too much into the situation? What he knew about women couldn't fill a thirty-second commercial. He knew they lied and manipulated. That they only thought about themselves. That given the chance, they would sell out anyone to get ahead.

Well, not Annie. She seemed to be genuine. He'd seen her with her students, with her cousins, hell, even with his uncle. She was exactly what she appeared to be. Open, honest, smart and funny. She led with her heart, which made her a fool, but everyone had flaws.

"You're here to plead Valentina's case?" he asked. "Did she offer to pay you?"

"No. It wasn't like that. She cried. She's desperately in love with you. I didn't want to believe her at first, but then she asked me if I'd ever been in love. If I'd ever known down to my bones that someone was the one. She meant it. Every word."

He was a whole lot less convinced. "She's a good actress, Annie. Don't let yourself get too caught up in her pain. It's mostly for show."

"It's not. She's your wife."

"Ex-wife. It's been three years."

"Can you honestly say you're not in love with her? That she doesn't matter, that she never mattered?"

"Of course I thought I loved her when we got married," he said, frustrated. "I was a fool."

"You owe it to her and to yourself to hear her out."

He stood up and crossed to the window overlooking the atrium below. Folding his arms across his chest, he faced Annie.

"She got to you."

Annie stood. Tears filled her eyes, but she blinked them away.

"She begged me to get out of the way and that's what I have to do. I'm not going with you tonight, Duncan. Take Valentina instead. Give her a chance."

"We have a deal."

"It's nearly over anyway. What does it matter if we stop things now?"

He'd known his relationship with Annie was finite. He'd designed it that way himself. But until now, he hadn't been willing to look past the holidays, to the days after. When she would no longer be with him.

She was leaving. Just like they all left. Her excuse was noble, but the outcome was the same. She would be gone and he would be left here, without her.

They all left. No one could be trusted. No *woman* could be trusted. Anger burned hot and bright, but he knew it was merely a shield to something else that would taunt him for a very long time.

"Our contract is clear," he told her coldly. "You walk out now and I throw your brother in jail."

He braced himself for the anger, the tears, the threats. Instead she smiled.

"Oh, please, Duncan. We both know you won't. You're not that guy." The smile quivered a little, then died. "Do you think this is easy for me? It isn't. I love you. But look at you and your life. I don't belong there. I've had a wonderful time and you're a great man. You deserve every happiness. That's why it's important for you to give Valentina a second chance. You loved her once. Maybe it was just the wrong time for the two of you."

Once again she was speaking the truth as she knew it. Duncan thought he understood Annie, but he'd been wrong. She loved him and she wanted him to be with someone else? The ridiculousness of it made him even more angry.

"If you loved me, you'd stay," he said, his voice practically a growl. "Next you'll tell me you want to be friends."

She winced, as if he'd slapped her. "You're upset."

"You're playing a game. I expected better. If you want to leave, then go. Don't give me any bullshit about it being for my own good. That's crap and you know it."

Now the tears fell, but unlike those in other women, these tears seemed to burn him. He felt the searing all the way down to his heart.

"You're everything I ever dreamed about. You're strong and gentle. You're giving and funny. I want to spend my whole life with you. I want to sleep in your arms and have your children and love you and worry about you. I want to spend fifty years with you and have the neighbors say things like, 'Those Patricks have been married forever.'"

She wiped her face with her fingers. "But it's not just about me. There's Valentina. So I'm doing the right thing. Because that's important. But all it would take is one word, Duncan. I'm not fighting this because I didn't think there was a point. I didn't think you loved me back. Tell me it's totally over with her and that you love me. That you want me to stay, and I will."

He finally knew her end game. To trap him. "I'd be a great meal ticket," he said. "And I'll give you points for originality. That was quite a speech."

She stiffened as the color faded from her face. She wiped at her tears again, then picked up her purse.

"There's no winning, is there?" she asked quietly. "You told me and told me and I didn't listen. Maybe you're right about Valentina and maybe I am. I hope you take the time to find out. As for me, if you can say those words, if you can really think I'm here because you're wealthy and successful, then you never knew me at all. And I guess I never knew you. Because the man I love can see into my heart and my soul. He knows who I am. And that's not you. Goodbye, Duncan."

And then she was gone.

Eleven

Duncan hadn't been mind-numbingly drunk in years. Probably not since college, when he'd been young and stupid. Now he was older, but apparently just as stupid. He'd avoided work, blown off the last of the holiday parties and had holed up in his condo for three days. Now, hungover, dehydrated and feeling like something that had been dead for a month, he forced himself to shower and get dressed before stumbling into the kitchen and making coffee.

He'd lost before. His first three fights had been a disaster. He'd barely gotten in a single punch. His coach had told him to go find another sport. Maybe baseball, where the only thing that could hit him was the ball. But he hadn't given up and by his senior year of high school, half a dozen colleges were offering him a free ride.

Taking over the family business hadn't been easy, either. He'd screwed up dozens of times, losing opportunities because of his youth and inexperience. But he'd persevered and now he had it all. But nothing in his life had prepared him for losing Annie.

Her words haunted him. "The man I love can see into my heart and my soul. He knows who I am. And that's not you." He would have preferred her to take out a gun and shoot him. The recovery would have been easier. Or at least faster.

He told himself that the bottom line was she'd left. She'd walked out. Telling him she loved him first only added a level of drama. He should respect that. And he could. The problem was he couldn't believe it. Annie didn't play games.

His doorbell rang. His head screamed at the sound. He made his way to the door and pulled it open. Valentina stood there, holding a package.

"This came for you," she said, handing over the flat box. "I told your doorman I'd bring it up myself."

She stepped into the condo and looked around. "It looks great, Duncan. I wish you'd kept our old place, though. There was so much room. Still, we can buy something else. Maybe a house, this time." She moved toward him and lightly kissed him. "How are you? Your assistant said you hadn't been feeling well. You're really pale."

He recognized Annie's neat writing on the package. As much as he wanted to open it, he wouldn't until he was alone. He set it on the dining room table, then returned to the kitchen. The coffee was ready.

He poured a cup and took a long drink. When he felt the heated liquid hit his belly, he turned back to face his ex-wife.

Valentina had dressed in winter-white. From her suede boots to her fuzzy sweater, she was a vision of sexual elegance. The woman knew how to wear clothes, he thought. And take them off for anyone interested.

"Why are you here?" he asked, taking another swallow.

"I want to talk to you, Duncan. About us. I meant what I said. I still love you. I want a second chance."

He looked her up and down. She was still preternaturally an ice queen if there ever was one. At one time she'd been all he'd wanted.

"And if I said I needed to test-drive the merchandise before I made a decision?" he asked.

She smiled. "Anytime."

"Kids?" She'd never wanted children. Too messy and she ran the risk of screwing up her figure.

"Of course." She tilted her head. "And a dog. Please. You can't have children without having pets. They need to learn about responsibility."

"The kids or the dog?" He reached for his coffee. "Never mind. You're serious about this?"

"Yes, Duncan. I still love you and am willing to do anything to prove that."

Uh-huh. "Including signing a prenup? One that gives you absolutely no part of my business or personal fortune. Now or in the future? You wouldn't get a penny, Valentina. Ever."

He would guess that Botox shots kept her from frowning, but there was no mistaking the tightening of her mouth or the stiffening of her body.

"Duncan," she began, then sighed. "Shit."

He wasn't even surprised. "So it is about the money."

"In part," she admitted. "And proving a point. Eric left me. *Me.* I was going to end things, but he beat me to it, the bastard. I wanted to prove a point. Show him what he'd lost."

Pride, he thought. He could respect that.

"Sorry I can't help," he said.

"Are you pissed?"

"More relieved."

"Excuse me?" she said, walking to the coffee and pouring herself a mug. "You would be nowhere without me. I took a rough, ill-mannered street kid and turned him into a gentleman."

"You screwed my business partner, on my desk."

"I know. I'm sorry about that."

"It doesn't matter anymore."

"But it was still tacky. I am sorry." She looked at him. "You look good. I mean that. You've come a long way."

They talked for a few more minutes, then Valentina left. Duncan closed the door behind her, relieved to have her out of his life. This time for good. Then he crossed to the table and opened the package from Annie.

Inside was a painting of two boxers. He knew the artist, had a larger piece of his work in his study.

There was a note inside. No, a Christmas card.

This made me think of you.

Duncan studied the masterful work and could guess the approximate price she'd paid. It was a whole lot more than she could afford. Why would she have done this? He checked the date. She'd had it shipped *after* she'd ended things. Who did that? What was she playing at?

He didn't have any answers, a circumstance he didn't like. He wanted his life simple—predictable. But Annie was anything but. She demanded too much. She wanted him to do the right thing, to be a better man. She wanted him to love her back.

Back. Meaning he believed she loved him in the first place? And if he did, what was he doing, letting her get away?

"Very upscale," Annie said, hoping it sounded more like a tease than nervousness. She sat across from Tim in a comfortable wicker chair on a patio behind the rehabilitation housing where her brother was staying.

"It's nice," he said.

He sat across from her, relaxed and tanned, more calm than she'd seen him in years. This was the first Saturday visitors had been allowed. Annie had arrived right at ten and Tim had been waiting for her. So far their conversation had consisted of greetings and the weather.

She picked at the wicker on the arm of the chair, then glanced across the broad lawn. Judging from the uneasy body language she saw in the other visitors, she wasn't the only one who didn't know what to say.

"Are you…" she began.

Tim leaned toward her and smiled. "It's okay. You did the right thing. I didn't believe that until a few days ago, but now I know you were right. I needed help. I still need help."

Relief rushed through her. She grabbed his hand and squeezed. "Yeah?"

He nodded. "I was chasing the dream, Annie. So sure that if I kept trying, I'd hit it big. It's what you always say about kids who cheat in school. If they would put half the effort into studying, they'd get a good grade. But instead they want to play the system. I want to play the odds. The trouble is, the odds are never in my favor."

"Which means what?" she asked.

"I have a gambling problem. I need to stay away from it. No blackjack, no Vegas, not even a raffle ticket. It's going to take a while, but I'll beat this, Annie."

She stared into her brother's blue eyes and felt relief. "I'm glad," she whispered.

"Me, too." He pulled free and shifted on his seat. "About what I said. I'm sorry."

"I know."

"I can't believe I stole that money. What an idiot. I really appreciate the deal you made with my boss. Anyone else would have let me go to jail."

"I couldn't do that."

"It's what I deserved."

"But not what you needed."

"I know. I've been in touch with Mr. Patrick. He says I can have my job back." Tim smiled self-consciously. "Sort of. I won't have access to any of the bank accounts. I'll have to earn his trust again, but I will. We worked out a payment plan for me to reimburse him."

Tim had talked to Duncan? Annie wanted to ask how he was. She missed him more than she had ever imagined, and she'd known it would be bad.

"I'm glad," she said.

"I want to pay you back, too," Tim told her.

"You don't owe me anything."

"Sure I do. Look what you did for me, Annie."

"I went to a bunch of parties. It wasn't work."

She'd also fallen in love and gotten her heart broken, but that wasn't anything Tim needed to hear right now. She would tell him later, when he was stronger.

"I'll make it up to you," Tim promised.

"All I need is for you to get your life back together," she said. "Be happy. That's enough."

Her brother stood and pulled her to her feet, then hugged her.

"You're the best," he said. "Thank you."

She hung on, willing him to heal. Because if he was all right, then this had been worth it. As for herself, and the aching emptiness inside, there was nothing to be done except hope that eventually she, too, would find her way back.

* * *

Duncan walked into the crowded Westwood restaurant. The hostess smiled at him. "Sir, do you have a reservation?"

"No."

"I'm sorry, we're booked. It's Christmas Eve and we're only having service until seven."

"I'm not here for dinner," he told her, looking into the dining room. "I want to see one of your servers. Jenny." He spotted her. "Never mind. There she is."

"Sir, you can't disturb our guests."

Duncan forced himself to flash her a smile. "Don't worry. I won't."

He wove through tables until he was next to Jenny. "We have to talk," he told her.

She barely glanced at him. "No, we don't."

She headed for the kitchen. He followed, grabbing her arm before she could disappear behind the swinging doors.

The restaurant hummed with conversation. Christmas carols played over the speakers. In the kitchen came the call for more turkey, as waiters and cooks battled for space.

Jenny glared at him, her blue eyes so much like Annie's. They were about the same height, too.

"I've been looking for her," he said. "I've been everywhere I can think of. Jenny, you have to help me."

The college student glared at him. "No way. You're nothing but a soul-sucking bastard. Do you know she cries every night? She doesn't want us to know, so she waits until she goes to bed. But we can hear her. She loved you and you hurt her."

"I know. I let her go and I'll regret that until the day I die. I was wrong. She's amazing and beautiful and so much more than I deserve. I love her, Jenny. I swear, I just want to take care of her. So please, tell me where she is."

Jenny hesitated, as if trying to decide.

"It's Christmas," he said. "A time for miracles. Can't you believe that I've changed?"

"I don't know," she admitted.

He stared into Jenny's eyes. "I love that she would sell her soul to save her brother. And when she's really stressed, she goes for M&M's. I love that she's never quite mastered the art of walking in high heels, so sometimes she has to grab the wall to keep from stumbling. I love how she sees the best in everyone, even me, and believes that everything is possible."

He cleared his throat. "I love how she let you and Julie and Kami live with her and that she would accept a new freezer because it would feed the three of you, but fought me on new tires that would keep just her safe. I love how she smiles at her students, how she worries about being a role model. I love how she takes care of the world. But who takes care of her? Who watches out for her and looks after her? Who takes over so she can rest? I want to be that guy, Jenny. I want to be the one."

He stopped talking, only to realize the restaurant had gone quiet. He glanced around and saw everyone was staring, listening. A couple of the men looked embarrassed, but the women were all smiling and nodding.

Jenny drew in a breath. "I swear, if you hurt her again…"

"I won't." He pulled the jewelry box out of his jacket pocket. "I want to marry her."

"Okay," she breathed. "She's at church. They called earlier and needed someone to help with the decorations. Apparently everyone has the flu and there's a midnight service." Jenny gave him the address. "Don't screw this up," she warned.

He kissed her cheek. "I won't. I promise."

Annie carried pots of poinsettias until her arms ached. When they were all in place, she adjusted the white lights, then plugged them in. The soft glow made the leaves seem to glisten. She'd already distributed the special booklets of Christmas carols, and attached beautiful sprays of roses and pine to the end of each pew. The candles were in place.

"You've done enough for twenty," Mary Alice, the minister's wife, told her. "Get along home, Annie. You need to rest a little or you'll be nodding off during the midnight service."

"All right. If you're sure."

"Thank you for answering my call for help. I hated to bother you, but I knew my old bones would keep me from getting everything done on time and Alistair is visiting with a member who's in the hospital. Everyone else…" Mary Alice smiled. "You were a blessing. Thank you."

"You're more than welcome. See you soon."

Annie turned to leave, telling herself she liked being able to help. And as everyone else had been busy in her family, it was a good thing she'd been home to receive the call. It was nearly Christmas. She refused to be sad. Or feel alone. She was lucky. Her brother was healing, her cousins were doing well. She had a great job and friends and so much to be thankful for. If there was an empty place inside, well, it would heal. By this time next year she would be her old self again.

She walked out a side door to the parking lot. It was already dark but still warm. This was going to be another Christmas with seventy-degree weather. One day she would spend the holidays where it was cold. A white Christmas. But for now, she would enjoy the fact that she didn't even need a coat.

She headed for her car, but before she got there, someone moved out of the shadows. A man. Duncan.

She came to a stop. Her heart pounded hard and fast, her chest got tight. She wanted to cry and laugh and throw her arms around him. She'd missed him so much.

"Annie," he said, then smiled at her.

And she knew. It was there in his warm gray eyes. The truth, the love. How he'd realized what was important, how he knew she was the one. Warmth and happiness flooded her. She felt as if she could float or even fly.

Without thinking, she threw herself at him. He caught her and pulled her against him, holding on as if he would never let go.

Home, she thought. She was finally home.

"Annie," he said again. "I love you."

"I know."

He laughed. "You can't know. I have a whole speech prepared. I have to tell you what I've learned and how I've changed and why you can trust me."

He slowly lowered her to the ground. Her feet hit the pavement, but she didn't let go. Instead she stared into his face, feeling the love spilling out of him.

"I already know all that."

He touched her cheek. "Valentina was in it for the money. Not that it matters. I was never interested in being with anyone but you."

"I want to say I'm sorry it didn't work out, but I'm really not." She laughed. "I guess that's bad, huh?"

"No. I feel the same way. Do you want to hear the speech?"

"Maybe later." Right now she just wanted to be with him, to feel him close and know that he loved her. This was perfect. She'd been given Duncan for Christmas.

"At least let me do this part." He pulled a small box out of his jacket pocket, then right there in the church parking lot, dropped to one knee.

"I love you, Annie McCoy," he said. "I will always love you. Please say you'll marry me. I'll spend the rest of my life making your dreams come true."

He opened the box and she gasped when she saw the huge diamond nestled there.

"Duncan? Really? You want to marry me?"

"Don't doubt me, Annie. You're the one. Now that I've found you, I'll never let you go."

She didn't know how or why she'd gotten so lucky, but she was grateful. She bent down and kissed him.

"Yes, I'll marry you."

He laughed, then stood and slid the ring on her finger. Then they hung on to each other as if they would never let go.

"I've missed you," he whispered. "I've been lost without you."

"Me, too."

"You've changed me. How did I get so lucky?"

"That's what I was thinking. That I got so lucky to find you," she admitted, then opened her eyes. A brilliant star winked in the sky. She pointed. "Look."

He turned. "It's just Venus."

"Don't tell me that. Can't it be a Christmas miracle?"

"If it makes you happy."

"It does."

"Then that's what it is." He kissed her. "Merry Christmas, Annie."

"Merry Christmas, Duncan."

* * * * *

Tonight he'd met the most beautiful woman he'd ever seen in his life.

A woman who looked totally out of place in Gamble, Wyoming. A woman whose voice alone could stir something deep inside of him.

A woman who was already taken.

There was no denying he was attracted to her, but wanting her was taboo. So why was he thinking about her even now? And why in the hell was he so eager to see her again tomorrow?

WESTMORELAND'S WAY

BY
BRENDA JACKSON

Published in Great Britain 2010
Harlequin Mills & Boon Limited,
Eton House, 18-24 Paradise Road, Richmond, Surrey TW9 1SR

© Brenda Streater Jackson 2009

ISBN: 978 0 263 88184 4

51-1110

Harlequin Mills & Boon policy is to use papers that are natural, renewable
and recyclable products and made from wood grown in sustainable forests.
The logging and manufacturing processes conform to the legal environmental
regulations of the country of origin.

Printed and bound in Spain
by Litografia Rosés S.A., Barcelona

Brenda Jackson is a die "heart" romantic who married her childhood sweetheart and still proudly wears the "going steady" ring he gave her when she was fifteen. Because she's always believed in the power of love, Brenda's stories all have happy endings. In her real-life love story, Brenda and her husband of thirty-six years live in Jacksonville, Florida, and have two sons.

A *New York Times* bestselling author of more than fifty romance titles, Brenda is a recent retiree who worked thirty-seven years in management at a major insurance company. She divides her time between family, writing and travelling with Gerald. You may write to Brenda at PO Box 28267, Jacksonville, Florida 32226, by e-mail at WriterBJackson@aol.com or visit her website at www.brendajackson.net.

To my husband, the love of my life and my best friend,
Gerald Jackson, Sr.
To everyone who enjoys reading a Brenda Jackson
novel, this one is for you!

Ponder the path of thy feet, and let all
thy ways be established.
—*Proverbs 4:26*

Dear Reader,

When I introduced the Westmorelands with Delaney's story almost eight years ago, I never thought that it would go beyond the twelve stories that included Delaney and her eleven siblings and cousins. Then I introduced Uncle Corey and had to acquaint him with the triplets he never knew existed. Twelve books then became fifteen books. And no, I'm not finished yet!

Meet the Westmorelands of Denver, Colorado, who are long-lost cousins to our Atlanta group. The men are just as hot and the women are just as stubborn. They are Westmorelands through and through, and I hope you have fun reading their stories and watching how they find true and everlasting love.

The oldest of the Denver clan is Dillon, a man who has tried marriage before, discovered it wasn't for him and has no intentions of trying it again. At least that was his intent before he met Pamela Novak. He finds staying a bachelor is no longer an option, but he's faced with numerous challenges before he can make her his. But this Denver Westmoreland won't let anything stand in his way—not even Pamela's fiancé.

Thank you for making the Westmorelands a very special family and I look forward to bringing you more books of searing desire and endless love and passion.

Happy reading!

Brenda Jackson

Prologue

"I know how much finding out everything there is about your grandfather means to you, and I wish you the best in that endeavor. If you ever need anything, you, your brothers and cousins should know that the Atlanta Westmorelands are here. Call on us at any time."

Dillon Westmoreland drained his wineglass before meeting the older man's eyes. He'd only met James Westmoreland eleven months ago. He had arrived in Denver, Colorado, with his sons and nephews, claiming to be his kin. They'd had the documentation to prove it.

"Thank you, sir," Dillon said. Their unexpected appearance at the Shady Tree Ranch had answered a lot of questions, but generated even more. After years of thinking they had no living relatives outside of Denver, it was nice to know there were others—others who hadn't hesitated to claim them as their own.

Dillon glanced around the wedding reception given for his cousin Reggie and Reggie's wife, Olivia. Dillon and the other Denver Westmorelands had officially met Reggie with a bunch of other Westmorelands from Atlanta at the family reunion a few months before. All it took was one look to know they were related. Their facial features, complexions and builds were practically the same. No surprise, given the fact their great-grand-fathers, Reginald and Raphel, had been identical twins.

Dillon now knew the story of how his great-grand-father, Raphel Westmoreland, had split from the family at the age of twenty-two. He'd left Atlanta, Georgia, with the wife of the town's preacher. It had been con-sidered a despicable act and Raphel had immediately become known as the black sheep in the Westmoreland family, never to be heard from again.

Many assumed he had died before his twenty-fifth birthday with a bounty on his head for wife-stealing. Few knew that Raphel had eventually made it to Denver, married and produced a son who had given him two grandsons, who in turn had blessed him with fifteen great-grands. Dillon was proud to say, at thirty-six, he was the oldest of Raphel's great-grandchildren. That left the Denver Westmoreland's legacy right smack on Dillon's shoulders.

It hadn't been easy, but he had done his best to lead his family. And he hadn't done too badly. All fifteen of them were successful in their own right, even the three that were still in college. But then you had to really try hard to overlook his youngest brother, Bane, whose occasional brush with the law kept Dillon down at police headquarters more than he would have liked.

"Are you still determined to find out the truth about whatever happened to your great-grandfather's other wives, or whether his previous relationships were even wives at all?" James Westmoreland asked him.

"Yes, sir. I'm taking time off from my company later this year, sometime in November, to travel to Wyoming," Dillon said.

Through James Westmoreland's genealogy research he had found Dillon's family. Now it was up to the Denver Westmorelands to find answers to the questions that still plagued them about their ancestry. That was one of the reasons why the trip to Wyoming was so important to him.

"Okay, Dillon, Uncle James has had your ear long enough."

Dillon couldn't help but chuckle when his cousin Dare Westmoreland walked up. If there had been a doubt in anyone's mind that the Atlanta and Denver Westmorelands were related, all they had to do was to compare him to Dare. Their features were so similar they could have been born brothers instead of cousins.

"I don't mind," he said truthfully. "I'm enjoying myself."

"Well, don't have too much fun," Dare responded with a huge grin. "As soon as Reggie and Olivia leave for their honeymoon, we're heading over to Chase's Place for a game of poker."

Dillon raised a brow. "The last time I played poker with you all, I almost lost the shirt off my back," he said, unable to suppress a grin.

Dare gave him a huge pat on that back. "All I can say to that, Dillon, is welcome to the family."

One

"Have you totally lost your mind, Pam? No matter what you say, we can't let you do it. You've given up so much for us already. We just can't."

Pamela Novak smiled as she glanced over her shoulder and saw the three militant faces frowning at her and quickly decided it would be best to give them her full attention. Drying her hands on a towel she turned away from the sink to face them.

She wondered what it would take to make her sisters see reason and understand that she had to do what she had to do. Not just for her own benefit but mainly for theirs. Fletcher was pushing for a Christmas wedding and here it was the first week in November already. So far they hadn't set a date, but he would bring it up every time she saw him. He'd let it be known that he didn't want a long engagement and, considering everything, a long engagement wouldn't be in her best interest, either.

She nibbled on her bottom lip, trying to come up with a quick yet effective strategy. If she could convince her sister Jillian of the importance of what she had to do, then Paige and Nadia would quickly come on board. But convincing Jillian was the big challenge. Jill didn't like Fletcher.

"And what makes you think it's something I'm being forced to do, rather than something I want to do?" Pamela finally decided to ask the three of them.

Of course, it was Jillian who stepped out to speak. Jill, as she was called by most people in Gamble, Wyoming, at seventeen was a senior in high school and was a spitfire. She was also smart as a whip. It was Pam's most fervent desire for Jill to leave Gamble next fall to attend the University of Wyoming in Laramie and pursue her dream of one day becoming a neurosurgeon.

And Paige, fifteen, and Nadia, thirteen, would soon be ready to pursue their aspirations. Pam wanted to make sure that funds were available for college when that time came. She also wanted to make sure that if her sisters wanted to return to Gamble, they would still have a home here. Pam felt certain that accepting Fletcher's marriage proposal made those things possible.

"You're sacrificing your happiness, Pam. We aren't stupid. What woman in her right mind would want to marry a jerk like Fletcher Mallard?" Jill boldly said.

Pam had to fight to keep a straight face when she said, "He is not a jerk. In fact, Fletcher is a nice man."

"When he's not being obnoxious and arrogant, which is most of the time. Already he thinks he can run things around here. We've been doing just fine without him," was Jill's bitter response.

Jill took a quick breather and then went on to say, "We don't care if we lose this house and it wouldn't bother us in the least if we don't get a college education. We refuse to let you marry the likes of *that* man to protect what you see as our bright futures. Speaking of futures, you should be back in California working on a real movie instead of spending your time teaching students at the acting school. You got a degree in drama, Pam. Being an actress has always been your dream. Your passion. You shouldn't have given it up for us."

Pam inhaled deeply. She had been through all of this before with her sisters. The problem was that they knew too much about the situation, something she wished hadn't happened. Unfortunately for her, they had been home that day when Lester Gadling, her father's attorney, had dropped by to deliver the bad news and they had overheard Lester's words.

"But I'm not in California. I'm perfectly satisfied being here in Gamble and running the acting school, giving others the same opportunity that was given to me," she countered.

She paused for a second and then said, "Listen, ladies, I've made these decisions because I love you."

"And we love you, too, Pammie," Nadia replied. "But

we can't let you give up the chance to one day meet a really nice guy and—"

"Fletcher is a nice guy," she interjected. However, all she received for her effort were three pairs of rolling eyes.

"No, he's not," Paige spoke up to say. "I was in the bank one day when he went off on one of the tellers for making him wait in line for so long. He thinks he's all that, just because he owns a chain of grocery stores."

"Okay, you saw his bad side just that one time," Pam said. "Deep down he's a kind person. He's willing to help us out, isn't he?"

"Yes, but look what he'll be getting. Our home and the most beautiful single woman in Gamble," Jill pointed out.

"A single woman who isn't getting any younger and who will be turning thirty in a few months. Don't you think it's time I get married?"

"Yes, but not to him," Jill implored. "Anyone but him."

Pam glanced at the kitchen clock that hung on the wall. Fletcher was coming to dinner and would be arriving any minute, and she needed to make sure her sisters put this behind them. They had to accept that she was now an engaged woman and move on.

She of all people knew that Fletcher had his flaws and could be arrogant at times, but she could deal with that. What she refused to deal with was letting her sisters lose the only home they knew and a chance to fulfill their dreams by attending the colleges they desired.

She couldn't help but wonder what her father had been thinking to put a second mortgage on their home—

a mortgage for which the full balance was due within a year of his death. There was no way she could come up with a million dollars. Fletcher, in the role of a friend, had made her an offer that she couldn't refuse. It would not be a love match, he was fully aware of that. She would, however, as agreed, perform her wifely duties. He wanted kids one day and so did she. And Pam was determined to make the most of their marriage and be a good wife to him.

"I want the three of you to make me a promise," she finally said to her sisters.

"What kind of promise?" Jill asked, lifting a suspicious brow.

"I want you to promise me that you will do everything I ask regarding my engagement to Fletcher. That, you will make me, as your oldest sister, happy by supporting my marriage to him."

"But will you be truly happy, Pammie?" Paige asked with an expression that said she really had to know.

No, she wouldn't *truly* be happy, but her sisters didn't have to know that, Pam thought. They must never know the extent of her sacrifice for them. With that resolve in mind, Pam lifted her chin, looked all three of them in the eyes and told a lie that she knew was going to be well worth it in the end.

"Yes," she said, plastering a fake smile on her lips. "I will truly be happy. I want to marry Fletcher. Now, make me that promise."

Jill, Paige and Nadia hesitated only for a moment and then said simultaneously, "We promise."

"Good."

When Pam turned back to the sink, the three girls looked at each other and smiled. Their fingers had been crossed behind their backs when they'd made their promise.

It was probably inconsiderate of him to show up without calling first, Dillon thought, as he turned into the long driveway that was marked as the Novak Homestead.

He had arrived in Gamble, Wyoming, earlier that day, with his mission on his mind. What had happened to his great-grandfather's other four wives, the ones he had before he married Dillon's great-grandmother, Gemma? According to the genealogy research James Westmoreland had done, Gamble was the first place Raphel had settled in after leaving Atlanta, and a man by the name of Jay Novak had been his business partner in a dairy business.

Dillon would have called, but he couldn't get a signal on his cell phone. Roy Davis, the man who owned the only hotel in Gamble, had explained that was because Gamble was in such a rural area, getting a good signal was almost impossible. Dillon had shaken his head. It was absurd that in this day and age there was a town in which you couldn't get a decent cell signal when you needed it.

He had finally gotten a signal earlier to contact his secretary to check on things back at the office. Not surprisingly, everything was under control, since he had hired the right people to make sure his billion-dollar real estate firm continued to be a success whether or not he was there.

Dillon parked his car behind another car in the yard and glanced up at a huge Victorian house with a shingle roof. It was very similar in design to his home in Denver and he wondered if that was a coincidence.

According to what he'd heard, four sisters occupied the house and the oldest was named Pamela Novak. He understood Ms. Novak had had an up-and-coming acting career in California but had moved back to Gamble upon her father's death. She was now operating the drama school a former teacher had recently willed to her.

When Dillon got out of the rental car he took time to stretch his legs. Like most Westmorelands he was tall, and because of his height he'd always enjoyed playing basketball. He'd been set to begin a career in the NBA when he'd gotten word of the plane crash that had claimed the lives of his parents and his aunt and uncle, leaving fourteen younger Westmorelands in his care.

It hadn't been easy and Tammi, his girlfriend from college, had claimed she would stick by his side no matter what. Less than six months into their marriage she had run back home hollering and screaming that she couldn't handle living on a ranch with a bunch of heathens.

That was after she had failed to convince him to put his youngest brother, Bane, who'd been eight at the time, his cousins—Adrian and Aiden—the twins who'd been ten, and Bailey, who'd been seven, into foster care because they were always getting into some kind of mischief.

He had understood that most of their antics had been

for the attention they'd needed after losing their parents. However, Tammi had failed to see it that way and wanted out of the marriage. One good thing that had come out of his divorce was that he'd realized it was meant for him to be single and, as long as he was the head of the family, he would stay that way.

Another good thing about his divorce was that the younger Westmorelands—all of them with the exception of Bane—had felt guilty about Tammi leaving and had improved their behavior. Now the twins and Bailey were in college. Bane…was still Bane.

"You lost, mister?"

Dillon quickly turned around to look into two pairs of dark brown eyes standing a few yards away. Twins? No, but they could pass for such. Now he could see that one of the teenage girls was a head taller than the other.

"Well, are you?"

He smiled. Evidently he hadn't spoken quick enough to suit them. "No, I'm not lost if this is the Novaks' place."

The taller of the two said, "I'm a Novak. We both are."

Dillon chuckled. "Then I guess I'm at the right place."

"Who did you want to see?"

"I want to see Pamela Novak."

The shorter of the two nodded. "That's our sister. She's in the house talking to *him*."

Dillon raised a brow. He had no idea who *him* was, and from the distasteful way it had been said, he really wasn't sure he wanted to find out. "If she's busy I can come back later," he said, moving back toward the car.

"Yeah, because he might get mad if he thought you'd come calling just to see Pammie," the taller one said.

A look of mischief shone in their eyes as the two girls looked at each other and smiled. And then, screaming to the top of their voices, they called, "Pammie, a man is here to see you!"

Dillon leaned against his car with arms across his chest, knowing he had been set up, and the two teens were having a little fun at his expense. He wasn't so sure how he liked it until the door to the house swung open. At that moment he literally forgot to breathe. A strikingly beautiful woman walked out. It didn't matter that she was frowning. The only thing that mattered was that she was definitely the living, breathing specimen of the most gorgeous woman he'd ever seen.

She couldn't have been any taller than five-eight, and was slim with just the right curves in the jeans she was wearing. She had shoulder-length black hair flowing around her shoulders and a medium brown complexion that complimented the rest of her features. Her eye color was the same dark brown as the two scamps, and she had a pixie nose that was perfect for her face. She was definitely a stunner. A raven-haired beauty that made him nearly breathless.

"Hey, you're trespassing. May I help you?"

He looked beyond her to a big hulk of a man standing directly behind her in the doorway who'd asked the question in a high-pitched and agitated tone. And he was glaring at Dillon as if his very presence annoyed the hell out of him.

Dillon quickly figured that this must be the "him" the girls had been referring to, and was about to open his mouth to speak when the taller of the two girls spoke up. "No, you can't help him because he didn't come to see you, Fletcher. He came to see Pammie."

A dark scowl covered the man's face at the same time a smile touched the teen's lips. It wasn't hard to see she was deliberately trying to get a rise out of the man.

"Paige and Nadia, shouldn't you be upstairs doing your homework?" the gorgeous woman asked the two before turning her curious gaze on Dillon. Unlike her male friend, she smiled brightly and had a cheerful look on her face.

"Pamela Novak?" he heard himself ask, trying to force air into his lungs. He'd seen beautiful women before, but there was something about her that was doing something to everything male within him.

"Yes," she said, still smiling while stepping down the steps toward him. He pushed away from the car and began moving toward her, as well.

"Wait a minute, Pamela," the hulk of a man called out. "You don't know this man. You shouldn't be so quick to be nice to people."

"Maybe you should follow her lead, Fletcher."

A new voice Dillon hadn't heard before had spoken up, entering the fray. He glanced behind the hulk to see a young woman, probably around seventeen or eighteen, stepping out the door. Another sister, he quickly surmised, due to the similarities in their features.

Pamela Novak continued walking and when she

came to a stop in front of Dillon, she offered her hand. "Yes, I'm Pamela Novak, and you are…?"

He accepted her hand and immediately felt a warmth that began to flow all through his body. Then a fluttering he felt in the pit of his stomach began to slide downward. Even the engagement ring he'd noticed her wearing couldn't stop the sensations engulfing him.

He watched her mouth move, fascinated with her lips and thinking they had a nice shape. He felt his stomach tighten when he raised his gaze from her lips to her eyes. "I'm Dillon Westmoreland."

He watched her brow lift ever so slightly, although she kept her smile in place. He could tell she was searching her memory for when, how and where she recalled the last name. He decided to help her. "I understand that my great-grandfather, Raphel Westmoreland, was once a business partner of your great-grandfather, Jay Winston Novak."

The smile on her lips transformed into a full chuckle. "Oh, yes, Raphel Westmoreland. The wife stealer."

He couldn't stop his lips from twitching in a smile. "Yes, so I've heard. In fact, that's the reason I'm here. I—"

"What does he want, Pamela?"

Dillon could tell by the stiffening of Pamela Novak's shoulders that she wished the hulk would keep quiet for once. "Is he your fiancé?" he couldn't help asking.

She met his gaze and studied it for a moment before saying, "Yes."

She then inclined her head to call back over her shoulder, "This is Dillon Westmoreland. Our great-grandfathers were once business partners so I consider him a friend of the family."

She quickly turned back to Dillon, presented him with another smile and whispered, "You know I say that loosely, don't you, considering your great-grandfather's reputation."

Now it was Dillon's time to chuckle. "The reason I'm here is to find out all I can about that reputation since I only recently discovered he had one and—"

"What does he want, Pamela?"

Before she could respond the shortest of the teen imps said, "We already told you. He wants Pammie."

The hulk's frown deepened and Dillon knew the young girl hadn't meant it the way it sounded, but basically she had spoken the truth. He *was* attracted to Pamela Novak. Encroaching into another man's territory had been Raphel Westmoreland's style, but was not his. However, at that moment Dillon didn't feel any guilt about the thoughts going through his mind, especially since it was apparent the woman was engaged to an ass. But that was her business, not his.

The man came down the steps and moved toward them and Dillon quickly sized him up. He wore a suit and an expensive pair of black leather shoes. His shirt and tie didn't look cheap, either, which meant he was probably a successful businessman of some sort.

When he stopped in front of him, Dillon offered the man his hand. "I'm Dillon Westmoreland, and like Ms.

Novak said, I'm a family friend. The reason I'm here," he decided to add, "is because I'm doing research on my family's history."

The man shook his hand. "And I'm Fletcher Mallard, Pamela's fiancé," he said, as if he needed to stake a claim by speaking his position out loud.

Dillon took it in stride and thought that you could tell a lot about a man from his handshake, and this man had all the telltale signs. He was using the squeezing handshake, often used to exert strength and power. A confident man didn't need such a tactic. This man was insecure.

Mallard looked at Dillon skeptically. "And just what is it you want to know?"

The smile dropped from Pamela Novak's lips and she actually glared at her fiancé. "There's no reason for you to ask all these questions, Fletcher. Mr. Westmoreland is a family friend and that's all that matters right now."

As if her words settled it, she turned to Dillon with her smile back in place. "Mr. Westmoreland, please join us for dinner, then you can tell me how we can help in your quest to learn more of your family's history."

It would have been so easy and less complicated to decline her offer, but there was something about Fletcher Mallard that outright irritated Dillon and pushed him to accept her invitation.

"Thank you, Ms. Novak, and I'd love to stay for dinner."

Two

Pam knew she had made a mistake inviting Dillon Westmoreland to dinner the moment he was seated at the table. She wished she could say Fletcher was in rare form, but she'd seen him behave this way before, when another man had shown interest in her.

But what was strange was that Dillon hadn't actually shown any interest in her, so she couldn't understand why Fletcher was being so territorial. Unless…he had picked up on her interest in Dillon.

She pushed such utter nonsense from her mind. She was *not* interested in Dillon. She was merely curious. What woman wouldn't be interested in a man like Dillon Westmoreland. He was at least six foot four with coffee-colored features. He had an angular face that boasted a firm jaw, a pair of cute dimples, full lips and the darkest eyes she'd ever seen on a man. She was engaged to be married, but not blind. And when he had sat down at the table to join them for dinner, his presence was powerfully masculine in a distracting way. She glanced around the table and couldn't help noticing her sisters' fascination with him, as well.

"So just where are you from, Westmoreland?"

Her spine stiffened with Fletcher's question. She hadn't invited Dillon to dinner to be interrogated, but she knew Fletcher wouldn't be satisfied until he got some answers. She also knew once he got them he still wouldn't be contented.

"I'm from Denver," Dillon answered.

Fletcher was about to ask another question when Dillon beat him to the punch. "And where are you from, Mallard?"

The question had clearly caught Fletcher off guard. He had a way of trying to intimidate people, but she had a feeling that Dillon Westmoreland was a man who couldn't be intimidated.

"I'm from Laramie," Fletcher said gruffly. "I moved to town about five years ago to open a grocery store here. That was my first. Since then I've opened over twenty more in other cities in Wyoming and Montana. It's my goal to have a Mallard Super Store in every state in the union over the next five years."

Pam couldn't help but inwardly smile. If Fletcher thought that announcement would get a reaction from

Dillon, then he was sadly mistaken. Dillon didn't show any sign that he was the least impressed.

"Where are you staying while you're in town?" Fletcher asked, helping himself to the mashed potatoes.

"At the River's Edge Hotel."

"Nice place if you can do without cable television," Jill said, smiling.

Pam watched how easily Dillon returned Jill's smile. "I can do without it. I don't watch much television."

"And what is it that you do?" Fletcher asked in a voice that Pam felt was as cold as the iced tea she was drinking.

Dillon, she saw, gave Fletcher a smile that didn't quite reach his eyes when he said, "I'm into real estate."

"Oh, you sell homes," Fletcher said as if the occupation was beneath him.

"Not quite," Dillon said pleasantly. "I own a real estate firm. You might have heard of it, Blue Ridge Land Management."

Pam saw the surprise that lit Fletcher's eyes before he said, "Yes, I've heard of it."

She had to force back a chuckle because she was sure that he had heard of it. Who hadn't? The Blue Ridge Land Management Company was a billion-dollar corporation, well known in the Mountain States, that had a higher place on the Fortune 500 list than Mallard Super Stores.

Seeing that Fletcher was momentarily speechless, she stepped in to say, "Mr. Westmoreland, you said that—"

"I'm Dillon."

He had raised his gaze to meet hers and she saw a friendly smile lurking in the dark depths of his eyes. Her heart rate began accelerating in her chest. "Yes, of course," she said quickly. "And I'm Pam."

After taking a sip of her tea, she continued. "Dillon, you said that you were here to research your family's history?"

"Yes," he said, his gaze still on her. "For years I was told by my parents and grandparents that my brothers, cousins and I didn't have any living relatives, and that my great-grandfather, Raphel Westmoreland, had been an only child. So you could imagine my surprise when one day, out of the clear blue sky, a man, his two sons and three nephews showed up at my ranch to proclaim they were my kin."

Intrigued by the story, Pam placed her fork next to her plate and gave him her full attention. "How did they find you?"

"Through a genealogy search. The older man, James Westmoreland, knew that his grandfather, Reginald Westmoreland, had an identical-twin brother. It was discovered that that twin brother was my great-grandfather, Raphel, who had left home at twenty-two and had never been heard from again. In fact, the family assumed he'd died. They had no idea that he had eventually settled in Denver, married and had a son, who gave him two grandsons and then a slew of great-grands—fifteen, in fact. I am the oldest of the fifteen great-grands."

"Wow, that must have been a shocker for you to

discover you had other relatives when you assumed there weren't any," Jill, who was practically hanging on to Dillon's every word, said. "What does your wife think about all of this?"

Pam watched Dillon smile and knew he hadn't been fooled by the way the question had been asked. Jill wanted to know if he was a married man. Pam hated to admit that she was just as curious. He wasn't wearing a ring, but that didn't necessarily mean a thing.

"She didn't have anything to say because I'm not married," Dillon replied smoothly. "At least not anymore. I've been divorced for close to ten years."

Pam glanced over at Jill and prayed her sister had the decency not to inquire as to what had happened to end his marriage.

Fletcher, disliking the fact he wasn't the center of attention, spoke up in an authoritative negative voice. "Sounds pretty crazy to me. Why would you care about a bunch of people who show up at your place claiming they were your relatives, or better yet, why would you want to find out your family history? You should live in the present and not in the past."

Pam could tell Dillon was fighting hard to hold his temper in check, and his tone was remarkably restrained when he finally responded. "Do you have a family, Fletcher?"

Again, by Fletcher's expression it was obvious he didn't appreciate being the one receiving the questions. "No, I was an only child. My parents are deceased, but they didn't have any siblings, either. I'm the only

Mallard around for now." He glanced over at Pam and smiled. "Of course, that will change once Pamela and I marry."

Dillon nodded slowly. "But until that changes, I wouldn't expect you to understand the significance of what a family means. I already do. Westmorelands are big into family and, after meeting my other relatives, my only regret is not having known them sooner."

He glanced over at her and, for a second, she held his steady gaze. And she felt it. There was a connection between them that they were trying to ignore. She looked down at her plate as she continued eating.

Nadia asked him a question about his siblings and just as comfortably and easily as a man who was confident with himself and who he was, he began telling her everything she wanted to know. Without even trying, Dillon was captivating everyone at the dinner table… with the exception of Fletcher.

"How long do you plan to stay in town?" Fletcher rudely cut into the conversation between Dillon and the sisters.

Dillon glanced over at Fletcher. "Until I get all the questions I have about Raphel Westmoreland answered."

"That may take a while," Fletcher said.

Dillon smiled, but Pam knew it was just for Fletcher's benefit and it wasn't sincere. "I got time."

She saw Fletcher open his mouth to make another statement and she cut him off. "Dillon, I should be able to help you with that. My great-grandfather's old business records, as well as his personal journal, are in the attic. If you want to drop by tomorrow and go up there and look around, you're welcome to do so."

"Thanks," he said, smiling. "I'll be happy to take you up on your offer."

"I don't want you meeting with that man alone, Pamela. Inviting him here tomorrow while your sisters are away at school wasn't a good idea. And tomorrow I'll be out of town visiting my stores in Laramie."

Pam glanced over at Fletcher as she walked him to the door. He was upset and she knew it. In fact, there was no doubt in her mind that everyone at the dinner table had known it since he wasn't a person who hid his emotions well.

"So," he continued, "I'll get word to him tomorrow that you've withdrawn the invitation."

Fletcher's words stopped her dead in her tracks just a few feet from her living room door. She stared at him, certain she had missed something, like a vital piece of their conversation, somewhere along the way. "Excuse me?"

"I said that since you agree that you shouldn't be alone with Westmoreland, I'll get word to him that you've withdrawn your invitation for tomorrow."

She frowned. "I don't agree to any such nonsense. The invitation I gave to Dillon Westmoreland still stands, Fletcher. You're acting controlling and territorial and there's no reason for it."

She saw the muscle that ticked in his jaw, indicating he was angry. "You're an attractive woman, Pamela. Westmoreland isn't blind. He noticed," he said.

"And what is that supposed to mean? I agreed to marry you but that doesn't mean you own me. If you're having seconds thoughts about this engagement, then—"

"Of course I'm not having second thoughts. I'm just trying to look out for you, that's all. You're too trusting with people."

His gaze then flicked over her before returning to her face. "And I think that you're the one having second thoughts," he said.

She lifted her chin. "Of course I'm having second thoughts. I agreed to marry you as a way to save my ranch. I appreciate you coming to my rescue but you deserve better than that. And that's why I plan to pay Lester Gadling another visit this week. I want him to go back over those papers. It's hard to believe Dad did not make arrangements for the balance on that mortgage to be paid off if anything happened to him."

Fletcher waited for a moment, then said, "If you feel that strongly about it then I agree that you should go back to Gadling, since he was your father's attorney, and ask him about it. But don't worry about what I deserve. I'll have you as my wife and that will make me a happy man."

Pamela didn't say anything. She and Fletcher weren't entering into their marriage under false assumptions. He knew she was not in love with him.

She took a moment to reflect on a few things. She had left home upon graduating from high school with a full scholarship to attend the University of Southern California Drama School. It was during her sopho-more year that Alma, her stepmother, had died. Her father had married Alma when Pam was ten, and Alma had been wonderful in filling the void after losing her mother.

She had thought about dropping out of college and returning home, but her father wouldn't hear of it. He was adamant about her staying in school and insisted that he would be able to care for her sisters, although Nadia had been only three at the time, the same age she'd been when she'd lost her own mother.

"Pamela?"

Pam blinked upon realizing Fletcher had called her name. "I'm sorry, Fletcher. I was just thinking about happier times, when Dad and Alma were both alive."

"And you will have even happier times once we're married, Pamela," he said, reaching out and taking her hand in his. "I know you don't love me now, but I'm convinced you will grow to love me. Just think of all the things I can give you."

She lifted her chin. "I'm not asking for you to give me all those things, Fletcher. The only things I've asked for, and that you've promised, are to make sure my sisters retain ownership of our home and to put my sisters through college."

"I promise all of that. And I'll promise to give you more if you would just let me," he said in a low, frustrated tone.

She didn't say anything for a long moment and knew her silence was probably grating on his nerves, but she couldn't help it. "I don't want anything more, Fletcher, so please let's just leave it at that."

Pam had met Fletcher four years ago on one of her trips back to Gamble to visit her family. After that, whenever she came to town, he would make it a point to ask her if she would go out with him.

After her father died and she'd moved back home, he had come calling on a regular basis, although she had explained to him that friendship was all there could ever be between them. At the time, he had seemed satisfied with that.

Then Lester Gadling had come visiting and dropped the bombshell that had changed her life forever. Fletcher had stopped by that evening and she had found herself telling him what had happened. He had listened attentively before presenting what he saw as an easy solution. She could marry him and her financial problems would be over.

At first, she'd thought he'd fallen off the deep end, certain he had taken leave of his senses. But the more she'd thought about it, the more his suggestion had taken shape in her mind. All she had to do was marry him and he would see to it that her ranch was saved and would establish a trust fund for her sisters, so when the time came for their college, everything would be set.

She didn't accept his offer at first, determined to handle things without Fletcher's help. She had gone to bank after bank trying to secure a loan but time and time again had been turned down. She had only accepted Fletcher's proposal when she'd seen she had no other choice.

Glancing down at her watch, she said, "It's getting late."

"All right. Don't forget to be careful around Westmoreland. There is something about him that I don't trust."

"Like I said, Fletcher, I'll be fine."

He nodded before leaning in closer to brush a kiss across her lips. As always she waited for blood to rush fast and furious through her veins, fire to suffuse her insides, but as usual, nothing happened. No stirring sensations. Not a single spark.

For months she had ignored the fact that she was not physically attracted to the man she was going to marry. It hadn't bothered her until tonight when she discovered she was *very* physically attracted to another man. And that man's name was Dillon Westmoreland.

Dillon eased his body into a huge bathtub filled with warm water. Whatever amenities the little hotel lacked, he would have to say a soak in this tub definitely made up for them. There weren't too many bathtubs around that could accommodate his height comfortably.

He closed his eyes and stretched out, thinking he'd never been able to relax in a tub before. It had been a while since he'd been able to sit in a tub and not worry about being disturbed by some family member needing his help or advice.

Family.

Damn, but he missed them already. He wasn't worried about the family he'd left in Denver since he'd left Ramsey in charge. He and Ramsey were only separated in age by seven months and were more like brothers than they were cousins. If truth be told, Ramsey was his best friend. Always had been and always would be.

He couldn't wait until he began digging into information about Raphel. He could have hired an agency to do it for him, but this was something he wanted to do himself. Something he felt he owed his family. If there was something in his great-grandfather's past, then he felt he should be the one to uncover it. Good or bad.

Dillon shifted his body. He kept his eyes closed while thinking that tonight he'd met the most beautiful woman he'd ever seen in his life. A woman who looked totally out of place in Gamble, Wyoming. A woman whose voice alone could stir something deep inside of him.

A woman who was already taken.

There was no denying he was attracted to her, but wanting her was taboo. So why was he thinking about her even now? And why in the hell was he so eager to see her again tomorrow?

He inhaled deeply, wondering how Fletcher Mallard could get so lucky. It was easy to see the man was a jerk, a pompous pain in the ass. But Fletcher was no concern of his, and neither was the man's engagement to Pamela Novak. Dillon was in Gamble for one thing and for one thing only. He was there to find out everything he could about Raphel, and not to encroach on another man's property.

He would do well to remember that.

Three

Glancing out the window Pam saw Dillon's car the moment it pulled up in front of the house. She took a sip of her coffee while watching him, grateful that the window was designed in a way that gave her a view of anyone arriving. From what she'd been told, her great-grandfather had deliberately built the house that way to have an advantage over anyone who came calling without their knowledge.

Today she was making full use of that advantage.

After he brought the car to a stop, she watched as he opened the car and got out. He stood for a moment to study her home, which gave her an opportunity to study him.

He was tall—she'd noticed that last night. But last night she hadn't had time to fully check him out. She couldn't help but appreciate what she saw now. Nice shoulders. Firm abdomen. Muscled chest. Taut thighs. He was wearing jeans and a blue western shirt that revealed strong arms, and a black Stetson was on his head.

She sighed deeply, thinking that inviting him to come back today might not have been a good idea after all, just as Fletcher had claimed. She glanced down at her hand holding the coffee cup and couldn't miss the diamond ring on her finger, the one Fletcher had put there a week ago.

Okay, so she was an engaged woman, one who would be marrying a nice guy in a few months. But being engaged, or married for that matter, didn't mean she couldn't appreciate a fine specimen of a man when she saw one. Besides, her best friend from college, Iris Michaels, would give her hell if she didn't check him out and then call to give her all the hot-tamale details.

She blinked as she nearly burnt her tongue on a sip of coffee when Dillon looked straight at her through what she'd always considered her secret window. How had he known about the side view? To anyone else it would appear to be a flat wall in the shadow of a huge oak tree.

There was only one way to find out. She pushed her chair away from the table and stood. As she made her way out of the kitchen toward the living room, she decided maybe it would be better for him not to know she'd been sitting here watching him since he'd arrived.

She slowly opened the door and was afforded an opportunity to watch him unseen some more when his attention was diverted by a flock of geese in the sky. While he studied the geese, she again studied him, taking in the angle of his face while his head was tilted slightly backward. He was standing with his legs braced apart and with his hands in his pockets. There was something about that stance, that particular pose—especially on him—that made her just want to stand there and stare.

While living in Los Angeles for five years she'd been surrounded by jaw-droppingly, stomach-stirringly handsome men, many from some of the world's most elite modeling agencies. But none could hold a light to the man presently standing in her yard. His features were distinct—sharp facial bones, firm jaw and full lips. His hair beneath his Stetson was close cut and trimmed neatly around his head.

A moment passed. Possibly two. When suddenly he turned his head and looked over in her direction.

She had been caught.

And she was immediately enveloped in his intense gaze. She was unable to do anything but return his stare while wondering why she was doing so. Why were her senses, her entire being, homed in on everything about him? This wasn't good, she thought.

At least that was what her mind was telling her, but her common sense hadn't gotten there yet. It was being held captive within the scope of the darkest pair of eyes she'd ever seen.

Somewhere in the not-too-faraway distance she

heard the sound of a car backfiring and the sound ripped right into the moment. It was only then that she was able to slide her gaze away from his to look over across the wide expanse of yard.

After taking a deep breath she returned her gaze to his, wrestled with those same senses she had lost control of earlier, placed a smile on her face and said, "Good morning, Dillon."

She wasn't just off the boat, and knew that during the brief moment when their gazes had held, something had happened. Just as it had last night. She wasn't sure of what, but she knew that it had. She also knew she would pretend that it hadn't. "It's a beautiful day, isn't it?" she added.

"Yes, it is," he said, turning to walk over toward her. Holy cow! she thought, swallowing deeply. The man's strides were sure, confident and deliberately masculine. He had one hell of a sexy walk, and what was so disturbing about it was that it seemed as natural as the sun rising in the morning.

He came to a stop in front of her and met her gaze fleetingly before glancing up at the sun. His gaze then returned to her. "It might rain later, though."

She nodded. "Yes, it might." She knew they were trying to get back in sync and to lessen the intensity of what had passed between them.

"I hope I'm not too early," he said in a deep, husky voice, breaking into her thoughts.

"No, you're fine. I was just having my morning coffee. Would you like to join me?"

With an ultrasexy shrug of his massive shoulders, he smiled as he removed his hat. "Umm, I don't know. I feel I'm taking a lot of your time already."

"No problem. Besides, you want to know about Raphel, right?"

"Yes. Is there something you can tell me other than he was your great-grandfather's partner and that he ran off with your great-grandmother, Portia Novak?"

Pam chuckled as she led him through the house and headed toward the kitchen. "Portia wasn't my great-grandmother," she corrected. "A few years after she'd run off, he met my great-grandmother and they married."

When he sat down at the table, she said, "I'm sure you've heard some stories about Raphel and Portia." She proceeded to pour him a cup of coffee.

"No, in actuality, I hadn't. I'd always assumed my great-grandmother Gemma was my great-grandfather's only wife. It was only after my Atlanta Westmoreland relatives showed up and explained how we were related that I found out about Portia Novak and the others."

Pam lifted a brow. "There were others?"

He nodded. "Yes, Gemma was his fifth wife."

Dillon was more than curious about what had happened to a preacher's wife, a woman by the name of Lila Elms. Although she was already legally married to the preacher, had she and Raphel pretended to be married for a spell before he dumped her for Portia, the wife of Jay Novak?

And then what happened to Clarice, wife number three? And Isabelle, wife four? All four women's names were rumored to be connected to Raphel in some say. If what they'd discovered so far was true, Raphel had taken up with the four women before his thirty-second birthday, and all had been married to another man or engaged to marry someone else. It seemed Raphel's reputation as a wife stealer was legendary.

Dillon took a sip of coffee, deciding for the moment not to inform her that the others, like Portia, were women who belonged to other men, legally or otherwise. But he would throw out the name of one she might have heard about already. "My goal is to find out what happened to Lila Elms."

"The preacher's wife?"

So, she had heard about Lila. "Yes." He took another sip and then asked, "How do you know so much about this stuff?"

She chuckled as she sat down at the table with him after refilling her own cup of coffee. "My grandmother. As a little girl we would spend hours and hours on the porch outside shelling peas, and she would fill my ears about all the family history. But the one subject she didn't shed a lot of light on was Portia. For some reason, any conversation about her was taboo. Jay wanted it that way and my great-grandmother respected his wishes."

Dillon nodded, trying to concentrate on what she was saying and not on how smoothly her lips would part each time she took a sip of her coffee. How the bottom lip would hang open a little and how the top one would fit perfectly around the rim of the cup.

He felt his gut tightening and took a sip of his coffee.

When he had been standing out in her yard and he'd turned and seen her staring at him, he had tried not to speculate just what was going on in her mind. He didn't want to even consider the possibility that it had been close to what had been going on in his.

Her gaze had touched him deeply, in a way he doubted she even realized. Something about Pamela Novak was calling out to him in the most elemental way, and that wasn't good. Since his divorce, he had dated on occasion. But if the truth be told, he'd made it a point to date only women who, like him, weren't interested in anything long term. All of those women had been unattached.

"Are you ready to go up to the attic?"

Her question reined his thoughts back and he glanced over at her and immediately wished he hadn't. Every muscle in his body immediately seemed to weaken yet at the same time fill him with an intensity that made him draw in a long breath. It was time to acknowledge it for what it was. Sexual chemistry.

He had heard about it but had never actually experienced it for himself. He'd been attracted to women before, but it never went further than an attraction. What he was beginning to feel was an element of something greater than a mere attraction. There were these primitive vibes he was not only emitting but was also receiving. That meant Pamela Novak was in tune to what was going on between them, although she might choose to pretend otherwise. Of course, he understood her reluctance to acknowledge such a thing. After all, she was an engaged woman. And she didn't come across as one who would deliberately be unfaithful to her fiancé.

But still…

"Yes, I'm ready," he finally said. "But first I want to clear the air about something." He watched her lips quiver nervously before she set her cup down and met his gaze. He tensed, trying to ignore the sensations rolling through him every time their eyes met.

"Clear the air about what?"

He'd been too busy watching her lips to pay any attention to the words flowing out of them. He fought back the urge to lift the tip of his finger and run it across those lips.

He cleared his throat. "About last night. My showing up here without calling first. I think I may have rattled your fiancé a little, and I regret doing that. It was not my intent to cause any problems between the two of you."

He watched as her shoulders gave a feminine shrug. "You didn't cause any problems. Don't worry about it."

She then stood. "I think we should go up to the attic and see what's there. There's a trunk that contains a lot of my great-grandfather's business records."

Dillon nodded. She had responded to his question and in the same breath, had effectively switched topics, which let him know the subject of her relationship with Fletcher Mallard was not up for discussion.

He pushed his chair back and then got on his feet. "I'm ready, just lead the way."

She did and he couldn't help but appreciate the backside that strolled in front of him as he followed.

* * *

With his long legs, it didn't take Dillon long to catch up with her, Pamela thought. Not that she was trying to leave him behind. But for a few moments she'd needed to get her bearings. The man had a way of making her not think straight.

He was silent as she led him up the stairs and she couldn't help looking sideways to gaze at his profile. What was it about him that affected her in a way Fletcher didn't? Her heart rate accelerated when she noticed he even climbed the stairs with an ingrained sexiness that made her senses reel.

When they reached the top landing he moved slightly ahead of her, as if he knew where he was going. "If I didn't know better I'd swear you've been here before," she said as they continued to walk toward the end of the hall that led to the attic stairs.

He glanced down at her and smiled. "This might sound crazy but this house is very similar to mine back in Denver. Was it built by your great-grandfather?"

"Yes."

"Then that might explain things, since the house I live in was built by Raphel. I'm thinking he liked the design, and when he decided to build his home he did so from his memory of this one."

"That would explain how you knew about our secret window." She regretted the words the moment they left her lips. She had just admitted to spying on him out the window when he'd arrived.

"Yes, that's how I know about it. I have one of my own just like it and in the same place."

"I see." But, in a way, she didn't see, which made her as eager to find out about Raphel as Dillon was.

She then walked on and he joined her. When they reached the door that led to the attic she opened it. Judging from the expression on his face, it was as if he'd seen the view before, and that made her determined to know why his home was a replica of hers.

Unlike the other stairs in her home, the attic steps were narrow and Dillon moved aside for her to go up ahead of him. She could feel the heat of his gaze on her back. She was tempted to glance over her shoulder but knew that wouldn't be the appropriate thing to do. So she did the next best thing and engaged him in conversation.

She broke into the silence by saying, "At dinner you mentioned that you were the oldest of Raphel's fifteen great-grands." She glanced briefly over her shoulder.

"Yes, and for a number of years I was the legal guardian for ten of them."

Pamela swung around so quickly, had she been standing on a stair she probably would have lost her balance. "Guardian to ten of them?"

At his nod, she blinked in amazement. "How did that come about?" She stepped aside when he reached her, noting there still wasn't a lot of room between them, but she was so eager to hear his answer she didn't make a move to step back any further.

"My parents and my aunt and uncle decided to go away for the weekend together, to visit one of my mother's friends in Louisiana. On their way back to Denver, their plane developed engine trouble and went down, killing everyone on board."

"Oh, how awful."

"Yes, it was. My parents had seven kids and my aunt and uncle had eight. I was the oldest at twenty-one. My brother Micah was nineteen and Jason was eighteen. My other brothers, Riley, Stern, Canyon and Brisbane, were all under sixteen."

He braced a hip against the stair railing and continued. "My cousin Ramsey was twenty, and his brother Zane was nineteen and Derringer was eighteen. The remaining cousins, Megan, Gemma, the twins Adrian and Aiden, and the youngest, Bailey, were also all under sixteen."

She also leaned against the rail to face him, still full of questions. "And family services didn't have a problem with you being responsible for so many little ones?"

"No, everyone knew the Westmorelands would want to stay together. Besides," he said, chuckling, "no one around our parts wanted to be responsible for Bane."

"Bane?"

"Yes. It's short for Brisbane. He's my youngest brother who likes his share of mischief. He was only eight when my parents were killed and he took their deaths pretty hard."

"How old is he now?"

"Twenty-two and still hot under the collar in more ways than one. I wish there was something holding his interest these days other than a certain female in Denver."

Pam nodded. She couldn't help but wonder if there

was a certain female in Denver holding Dillon's interest, as well.

"Do all of you still live close to one another?" she asked.

"Yes, Great-Grandpa Raphel purchased a lot of land back in the thirties. When each Westmoreland reaches the age of twenty-five they are given a hundred-acre tract of land, which is why we all live in close proximity to each other. As the oldest cousin, I inherited the family home where everyone seems to congregate most of the time."

He then asked her, "How old were you when your great-grandfather passed?"

"He died before I was born, but I heard a lot about him. What about Raphel? How old were you when he passed?"

"He died before I was born, too. My great-grandmother lived until I was two, so I don't rightly remember much of her, either. But I do remember my grandparents, Grampa Stern and Gramma Paula. It was Grampa Stern who used to tell us stories about Raphel, but never did he mention anything about past wives or other siblings. In fact, he claimed Raphel had been an only child. That makes me wonder how much he truly knew about his own father."

Pam paused for a moment and then said, "I guess there are secrets in most families."

"Yes, like Raphel running off with the preacher's wife," he said.

"And you think Raphel eventually married her?"

"Not sure of that, either," Dillon replied. "Since she was legally married to the preacher, I don't see how a marriage between them could take place, which is why I'm curious as to what happened to her once they fled Georgia."

"But her name, as well as Portia's, are shown as former wives on documents you've found?" she asked, trying to get a greater understanding of just what kind of life his great-grandfather may have led.

"Two of my Atlanta cousins, Quade and Cole, own a security firm and they did a background check, going as far back as the early nineteen-hundreds. Old land deeds were discovered for Raphel and they list four separate women as his wives. So far we know two of them—the preacher's wife and Portia Novak—were already legally married. We can only assume Raphel lived with them pretending to be married."

He paused a moment and then glanced around and asked, "Do you come up here often?"

His question made her realize they had been standing still long enough and were awfully close, so she shifted toward the attic door. "Not as often as I used to. I just moved back to Gamble last year when my father passed. Like you, I'm the oldest and I wanted to care for my sisters. I am their legal guardian."

Dillon nodded and stepped back when she opened the attic door. He had noticed the way she had interacted with her sisters last night at dinner. It was obvious they were close.

"That's my great-grandfather's trunk over there. It's my understanding that he and your great-grandfather were partners in a dairy business, which was very profitable at the time. I know there are a lot of business records in there, as well as some of Raphel's belongings. It seems he made a quick getaway when he left Gamble."

Dillon shot her a glance. "You have some of Raphel's belongings?"

"Yes," she said, moving toward the trunk. "I didn't mention it at dinner last night."

He understood the reason she hadn't done so. Her fiancé probably would have had something to say about it. It was quite obvious the man could make an argument out of just about any subject.

Instead of immediately following her over to the trunk, Dillon stood back for a moment and watched her go. His gaze was focused on her. The possibility that some of his great-grandfather's belongings might be inside that trunk intrigued him. But she intrigued him more.

She was wearing jeans and a pretty pink blouse that added an ultrafeminine touch. He couldn't help but notice the seductive curves outlined in those jeans. Walking behind her up the stairs to the attic had been hell. He was certain sweat had popped out on his brow with every step she'd taken.

When she saw he hadn't followed her, she turned and slanted him a glance. "Are you all right?"

No, he wasn't all right. One part of his brain was trying to convince him that, although she was an engaged woman, she wasn't married yet, so she was still available. But another part of him, the one looking at the ring on her finger, knew to make a pass in any way would be crossing a line. But hell, he was tempted.

She held his gaze, and he realized at that moment he hadn't given her an answer. "Yes, I'm fine. Just overwhelmed." If only she knew how much and the reason why.

"I understand how you feel. What you said last night at dinner is true for me, as well. I consider family important. Although you never knew him, you want to know as much about your great-grandfather as you can learn. I think it is admirable that you want to do so."

She glanced down at the trunk and then back at him. "I just hope you don't think you're going to find out everything there is to know about your great-grandfather in one day, Dillon. Even after I open that trunk it might spur you to ask more questions, seek more answers."

"And if I need to come back here?" he asked, knowing she knew where he was going with the question.

"You're welcome to come back for as long as it takes."

His gaze held hers intensely as he asked, "Will Fletcher be okay with it? Like I said earlier, I don't want to cause any problems between the two of you."

"There won't be any problems. Now, aren't you going to open this trunk? I've been dying to do so for years, but growing up we were always told it was off limits." Her lips curved at the corners. "But I will admit to defying orders once and poking around in there. At that time, I didn't see anything that held my interest."

Dillon smiled as he crossed the floor toward her. Like his at home, the attic here was huge. As a boy, the attic had been one of his favorite places to hide when he wanted some alone time. This room was full of boxes and trunks, but they had been arranged in a neat order, nothing like the way his attic looked back home. And there was that lone, small rectangular window that allowed just enough sunlight to shine through.

Kneeling, he pulled off a key that was taped on the side of the trunk and began working at the lock. Moments later he lifted open the lid. There were a lot of papers, business books, a couple of work shirts that had aged with time, a bottle of wine, a compass and a tattered looking journal.

He glanced up at Pam. "Mind if I take a look at this?"

"No, I don't mind. In fact, there's a letter inside."

He lifted a brow as he opened the journal and, sure enough, a letter whose envelope had turned yellow, lay on the front page. The name on the envelope was still legible. It simply said *Westmoreland*. He glanced back over at her.

"Like I said, although the trunk was off limits, I couldn't help but snoop that one time. That's how I knew about that letter."

Dillon couldn't hide his smile as he opened the sealed letter. It read, *"Whomever comes to get Raphel's belongings just needs to know that he was a good and decent man and I don't blame him for leaving and taking Portia with him."*

It had been signed by Pam's great-grandfather Jay. Dillon put the letter back in the envelope and glanced up at Pam. "This is all very confusing. Think you can shed some light on it?"

She shook her head. "No, sorry. For a man not to hold

any animosity against the man that took his wife is strange. Perhaps Raphel did Jay a favor if he didn't want to be married to her anyway. But that theory is really stretching it a bit. A man's wife is a man's wife, and Portia had been Jay's wife."

"And what about Lila Elms?"

She shrugged. "I can't tell you anything about her, other than they must have parted ways between Atlanta and here, because from all I've heard when Raphel arrived in Gamble he was a single man."

She glanced at her watch. "There are a few phone calls that I need to make, so I'm going to leave you for a while. Take as much time as you like up here, and if you need me for any reason, I'll be downstairs in the kitchen."

"All right."

She moved toward the attic door.

"Pamela?"

She glanced back around. "Yes?"

He smiled. "Thanks."

She smiled back. "Don't mention it."

Dillon released a deep breath the moment Pam left, closing the attic door behind her. Pamela Novak was a temptation he had best leave alone. All the while she had been in this room, he had tried keeping the conversation going, anything to suppress the desires that had run rampant through him.

What was there about her that ruffled his senses every time she was within ten feet of him? What was there about her that made a number of unnamed and undefined sensations run through him? It had been hard as hell to maintain his composure and control around her.

Perhaps his dilemma had to do with her understanding of his need to delve into his family's history, his desire to know as much about Raphel Westmoreland as he could find out. Even some of his siblings and cousins didn't understand what was driving him, although they did support him. He appreciated them for it, but support and understanding were two different things.

However, he had a gut feeling Pamela did understand. She not only understood but was willing to help him any way she could…even if it meant stirring her fiancé's ire.

Deciding he needed to do what he'd come to Gamble to do, he pulled a chair out of a corner and placed it in front of the trunk. Picking up Jay Novak's journal, he began reading.

Four

Pam glanced at the clock on the kitchen wall. Dillon had been up in the attic for over an hour, and she couldn't help but wonder how things were going. More than once she'd thought about going up to find out but had talked herself out of it. Instead she got busy looking over scripts for new plays her students had submitted.

The ringing of her phone interrupted her thoughts and she had a feeling who the caller was without bothering to look at caller ID. Sighing deeply, she picked up the phone. "Hello?"

"How are you, Pamela? This is Fletcher."

"I'm fine, Fletcher. How are things in Laramie?"

"They are fine, but I received a call and I'm going to have to leave here and go to Montana and check on a

store there. A massive snowstorm caused a power failure
that lasted a couple of days, and a lot of our refrigerated
items were destroyed."

"I'm sorry to hear that."

"So am I. That means I'll be flying to Montana to
meet with the insurance company representative. It
may take a few days and I might not be back until the
end of the week."

She could lie and say she was sorry to hear that, but she
really wasn't. She had felt the two of them needed space
and this was a way she could get it. Since agreeing to marry
him, he'd made it a point to see her practically every day.

"You can make me happy and come spend some time
with me here." His words intruded into her thoughts.
The two of them hadn't slept together. Although he had
brought up the idea several times, she had avoided the
issue with him.

"Thanks for the invite, but I have a lot to do here.
Besides, I need to be here for my sisters."

She didn't have to see him to know his jaw was
probably tight from anger right now. This was not the
first time he had tried to talk her into going out of town
with him since they'd become engaged.

He didn't say anything for a moment and when he
did speak again, she was not surprised by his change in
subject. "And where is Westmoreland? Did he show up
today?"

She had no reason to lie. "Yes, he showed up. In
fact, he's still here, upstairs in the attic going through
some things."

"Why couldn't he take the stuff with him and go through it back at the hotel?"

Fletcher's tone, as well as his words, annoyed her. "I saw no reason for him to take anything back to the hotel. I regret you evidently have a problem with it."

"I'm just looking out for you, Pamela," he said after a brief pause. "I still feel you don't know the man well enough to be there alone with him."

"Then I guess you just need to chalk it up as bad judgment on my part. Goodbye, Fletcher."

Without waiting for him to say anything else, she hung up the phone. He would fume for a few hours and then he would call her back later and apologize once she realized just how controlling he'd acted.

Pam eased back to the table and picked up the papers once again, determined to tuck Fletcher and his attitude away until later. She had agreed to marry him and she *would* marry him, since her sisters' futures and not losing her family home meant everything to her.

Dillon closed the journal and stood to stretch his legs. He was used to being dressed in a business suit every day, instead of casual jeans and a shirt. That morning he had checked in with Ted Boston, his business manager, to see how things were going at his real estate firm and, not surprisingly, Ted had everything under control. He had made his firm into a billion-dollar company with hard work and by hiring the right people to work for him.

He glanced at his watch, finding it hard to believe that

two hours had passed already. He looked down at the journal. At least part of his curiosity had been satisfied as to what had happened to Lila, the wife of the preacher from Georgia.

According to what Raphel had shared with Jay, the old preacher had been abusing his young wife. Church members had turned their heads with the mind-set that what went on behind a married couple's closed doors was their business, especially when it involved a preacher.

Evidently, Raphel hadn't seen it that way. He had come up with a plan to rescue Lila from the clutches of the abusive preacher—a plan his family had not supported. After taking Lila as far away as Texas, Raphel had helped her get established in the small Texas town of Copperhead, on the outskirts of Austin. Raphel had been her protector, never her lover, and before moving on he had purchased a small tract of land and given it to her to make a new beginning for herself.

Dillon smiled, thinking, at least in the case of Lila, Raphel had been a wife saver and not a wife stealer. Given the woman's situation, Dillon figured he would have done the same thing. He'd discovered that when it came to the opposite sex, Westmoreland men had this ingrained sense of protection. He just regretted that Raphel had severed ties with his family.

At that moment Dillon's stomach started to growl, reminding him that he hadn't eaten anything since early that morning and it was afternoon already. It was time for him to head back over to the hotel.

* * *

Pam had been intensely involved in reading one of her students' scripts when suddenly she felt sensations curl inside her stomach at the same time chill bumps began to form on her arms.

She glanced up and met Dillon's gaze as he stepped into the kitchen. She wondered how her body had known of his presence before her mind. And why even now the sensations curling her stomach had intensified. She decided to speak before he had a chance to do so, not sure what havoc the sensations combined with his deep, disturbingly sexy voice would play on her senses.

"How did things go? Did you discover anything about your great-grandfather that you didn't know before?" she asked, hoping he didn't hear the strain in her voice.

He smiled, and the effect of that smile was just as bad as if he'd spoken. He had a dimpled smile that showed beautiful white teeth. "Yes. At least, thanks to your great-grandfather's journal, I was able to solve the mystery of Lila, woman number one."

"Did they eventually marry?" she asked, curiously.

"No, from what I read, Lila's preacher husband was an abusive man and Lila sought out Raphel's help to escape the situation. He took her as far as Copperhead, Texas, hung around while she got on her feet, established her with a new identity and then moved on."

Pam nodded. "That explains why he wasn't married when he arrived here in Gamble."

"Yes, but it doesn't explain why he would run off with your great-grandfather's wife. And so far nothing

I've read explains it, but then I didn't get through the entire journal. Not even halfway. Jay would digress and talk about the dairy business and how it was doing. But from what I've read so far, it seemed that he and Raphel were close, which doesn't explain how my great-grandfather could betray him the way he did."

Pam didn't say anything for a moment and then she asked, "So, are you taking a break before reading some more?"

"No, it's getting late and I think it won't be a good idea to be here when your fiancé arrives this evening. I've outstayed my welcome today anyway, and I appreciate you giving me a chance to read the journal."

"You're welcome." And before she could think better of her actions, she said, "And I'd like to invite you to stay for dinner. I'm sure my sisters would love hearing what you've discovered today. I think you piqued their interest at dinner yesterday and they see this as some sort of family mystery needing to be solved. At some time or another everyone has heard about Raphel Westmoreland and how he ran off with my great-grandfather's first wife."

Dillon leaned against the kitchen cabinet. "I'm surprised no one in your family has been curious enough to find out what really happened."

Pam shrugged. "I guess you have to understand how some women think, namely my great-grandmother. I'm sure she could have cared less why her predecessor ran off with another man, and the less the family talked about Portia, the better."

She tilted her head and looked up at him. "So will you take me up on my invitation and stay for dinner?"

Pam's words intruded into his thoughts and he looked up and over at her, holding her gaze a moment. "And what about Fletcher? How is he going to handle me sitting at your dinner table two evenings in a row?"

He watched as she nervously bit her bottom lip and then lifted her chin. "There's nothing wrong with me inviting someone I consider a family friend to dinner. Besides, Fletcher is out of town for a few days."

He nodded, considered her words and decided not to read anything into them. It was an invitation to dinner, nothing more. As long as he remembered she was an engaged woman, everything would be all right.

Only problem with that was that the more he saw her, and the more he was around her, the more he was attracted to her. And the more he was attracted to her, the more he could admit, whether it was honorable or not, that he wanted her.

He swallowed and intentionally glanced out the window, needing to break eye contact with Pam. What he'd just inwardly admitted wasn't good, but he was being honest with himself. That meant as soon as he could find out all the answers he wanted about Raphel, he hoped in the next couple of days, he would return home.

He glanced back at her, met her gaze, felt the pull, the attraction, and although she might never admit it to anyone, not even to herself, he knew it was mutual. He knew he should ask if he could take the journal back to the hotel and spend the next several days reading it, out of such close proximity to her and this unusual sexual chemistry he felt whenever they were near each other.

But for some reason he couldn't. "If you're sure it will be okay then, yes, I'd love to join you and your sisters for dinner."

"And you're sure he's coming back for dinner, Pammie?" Nadia asked with excitement in her voice as she helped her oldest sister set the table.

Pam lifted a brow. She couldn't remember the last time Nadia or Paige had gotten excited about someone coming for dinner, least of all a man. The first time she had invited Fletcher, they had almost boycotted dinner until she'd had a good, hard talk about being courteous and displaying Novak manners.

"Yes, he said he was going back to the hotel to change clothes and would be coming back."

"And don't you think he's very handsome, Pam?" Paige chimed in to ask.

Pam turned after placing the last plate on the table and faced her three sisters. Although Jill hadn't voiced her excitement, Pam knew it was there—she could clearly see it on her face. The one thing she didn't want her sisters to think was that Dillon's presence at dinner had anything to do with her engagement to Fletcher. She knew what they were trying to do, and it was time she made sure they understood that it wasn't working.

"Yes, he is handsome, Paige, but so is Fletcher. But I'm not marrying a man because of his looks. I'm not that vain and I hope the three of you aren't, either. To set the record straight, so the three of you fully know that what you're doing isn't working, I *will* be marrying Fletcher."

Jill smiled. "We have no idea what you're talking about, Pam."

Pam rolled her eyes and was about to give them a good talking-to when the sound of the doorbell stopped her. "Okay, that's our guest and I want you on your best behavior, and please keep in mind that I am engaged to marry Fletcher."

Jill made a face and then said, "Please, don't remind us."

"We're glad you found out something about your great-grandfather today, Dillon," Nadia said, smiling.

Dillon couldn't help but return her smile, thinking she reminded him a lot of his cousin Bailey when she'd been Nadia's age. There was an innocence about her, while at the same time if you looked into her eyes long enough, there was mischief there, as well. The same thing could be said about Paige, but Jill was a different story.

There was something about her and her antics tonight that reminded him of Bane. The thought of a female Bane made him cringe more than a little. Her eyes twinkled when she encouraged him to talk about his family. He couldn't help but wonder if she was truly interested, or if her inquisition was a ploy. And he was smart enough to figure out it all came back to the same thing as last night. For some reason Pam's sisters were not happy with the man she had chosen to marry. It didn't take a rocket scientist to see that.

"Would you like something more to eat, Dillon?"

He glanced over at Pam. Their gazes met across the table and he smiled while at the same time fought down the tightening of his gut. He'd never been a man easily distracted by a beautiful face, but in the last forty-eight hours he'd known the real experience of feeling weak in the knees and having his heart thud mercilessly in his chest.

"No, and I appreciate your invitation to dinner."

"Tell us some more about Bane. He sounds like someone I'd like to meet one day," Jill said.

"No, he's not," both Dillon and Pam said simultaneously, and then they couldn't help but glance across the table at each other and laugh. They agreed with each other on that point.

Pam excused herself to go get dessert, a chocolate cake she had baked earlier. Dillon smiled at the three females staring at him and, as soon as Pam left the room, he was surprised when they lit into him with questions they dared not ask while their older sister was still in the room.

Nadia went first. Her dark eyes, as beautiful as her older sister's, stared him down. "Do you think Pammie is pretty?"

He smiled. That was easy enough for him to answer and do so truthfully. "Yes, she's pretty."

"Do you have a girlfriend?" Paige quickly asked.

He chuckled. "No, I don't have a girlfriend."

"Would you be interested in Pam if she wasn't engaged?"

Jill's question would have shocked the hell out of him if he hadn't gotten used to her tactics by now. She shot straight from the hip and he intended to answer her the same way.

"The key point to remember is that your sister *is* engaged, so whether I would be interested is a moot point, now, isn't it? But to answer your question, my answer would be yes, I would be interested."

"Interested in what?" Pam asked, returning and toting a plate with a huge chocolate cake.

"Nothing," three voices said at once.

Pam lifted a brow as she glanced at her sisters. She then looked over at Dillon and he couldn't help but smile and shrug his shoulders. Joining Pam and her sisters for dinner made him feel right at home and he wasn't sure that was a good thing.

"I think I need to apologize for anything my sisters might have said that could have grated on your nerves tonight," Pam said, walking Dillon out to his car. She had convinced herself this would be the only way she could get a few private words in without her sisters' ears perking at each and every word.

He chuckled. "Hey, it wasn't bad. I enjoyed their company. Yours, too. And dinner was wonderful."

"Thanks."

They didn't say anything for a few moments and then she asked, "Will you be coming back tomorrow? To continue reading Jay's journal?"

When they came to his car he leaned against it to face her. "Only if you say it's okay. I don't want to wear out my welcome."

She chuckled. "You won't be. Besides, finding out more about Raphel and Portia is like a puzzle waiting to be pieced together."

Pam knew she probably should suggest that he take the journal with him—that way he wouldn't have to bother coming back tomorrow—but for some reason she couldn't do that.

"Well, I guess I'd better let you go now. See you tomorrow," she said, backing up, putting proper distance between them.

"Good night," he said.

Dillon opened the door and got into the car but sat there until Pam had raced up the stairs, let herself inside and closed the door behind her. He saw three pairs of curtains automatically fall back into place in upstairs windows, and couldn't help but chuckle at the notion that he and Pam had been spied on. To be honest, he wasn't surprised.

As he drove off, he could only shake his head when he remembered his siblings' and cousins' reaction to Tammi when he'd brought her home, a year before they'd married. Although his parents and aunt and uncle had tried making the Westmoreland clan behave, it had been pretty obvious that Tammi hadn't been too well received. But that hadn't stopped him for marrying her the following year and bringing her home as his wife. Now he wished that it had.

He shifted in his seat to pull his cell phone out of his jeans pocket, hoping tonight he could pick up a signal. He smiled when he did and immediately placed a call home.

Ramsey answered on the second ring. "The West-morelands."

"Hey, Ram, it's Dillon. How are things going?"

"As well as can be expected. Bane's been behaving, so that's good."

Yes, that was good, Dillon thought.

"I went up to the big house and got all your mail," Ramsey was saying.

"Thanks."

"You find out anything on Raphel yet?" Ramsey asked.

"Yes." Dillon then spent the next half hour bringing his cousin up to date on what he'd uncovered that day from Jay's journal.

"And Jay Novak's great-granddaughter is actually nice to you? After Raphel ran off with her great-grandfather's wife?"

Dillon chuckled. "Yes, she's operating on the premise of good riddance. If Portia hadn't left then Jay would never have met and married her great-grand-mother. Needless to say, Pam has no problem with Raphel running off with the woman."

"Pam?"

Dillon heard the curiosity in Ramsey's voice and knew why. Ramsey of all people knew how hard it had been in making the real estate firm he had inherited from his father and uncle into the billion-dollar com-pany it was today, taking care of the Westmoreland stronghold and being responsible for all those West-morelands who were still dependent while they were away at college.

"Yes, Pam is her name, and before you ask, the answer again is yes, she is beautiful. The most beautiful woman I've ever set eyes on."

And before Ramsey could say anything, he quickly added, "And she's engaged."

"Umm, have you met her fiancé?" Ramsey wanted to know.

"Yes, and he's an ass."

Ramsey chuckled. "How did a beautiful woman get engaged to an ass?"

"Beats me and it's none of my business."

"That's the difference between me and you, cuz. I would make it my business, especially if she was the most beautiful woman I'd ever seen. You know what they say about it not being over until the fat lady sings? Well, in this case, she's not off limits until the wedding is over."

"That's not my style, Ram."

"Typically, it's not mine, either, being the loner that I am, but I've learned that with some things you need to know when and how to adjust your thinking, be flexible and restructure your thought process. Especially if it's a woman you want."

Dillon blinked, taken aback by Ramsey's statement. "What makes you think she's a woman I want?"

"I can hear it in your voice. Do you deny it?"

Dillon opened his mouth to do that very thing and then closed his mouth shut. No, he couldn't deny it, because his cousin who knew him so well had just spoken the truth. And the question of the hour was whether or not he intended to do anything about it.

Five

Pam was trying, desperately so, to convince herself that the only reason she was sitting at the kitchen table and staring out the window was to study all the Indian paintbrushes that were still blooming this late in the year.

It wasn't working.

Just like it wasn't working to try and convince herself the only reason she'd gone to bed with thoughts of Dillon on her mind instead of the man she was engaged to marry was because Dillon had been to dinner the last couple of nights. The reason that argument wouldn't hold up was because, although Fletcher had been dropping in for dinner quite often, she had yet to take visions of him to her bed. She had yet to remember, in vivid detail, what he'd been wearing the last time she'd seen him, and yet to hear the sound of his voice in her head in the wee hours of the morning.

So why was Dillon Westmoreland causing so much havoc in her life when she should be concentrating on setting the best date to marry Fletcher? The main thing that had been nagging at her since meeting Dillon was the fact that he could arouse feelings and sensations within her that Fletcher didn't. Was that something she should be concerned about, she wondered.

She quickly decided that it didn't really matter if she should be concerned, since Fletcher was the only one capable of getting her out of such a dismal situation. Their marriage would not be one of love and, the way things were looking, it wouldn't be one of passion either. But she would make do. She really didn't have a choice.

The ringing of the phone intruded her thoughts. Getting up from the table she quickly crossed the room to pick it up, but turned to make sure she still had a good view out the window. "Hello."

"I called to see if you've come to your senses and called off your engagement."

Pam couldn't do anything, but shake her head and smile. She wasn't sure who was worse, her sisters or her best friend from college, Iris Michaels. From Iris's initial meeting with Fletcher, he had rubbed her the wrong way and she hadn't gotten over it yet. "No, sorry, the wedding is still on, so I hope you haven't forgotten your promise to be my maid of honor."

Pam could picture Iris sitting behind the desk of the PR company she owned in Los Angeles with a beautiful view of the Pacific. Iris would be tapping a pen either on her desk or to the side of her face, trying to think of a way to get out of the promise she'd made their second year in college together over a peanut butter and jelly sandwich. Their days in college had been hard. Money had been tight, so they had made do, shared practically everything and had become best friends for life.

Right out of college, Iris had met, fallen in love with and married Garlan Knight. Garlan, a stuntman, had been killed while working on a major film less than a year into their marriage. That was four years ago and, although Iris dated on occasion, she had long ago proclaimed that she would never give her heart to another man because the pain of losing the person she loved wasn't worth it.

"I'm trying to forget I made that promise. So what's been going on with you lately?"

At first Pam couldn't decide whether she should mention anything about Dillon and then thought, why not? Chances were, when Iris came to visit, her sisters would tell her about him anyway, and then Iris would accuse her of holding secrets. "Well, there is something I need to tell you about. I had a visitor this week."

While periodically glancing out the window, Pam told Iris how Dillon had shown up two nights ago. Surprisingly, Iris didn't ask a lot of questions; she listened attentively, giving Pam the chance to finish. "So, there you have it," Pam finally said, glad it was over and done with. She made an attempt to move to another subject—about how things were going at the drama school—when Iris stopped her.

"Hey, not so fast, Pam. What aren't you telling me?"

Pam rolled her eyes. "I've told you everything."

"Then why did you deliberately leave out any details about how this guy looks? You know I'm a visual person."

Pam breathed in deeply. "He's good-looking."

"How good-looking?"

"Very good-looking, Iris," she said, hoping that would be the end of it.

"On a scale of one to ten with ten being the sexiest, how would you rate him?" Iris asked.

"Why do you want to know?"

"Just answer the question, please," Iris demanded.

When Pam didn't say anything for a moment, deciding to keep her lips sealed, Iris said, "I'm waiting."

Pam rolled her eyes again and then said, "Okay, he a ten."

"A ten?"

"Yes, Iris, a ten. He is so darn pleasing to the eyes it's a shame," she said, inwardly blaming Iris for making her tell all.

"What about his personality?"

Pam thought about how dinner had gone yesterday and how pleasant it had been for her sisters to feel included in the dinner discussions. Dillon had held their focus because he had paid attention to them, as if what they had to say was important, not trivial like Fletcher would often do. Yes, she would have to say he had a nice personality.

"He's nice, Iris, and his personality goes right along with it."

"Would he be someone that would interest you if you weren't engaged to Fletcher?"

Pam frowned. "Why would you ask me something like that when I *am* engaged to Fletcher?"

"Cut all the drama, Pam, and answer the question."

Pam's frown deepened because she knew the answer to Iris's question without thinking much about it. "Yes, he would be. In a heartbeat." And then because she had to tell someone and Iris, being her best friend, was the likely candidate, she said, "I'm attracted to him. Isn't that awful?"

"Why is it awful? You and I both know why you're marrying Fletcher, which I still think is a mistake. I refuse to believe there is not a bank anywhere that will loan you the money you need to pay off that second mortgage."

"We're talking about a million dollars, Iris. You know how much hassle you got from the banks when you wanted to borrow half that much to start your PR business. I have very little in savings and what I do have Jill will need for college next year. And Paige and Nadia need a home. I can't expect them to move away from the only home they've known. A home that's been in the Novak family for over a hundred years." Pam sighed in frustration. "I still can't believe Dad didn't take all that into consideration when he took out that second mortgage."

"If Fletcher was really a nice guy, he would cosign for you to get that money without any strings attached," Iris said. "For him to put stipulations on his help by asking you to marry him is just downright underhanded, if you ask me."

Pam didn't say anything since she had heard it all from Iris before, several times. When Iris finally ended her spiel, Pam said, "Marrying Fletcher won't be so bad, Iris."

"It will be if you're sentencing yourself to a life without love and passion, and we both know that you are. I loved Garlan and the passion we shared was wonderful. I can't imagine being married to a man I didn't love or who didn't do anything for me sexually."

Pam was silent for a moment and then said quietly, "Well, I can. I don't have a choice, Iris."

For a short while Iris didn't say anything, either. "Then maybe now is the time to enjoy passion while you can."

Pam blinked. "Just what are you suggesting?"

"You've admitted you're attracted to Dillon Westmoreland, so take advantage of that attraction and think about yourself for a change, not the house or the land or your sisters. Think about Pamela."

"I can't do that," Pam said.

"Sure you can. Are you going to deny you haven't been thinking about Dillon Westmoreland in the wee hours of the night?"

Pam almost dropped the phone. "How did you know?"

Iris laughed. "Hey, you said the man is a ten. Men who are tens can't help but find their way into a woman's nightly dreams, regardless of whether she's single, engaged or married. It happens. My advice to you is to bring him out of your dreams into your reality. You will be married to Fletcher until death do you part. Do you want to go through the next fifty, sixty or seventy years without feeling any passion again?"

"I told you about my past experiences with passion, Iris," she said, remembering the couple of times she had slept with guys and the disappointment she'd felt afterward. She hadn't heard the bells and whistles, nor had she felt any earthquakes like Iris had claimed she would.

"That's why you owe it to yourself to try things out one more time. I bet Mr. Ten will deliver."

At that moment Pam saw Dillon's car pull into her yard. Moments later she watched him get out. Today he was wearing a pair of khakis and a dark green shirt. And just like yesterday and the day before, he looked handsome and utterly sexy.

Her gaze scanned over his body and, as if he knew she was staring out the window, he turned and looked directly toward her. She immediately felt heat suffuse her body at the same time blood gushed through her veins. Yes, there was no doubt in her mind that if given the chance he could deliver.

"Pam?"

"Yes?"

"When will you be seeing him again?"

Pam licked her lips as she continued to stare. Dillon hadn't moved. He was still standing in that same spot gazing through the window. He couldn't see her, although she could see him. Yet it was as if he knew she was there, knew he was holding her attention. She wondered if he had any clue about the thoughts flowing through her mind at that particular moment. If he did, he would probably jump back into the car and hightail it off her property.

"Pam?"

"I see him now, Iris. Through the kitchen window. He just drove up and has gotten out the car."

"Then the ball is now in your court, Pam. And you owe it to yourself to play it."

Dillon leaned back against his car as he stared into what he knew was Pam's secret window. Somehow he knew she was there, looking at him, with the same intensity with which he was looking at her.

Ramsey's words of last night rang in his ears, and the thought of wanting her made his breathing quicken and his guts clench. If she knew what he was thinking she probably wouldn't let him within a foot of her, and definitely not inside her house.

He had soaked in the bathtub in his hotel room last night with his eyes closed and thought about her. He had gone to bed thinking about her. And he had awakened that morning thinking about her. A woman who belonged to another man.

Not yet though, as Ramsey had pointed out to him last night.

He would be out of line to make a pass at her, so he wouldn't. But he intended to do everything to incite her to make a pass at him…if she was interested. If she wasn't, then he knew he would have to control his urges. But if she *was* interested, then those urges would be set free.

There was a chance that he was reading too much into the looks they had exchanged across the dinner table last night, or the heat that he'd felt. But there was only one way to find out. If she decided to indulge in this thing he felt between them, then that meant her relationship with Fletcher wasn't as tight as it needed to be.

Deciding he couldn't stay outside and stare into the window for the rest of the day, he drew in a deep breath before shifting his eyes away to move toward her front door. He took his time walking up the steps and by the time he lifted his hand to knock, the door had opened and she stood there.

His guts clenched harder as he lowered his hand to his side. She looked as beautiful as usual, but today she was wearing her hair differently. It appeared fluffed up and it billowed around her shoulders like she had used one of those curling irons on it.

His gaze moved from her head to her eyes and saw her watching him as intently as he was watching her. He then moved his gaze lower to her lips. They were the same lips he had dreamed about last night. Many times.

Then his eyes followed the hand that she nervously ran down her throat to the V of her knit top. He couldn't help but notice how her breasts swelled in perfect formation against the blouse.

"I've been waiting for you," she said, snagging his attention as his gaze shifted back to her face. Captured her eyes.

"I know," he said in a voice that sounded husky to his own ears.

He didn't think he needed to explain. For some reason he sensed that she fully understood. "Am I allowed in today?" he asked as a smile touched his lips. She had yet to move from in front of the door.

She blinked as if she'd just realized that fact. "Oops. Sorry about that. Yes, please come in," she said before stepping aside.

He strolled past her, took a whiff of her scent and felt his entire body respond. Instantly. Why was the sexual chemistry between them stronger today than yesterday? More potent. Today, they seemed to be on instinct, with little or no control.

When she closed the door behind her and leaned back against it, she eyed him warily. He didn't say anything for a while. "And how are you doing today, Pam?"

"I'm doing fine," she said, in what sounded like a strained voice. "What about you?"

"I'm doing okay," he said. No need to tell her about his restless night, in which he had dreamed endlessly of her and all the things he wouldn't mind doing to her.

"I guess you're eager to get back to reading that journal."

He chuckled. He was eager all right, but that journal wasn't what was driving his eagerness. "Sort of."

Again he wasn't entirely sure just what was going on between them. What had happened since yesterday to make them so sexually charged that the very air they were breathing sizzled. He pulled in a deep breath, both feeling it and fighting it.

"I'm going up to the attic now," he said in a low voice, just loud enough for her to hear. "You probably have a lot to do, so forget that I'm here."

She smiled in a way that sent blood rushing all through him. "I doubt I'll be able to do that."

"Do what?" he asked.

She held his gaze. "Forget that you're here."

He wanted to ask why, but decided not to do so. She was the one who was engaged. If any boundaries were going to be crossed, she would have to be the one to take the first step over. "You can try," he suggested.

"And if I can't?" she asked in a somewhat shaky tone.

Holding her gaze, he breathed in and pulled more sexually charged air into his lungs. He felt it stirring in his chest and flowing in his extremities, causing the lower part of him to harden. Throb. He even felt a sheen of sweat form on his brow, which compelled him to say, "Then you know where I am."

Without saying anything else, he turned and headed slowly up the stairs to the attic.

Pam leaned against the door and watched as Dillon disappeared up the stairs before releasing the breath she'd been holding. She was too shaken to think straight, and too tempted to follow him up those stairs to move away from the door.

She glanced down at the ring on her finger, the ring Fletcher had placed there. Instead of feeling guilt, she felt desperation as Iris's words rang loud in her ears. *"Then the ball is now in your court, Pam. And you owe it to yourself to play it."*

If only Iris knew just how much she wanted to play it. Maybe her best friend did know, which was why she'd said what she had. Iris did know love and she understood passion. She had been happy with Garlan and when Garlan had been taken away from her so suddenly and unexpectedly, Iris's life had nearly fallen apart.

She had been there for Iris, to encourage her to go on with life, and now Iris was there for her, encouraging her to do something for herself before it was too late. Before she legally became Mrs. Fletcher Mallard.

But still, she needed to pull herself together and wondered why she would even consider following her impulses with a man she'd met only three days ago. What was there about Dillon that drew her to him, made her feel things she'd never felt before? Made her desire things she'd never before wanted?

Something you'd tried twice and left you disappointed.

Why did she think with him it would be different? Why did a part deep inside of her know that it would? It might be the way he looked at her, the heated intensity she felt from his gaze, the desire she saw even without him speaking a single word.

Those were the things that were urging her to move away from the door and propelling her to walk up the stairs, one step at a time.

Dillon stared at the words written in the journal, his eyes feeling the strain of seeing the words but not comprehending them. He had read the same sentence three times, but his mind was not on what Jay Novak had written close to a century ago. Instead his mind was on the woman he had left downstairs.

Why did some things have to be so complicated? Why had the Novaks' homestead been the first place on his list in his quest to find the key to his heritage as the eldest son of the Denver Westmorelands? And why was he lusting after a woman who another man had already claimed?

Dillon closed the journal and rubbed his hand down his face. Fletcher Mallard was a successful businessman and probably a prime catch for any woman in these parts. Evidently there was something about the man Pam had found to her liking.

And there was evidently something about him that she'd also found lacking.

No matter how things appeared, and regardless of the fact he'd only known her for three days, he refused to believe, or even consider the possibility that Pamela Novak was the type of woman who could love one man and mess around with another. So he could only come to the conclusion that she was not in love with Fletcher. Then why was she marrying him, Dillon wondered.

Wealth? Prestige? Security?

It hadn't been hard to figure out that Tammi had only been interested in him because he had made the pros, and the thought of being the wife of a professional basketball player had stroked her fancy. When he had given it all up, had walked away to handle his family's business, he'd known she assumed it was only short term, although he'd always told her differently. When she couldn't get him to walk away from family obligations, she had left.

Dillon's thoughts were interrupted by the soft sound

of footsteps approaching. He felt a quick tightness in his stomach. His entire being tensed in anticipation, knowing it could be only one person. He could no longer sit, so he stood and had placed the journal aside by the time Pam crossed the threshold.

His heart began beating wildly in his chest and his body automatically hardened at the sight of her standing there. She had come to him. He hadn't been certain that she would, but she had.

His gaze scanned her body. He had meant to tell her earlier that he thought the outfit she was wearing, a white blouse and a dark blue skirt, looked good on her. It had been the first time he'd seen her legs and they were definitely a beautiful pair.

"Looks like it might rain later," she said. She strolled over to the window to glance out. While she looked out the window, he was looking at her. The sun was still shining so he wondered how she figured it might rain later. If anything, he figured it might snow. Like Denver, Gamble had its sunny days and cold nights, especially this time of the year. But at the moment he didn't care about either. The only thing on his mind right now was Pam.

She glanced over at him and he realized he hadn't responded to her earlier comment about the weather. "Yes, it just might rain," he said quietly.

She nodded and turned back to the window. His throat had started to go dry, while at the same time liquid fire raced through his veins. At that moment he decided she had made the first move and now it was time to make his.

Helplessly and with an urgency he felt all the way to the bottom of his feet, he slowly crossed the room, knowing each step was taking him closer to the woman he wanted. When he came to a stop behind her, she turned and looked up at him.

He gazed down into her face thinking she looked uncertain and indecisive. "You give. I take. No regrets," he said in a thick voice.

Dillon hoped she understood because he meant every word. She glanced down at the engagement ring on her hand and his gaze followed hers. And while he watched, she twisted the ring off her finger and then placed it on the windowsill.

Then she looked up, met his gaze and said in a soft, barely audible voice the exact same words he'd spoken to her. "You give. I take. No regrets."

Her words touched an inner coil within him, made desire drum through his entire body at a pace that had him breathing in deeply.

He took another step toward her and heard himself groan low in his throat at the same moment he reached out and pulled her into his arms. And with a hunger that he felt all the way to his toes, he lowered his mouth as she parted her lips. The connection was explosive, and sensations rocked through him as his mouth greedily took hers, desire flooding him from all corners and settling in his body part right below his belt.

His hands tightened around her waist when she began to tremble in his arms, and she kissed him back in a way that made everything within him, every single molecule, feel new, revitalized and energized. He couldn't recall the last time he had feasted on a woman's mouth the way he was feasting on hers.

He didn't want to take the time to pause to pull air into his lungs. He just wanted to keep kissing her, continue pressing against her middle to let her feel the hard, solid evidence of just what she was doing to him, how she was making him respond.

The kiss went on, seemed unending until the cell phone in his pants pocket sounded. Of all the times to get a damn signal, he thought, and for a moment he refused to release her mouth, needing to ply it over and over again with strokes of his tongue, although each flick inside her mouth was causing his muscles to contract in a way they had never contracted before.

He hoped the phone would stop ringing but when it didn't, he reluctantly pulled his mouth away from hers, after he'd swept his tongue against her already moist lips.

The ringing had ceased by the time he snatched the phone from his pocket and saw the missed call was a text from Ramsey. He checked the message and it said one word. Bane. Dillon gritted his teeth, wondering what the hell his baby brother had gotten into now.

He glanced over at Pam and thought at that moment he really didn't care, since Ramsey's message had interrupted the most passionate kiss of his entire life. Never had a kiss left him with his senses spiraling out of control and his entire body feeling like it had been torched into flames.

He knew Pam had been as affected by the kiss as he

had. She seemed to be trying to pull herself together. They had done more than just grasped the moment, they had taken total control of it in a way that had them both still scraping for breath.

He watched as she slowly moved away from him to return to the window. She gazed out and he couldn't help wondering if she had reneged and now had regrets. He tensed, refusing to let her off his hook that easily. "Come to my hotel room tonight, Pam."

She swirled around and met his gaze but before she could open her mouth to say a single word, he reached out, pulled her back into his arms and took control of her mouth all over again.

The last time, he had kissed her with a need. This time it was with desperation. He refused to let her incriminate herself in any way, and if kissing her was the way to keep it from happening, then so be it. He would stand here and ply her mouth with his kisses forever if that's what he had to do.

A short while later, when he finally released her mouth, she looked somewhat dazed and her lips appeared slightly swollen. He lifted his hand and pushed her hair from her face, tempted beyond reason to sink his mouth onto hers again. Just the thought of doing so made his hand tremble. He hoped she knew this wasn't the end. Just the beginning.

And to make sure of it, he repeated the words he'd said earlier. "Come to my hotel room tonight, Pam."

Again she looked up and met his gaze. Her lashes fluttered just seconds before she replied, "No."

But before his heart could drop to the floor, she added, "Mr. Davis, the owner of the hotel, knows me, so that won't be a good idea. However, my drama school is only a few blocks away on Durand Street. Will you come there?"

He nodded quickly. "What time?"

"Eight," she said almost in a whisper. "I have a class tonight and everyone should be gone by then."

A moment of silence purred between them and then she searched his eyes. "So, will you come?"

A smile touched his lips and he reached out and stroked her cheek with the back of his hand, leaned closer to her and responded in a low, husky voice, "Sweetheart, nothing short of death is going to keep me away from you tonight."

Six

Pam glanced around at the excited faces of her students. Practice had gone perfectly, with all of them knowing their lines. There was no doubt in her mind that nine-year-old Shauna Barnes had an acting career in her future. Everyone was gearing up for the play Dream Makers Drama Academy would be presenting next month, Charles Dickens's classic *A Christmas Carol*.

"Do you need me to stay behind and help you straighten things up?" Cindy Ruffin asked a short while later, after all the students had been dismissed and were rushing out the door. It hadn't rained as Pam had predicted, but a light layer of snow flurries were coming down.

"No, I'm fine," she said smiling.

Cindy had been a godsend. Her husband, Todd, had

been a classmate of Pam's and, like her, Todd had left Gamble for college. He'd played pro football until an injury ended his career. A few years ago, after Hurricane Katrina, Todd had decided to move his family from New Orleans and back to his hometown. Everyone in town was glad for Todd's return and within a year had talked him into running for mayor.

"I think the kids did an awesome job at practice tonight, don't you?" Cindy asked as a bright, cheery smile touched her lips.

"Yes, and I have to thank you and Marsha for it. You're the ones who have been working tirelessly with them while I've been dealing with paperwork," she said.

"Yes, but having you here is such an inspiration to them since it shows how successful you can be with hard work. You graduated from high school and went off to California to pursue your dream of acting. Do you miss it? All the glitz and glamour of Hollywood?"

Pam thought about Cindy's question. A part of her did miss it, but since she hadn't yet become a part of the "Hollywood crowd" there wasn't a lot she'd had to give up. She had gotten parts in a few low-budget movies, and her dates were mostly those planned by her agent for publicity purposes. She'd spent most of her free time studying her lines for auditions.

"No, I really don't miss it," she said honestly. "At least not as much as I thought I would. I have so much going on for me here."

"Yes, I can see that," Cindy said, glancing down at Pam's engagement ring. "You didn't make an official announcement about your engagement, but I gather a wedding is coming soon. Have you set a date yet?"

Pam swallowed deeply as she looked down at her hand. She had put the ring back on after Dillon had left. Whenever she thought about the kiss they had shared, she could feel her eyes glaze over and her cheeks burn. She had never been kissed that way before. Never.

Clearing her throat she said, "No, not yet."

After a few minutes more of conversation, Cindy left, leaving Pam all alone in the spacious residence that now housed the acting school. Several of the bedrooms downstairs had been converted into office space and classrooms, and the walls had been removed from the entire upstairs area to transform it into one vast studio.

The huge basement had been transformed into a mini-movie-set where scenes could be filmed. It was here at Dream Makers that she had starred in her first low-budget movie for the Gamble theater group. She would always appreciate her very humble beginnings here.

She glanced at her watch. It was a little past seven. She would have a chance to be by herself for a while before Dillon arrived, she thought.

Dillon.

She couldn't think about him without remembering the kiss they had shared earlier that day. And every time she did sensations too numerous to count would invade her body, sending a thrill through her. She'd heard of a man pushing a woman's buttons but, in Dillon's case, he not only pushed them, he had leaned right on them and pretty heavily at that. He had pressed them into another zone. She still felt wired up.

He had left her home shortly thereafter, saying he thought it would be best if he did so, fearing if he were to stay he might not be able to control himself. So she had watched him leave, Jay's journal tucked under his arm, while flutters of desire had overtaken her stomach.

Fletcher had called before she'd left home to tell her he had arrived in Montana safely but wouldn't be returning to Gamble at the end of the week as he'd planned. The insurance company was being difficult, so it would be the first of next week before he got back.

He had asked about Dillon, wanting to know if he was still hanging around town, and she had been upfront with him. Pam had informed him that Dillon had been invited back to dinner and had come to the house to finish going through the items in the attic. She could tell from the tone of Fletcher's voice he hadn't been pleased.

She had dropped by Lester Gadling's office before arriving at the academy and asked him to recheck her father's papers to make sure he hadn't missed something the first time. The attorney had seemed agitated by her visit, and had told her that he would do as she requested, but was confident that nothing would change. She had been hoping that somehow he had made a mistake.

After phoning in and checking on her sisters to make sure everything was okay and all their homework was done, she began walking through all the rooms, tidying up as she went along. As it got closer to eight o'clock, she began to feel a nervousness tugging at her insides. And that same outlandish bout of desire that had overtaken her earlier that day was working its way upward from her toes to her midsection.

There was no doubt in her mind that tonight she and Dillon would do more than just kiss. She knew they would be sharing passion of the most intense kind. They would both give, they would both take and she was truly counting on neither of them having any regrets. Now that she'd thought everything through and was comfortable in her decision, she would admit that she needed him tonight. She wanted him. And she intended to have him.

After pulling into the empty parking lot, Dillon switched off the ignition and checked his watch. Noting it wasn't quite eight o'clock, he decided to stay put for a while.

Adjusting the car seat to accommodate his long legs, he stretched them out in front of him as he released a deep sigh. It seemed as if time had done nothing but drag by since he had seen Pam earlier. He'd nearly gone crazy waiting so he had tried reading more of the journal. So far all Jay Novak had written was information about the dairy business and how well he and Raphel worked together. Apparently, Jay hadn't been suspicious of the relationship between Raphel and Portia.

Dillon's thoughts shifted back to Pam. On the drive over from the hotel he had given himself a pep talk. Getting hyped up over a woman wasn't his typical style, but he'd discovered nothing about him was the norm when it came to Pamela Novak. From the moment he had first laid eyes on her, she had touched him in a way no other woman had ever done before, and that included Tammi.

He checked his watch again and as each minute ticked by so did his need to see her, be with her, hold her in his arms once more. He wanted to run his hands all over her and to taste her with his lips and tongue. He shifted in the seat as he felt his body get hard. It was cold outside, but the inside of his car was getting pretty damn hot.

Dillon tried to switch his concentration to something else, anything else, as he waited. His thoughts drifted to the conversation he'd had with Ramsey a few hours ago regarding the text message he'd sent. Ramsey had gotten an angry call from Carl Newsome. It seemed that Bane was hanging around the man's daughter again and making her dad downright unhappy to the point he'd threatened to do bodily harm to the youngest Denver Westmoreland if he didn't leave Crystal Newsome alone.

Dillon shook his head. For as long as he could remember, Crystal Newsome had been an itch his baby brother just had to scratch. If Bane didn't wise up and leave Crystal alone, that scratch might get him into hot water.

Dillon checked his watch again and after releasing a long breath, he opened the car door and got out. He couldn't recall the last time he'd sneaked around to meet a woman under the cover of night, but as he headed toward the entrance to the Dream Maker

Drama Academy, he had a feeling that tonight such a move would be well worth it.

Pam's feet had touched the bottom stair when she heard the knock on the door. Without wasting any time, she moved in that direction. It was exactly eight o'clock.

As she got closer to the glass door, she could see Dillon through it. He was standing there staring at her with an intense look on his face. That look sent ripples through her body and made her shiver, although the temperature was warm inside. She nervously licked her lips as she opened the door and shivered even more when she felt a blast of cold air.

She quickly stepped back when Dillon walked in, and when he closed the door and gave her his dimpled smile, she felt heat bubbling up inside of her. As usual, he looked good. He had changed clothes and was now wearing dark slacks and a blue buttoned-up shirt. In place of his long coat he now had on a black leather bomber jacket.

She felt ridiculously happy to see him and for lack of anything else, she said, "It didn't rain today like I thought it would."

"No, it didn't rain." The warmth of his response matched the look in his eyes. As she stared deeper she saw that his dark depths seemed more hot than warm.

He glanced around and sensing his curiosity, she said, "Come on, let me show you around." She started to reach out and take his hand and then thought better of it. If she were to touch him now, any part of him, she would probably lose the little self-control she still had. For the next five minutes she took him on a tour of the academy and she could tell he was impressed with everything he saw.

"And the woman who used to live here was once a teacher of yours?" he asked, after she had completed her tour of the upstairs and was ready to show him the basement.

"Yes. Louise Shelton used to be my drama coach and was instrumental in my getting a scholarship to attend college in California. She died within a few months of my returning home after my father died. When she died she willed this place to me, with stipulations."

He lifted a brow. "What kind of stipulations?"

"That I could never sell it and that it would always be used for what it was intended, which was to be a drama academy. I don't have to stay here and run the school per se, but I have to make sure it is managed the way I know Louise would have wanted."

He nodded as he kept walking beside her. A part of her was aware they were wasting time when they both knew exactly what they wanted to do and why they had arranged to meet here at eight o'clock. She was willing to draw things out if he was; however, she doubted he had any idea of how being close to him, walking beside him, was messing with her senses and was stretching what little self-control she had to the limit. When they reached the basement stairs he slowed his steps to let her go first, and she could feel the intensity of his gaze on her again.

It took all she had to put each foot in front of her, being careful not to slip, knowing he was so close behind her, watching her every step. When she reached the bottom floor she turned to wait for him to join her.

And to kiss her.

She had a feeling he knew it. He probably had detected that fact by the way she was breathing, or by the way she was now looking up at him as he moved down the stairs toward her. No doubt it wasn't just one, but all of those things. And really, it didn't matter. What mattered was that he was intuitive enough to pick up on what she wanted and needed, and as soon as he joined her on the bottom floor, he placed his hands at her waist and pulled her into his arms. Before she could draw in her next breath, he leaned down and connected his mouth to hers.

Dillon figured he could stand there and sip on her all night.

Then, maybe not.

Plummeting into her mouth, tasting her like this, with such intensity, such greed and hunger, was making his entire body throb. Desire as thick as it could get, was spreading through him at a rate he could barely control.

He shifted his body, needing her to feel how aroused he was, which equated to just how much he wanted her. And just how much he needed her. He knew she was getting a clear picture when she wrapped her arms around his neck and shifted her body, adjusting it to his so that his erection was resting between the juncture of her thighs. And damn, it felt just like it was where it belonged, he thought.

Well, not quite.

Where it really belonged was deep inside of her. Hell, he was a man, a Westmoreland at that. He knew his male brothers and cousins that he'd grown up with, and he had met the male cousins from Atlanta. So there was no doubt in his mind they all had something in common when it came to basic primitive instincts. They all enjoyed making love to women.

He could imagine taking her all over the place. He wanted to make love to Pam in every room and every single position he could think of and then some. He could certainly get creative rather quickly. But first, this way, starting at her mouth, kissing her with a yearning that made him wonder where in hell a damn bed was when you needed one.

As if she sensed his agitation and the reason for it, she pulled her mouth away, took hold of his hand and led him through an area that looked like a soap-opera film set. They walked through a living room and dining room, caught a glimpse of a kitchen before going around a movable wall that led to a bedroom, one that was decorated with billowy white curtains at a fake window.

On a shuddering sigh she stopped by the bed, and Dillon gazed deep into her eyes. He could tell that she was about to get all nervous on him and decided to say the same words he'd spoken earlier that day. Words she seemed to understand and accept. "You give. I take. No regrets."

She stared at him for a moment and then he watched

as her mouth curved into an easy smile. They would go through with their plans for tonight. No questions asked, no discussions needed. The main thing on his mind was getting inside of her, feeling her wetness surround him, clench him and milk him, which made him decide there was one subject open for discussion and he would initiate it. Birth control.

"I brought condoms," he said, patting the pocket of his slacks. There was no need to tell her just how many since it might scare her.

"And I'm on the pill." She bit nervously on her bottom lip and then added, "And I am not sleeping with Fletcher. I've never slept with him, in case you're wondering about that for health reasons."

Fletcher.

It was only then that he remembered the other man, which made him glance down at her hand. She had taken the ring off again. He wondered why she and her fiancé had never been intimate. Not that he was complaining.

He truly believed she was not a woman who could be in love with one man and sleep with another. That meant there was something about her engagement to Mallard that wasn't on the up-and-up. Sooner or later he intended to get some answers. But not now.

The only thing he wanted to get right now was some of her.

He suddenly detected that her scent had changed and, like a man acutely honed on the woman he wanted, he breathed her into his nostrils, a potent blend of perfume and body chemistry. It was an aroma that could drive a man wild and would make him want to get inside of her real quick and explode all over the place. But only after making sure she was ready to detonate right along with him.

For a long time after Tammi had left he had kept his guard up around women, and had only dated when he got a physical urge to mate as a way to relax, relieve stress and keep his abundance of male hormones in check. But there was something different about Pam, something he'd picked up on the first moment he'd seen her.

She sparked to life something inside of him and he knew making love with her was about more than just blowing off steam. More than great sex. It was about a connection he had never felt before with a woman. A connection on a plane so high it had his insides throbbing.

On a deep, shuddering breath he reached out and tilted her chin up, needing to plunge into her mouth once more, to intensify the connection he already felt. And when she automatically pressed closer to him, he deepened the kiss and slid his arms around her, holding her in a tight grip, as if he never wanted to let her go.

He gave full concentration to her mouth, just as he had done earlier that day. He'd once heard a woman say that you hadn't been kissed unless you'd been kissed by a Westmoreland. Dillon wanted to make sure after tonight that Pam thought the same thing.

So with thorough precision and a masterful meticulousness, Dillon took his time and put his tongue to work. He penetrated it into areas of her mouth that had her groaning, and then he flicked it around in a way that seemed to jar her senses—if the sounds she was making were any indication. He enjoyed kissing her, but moments later he knew he wanted more. Pulling his mouth from hers he took a step back to remove his jacket.

After tossing it across a chair he whispered, "Undress me and then I will undress you." He intended to save her—the best—for last.

A pair of uncertain eyes stared up at him in a way that had him asking, "You have done this before, right?"

He watched a lump appear in her throat as she swallowed, and then she said in a strained voice, "Which part?"

Which part? He lifted a curious brow before responding. "Any of it."

She shrugged her feminine shoulders. "I've had sex before, if that's what you're asking. While in college. Twice. But it wasn't good. Both times it was over before it got started. And I've never undressed a man."

She then lowered her gaze for a second before returning her eyes to his with a flush on her face. "I've said too much, haven't I?" she asked softly. "Given too much information?"

As far as Dillon was concerned, it definitely hadn't been too much information. What she'd just said was something he needed to know. Now he was aware of just what she needed and how she needed it. If any woman deserved to be made love to the Westmorelands' way, it was her. And he intended to do the honors. Proudly. Gladly. Tonight would be a night she wouldn't easily forget. In fact, he planned on taking things slow and making sure every aspect of the evening stayed in her memory forever.

"No, you've told me what I needed to know," he said. In fact, he was sure there had to be more, like why the man she intended to marry hadn't done his job. But they would talk about Fletcher later.

"I'm going to make undressing me worth your while," he said, smiling at her, already imagining her hands on him, all over him. "Go ahead, baby, and do your thing."

She gave him a hesitant smile before reaching out, and the moment her fingers began working on the buttons of his shirt his stomach knotted, and it was all he could do to remember he was supposed to go at a slow pace and not be tempted to speed up the process. This first round would be hers and he intended to make it special for her, even if it killed him.

Pam pushed the shirt off Dillon's shoulders and marveled at how broad they were. She couldn't resist the temptation to touch them, amazed at the strength she felt in them. Then her hands slid to the dark hairs of his chest and she glanced down and saw his hard, flat abdomen. Dillon had a beautifully powerful body, she thought.

Deciding she wanted to check out other areas of that body, she trailed her fingers downward. The moment she did so, she heard his sharp intake of breath and glanced up to his face. The eyes watching her beneath lowered lashes were dark, smoky, sensuous.

Knowing they didn't have all night, she unhooked his belt and pulled it through the loops before tossing it to join his jacket and shirt on the chair. She glanced back up at him. "I need to take your boots and socks off before going any further," she said softly.

He smiled before sitting down on the bed so she could remove his boots and socks. When that was finished, she stepped back as he stood again. Instinctively, her hands went to his waist and she eased down his zipper. Tugging it down wasn't as easy as she'd thought it would be, mainly because of the size of his erection. It was hard to believe that he wanted her *that* much.

"Need help?"

She glanced up at him. "I'll be okay once I get this zipper past here."

He chuckled. "Here where?"

She couldn't help chuckling with him before replying, "You know where. And why do you have to be so big?" Too late. She couldn't believe she'd actually asked that.

Embarrassed to the core, she peered back up at him and saw the huge smile on his face. "This isn't funny, Dillon Westmoreland."

"No, sweetheart, that is the most precious thing anyone has ever said to me."

She knew he was teasing, of course, and after working with his zipper a few moments more it finally cooperated. She was able to tug his pants down his legs as he stepped out of them. Satisfied, she took a step back. There was only one piece left, his briefs. She frowned, wondering why she hadn't thought to remove them with his pants.

"It's not all that serious," he said in a deep, husky voice.

"Maybe not for you, but it is for me," she said, giving him a playful pout. "This is my first time and I have to get it right."

A smile curved his lips. "No, you don't. You can get it all wrong and I will still make love to you tonight."

His words, as well as the determined look in his eyes, did something to her, made her eager to remove his final piece of clothing. She was curious to unveil that part of him that had given her the most trouble. From the way the briefs fit him she had a pretty good idea of just how well-endowed he was. The rest of him was exceedingly toned, definitely virile and oh-so-male.

She inserted her fingers into the waistband of his briefs and gently tugged them down his hips, having no easier time getting them off than she had his slacks. But what removing them fully exposed to her eyes had been well worth the trouble. The man's body was perfect in clothes, but she was particularly enjoying this view of him out of clothes. She had seen a naked man before, but not one this well put together. Not one this large and hard.

"Is there a problem?"

She glanced up and met his gaze, suddenly feeling shy, awkward and unsure of her capabilities where he was concerned. "I hope not," she said softly.

"There *is* not," he countered. "Go ahead, feel your way. Touch it." And then in a lower voice he said, "Get to know it."

Get to know it? She had never fondled a man before in her life but, doing what he suggested, she reached out and first ran her fingers over the tip, fascinated by the feel of the smooth head. Then she traced with her fingertips a path along the sides, marveling at the swollen veins. And when she finally got the nerve to close her hand around him, he moaned out loud.

She quickly loosened her hand. "Sorry, I didn't mean to hurt you."

"It didn't hurt. In fact, just the opposite. Your touch feels good."

She smiled at that. "Really?"

"Yeah."

"Umm, in that case…" She began stroking her hand up and down the length of his thick erection. Her gaze held tight to his face and watched how his eyes became glazed and his lips seemed to tremble. She smiled, satisfied with her efforts and what they were doing to him.

"Not so bad for an amateur, wouldn't you say?" She beamed, feeling like she had accomplished something monumental and proud of herself for doing so. She allowed her hands to get more brazen while watching his erection get harder, and feeling it thicken in her hands.

"I have no complaints," he said in what sounded like a tortured moan. His physical reaction fascinated her, brought out a level of womanly pride that drove her boldness.

"When you're through having your fun then it's my turn," he said in a voice that to her ears sounded like an intoxicated slur.

She considered the wisdom of continuing what she was doing for too long and stole a peek at him from under her lashes. His eyes were closed and his head was tilted back at an angle that showed the veins in his neck. They looked like they were straining. Almost ready to pop.

"Hey, I'm merely doing what I was told. You said to get to know it," she said defensively, but couldn't hide her smile.

Deciding she'd gotten to know him very well, she released him and stepped back and watched as he slowly regained control. Then he stared at her and muttered in a low, throaty voice, "Now it's my time to get you naked."

Getting her naked would be just the start, Dillon thought, looking at her and imagining just how she would look without her jeans and sweater. Even now she looked sexy, with her raven-black hair spilling around her shoulders, a few loose tendrils cascading around her face. Making love to her had been on his mind since leaving her house, and now that he was here, standing stark naked in front of her, knowing that soon, very soon, he would be inside of her sent his entire body into an intense throb mode.

"Come here, Pam," he murmured in a breathless tone, and watched as she didn't hesitate to cover the short distance between them.

When she was within close range, he reached out and snagged her by the waist and brought her closer to the fit of him, and was sure, without a doubt, that she could feel his hardness and his heat, through her jeans.

But he wanted more. He wanted to give her more. Wanted to let her feel more. And with that thought firmly planted in his mind, he reached out and pulled her sweater over her head. Moments later he slung it onto the chair. Her lacy black bra was sexy, but also needed to come off, and he proceeded to remove it. Like her sweater, he sent it flying to the chair.

"Good aim," she leaned closer to say, her breath warm against his throat.

"Thanks," he uttered raspily, his gaze giving her breasts full attention. Her breasts were full, firm twin mounds supported by delicate, feminine shoulders. As if a magnet was drawing his gaze, his eyes were pulled to the nipples and, unable to resist temptation, he took the pad of his finger to flick across both hardened tips.

But he wanted to do more than just look and touch. He wanted to taste them and, with that thought in mind, he leaned in and lowered his mouth to close over a quivering, delicious-looking peak.

"Dillon."

The moment she said his name he stuck out his tongue to run it across a nipple before pulling it into his mouth to suck in all earnestness. He didn't even try to change his stance when she lifted her hand to support the back of his head to keep right where he was, to continue what he was doing. Not that he intended to stop. The taste of her breasts was arousing him and, with an easy movement, he shifted his mouth to the other nipple to greedily ply it with the same attention.

By the time he lifted his head and met her gaze he could barely keep his entire body from trembling. A need for her, to make love to her, surged through him and he stooped down on bended knees to remove her shoes and socks. To maintain her balance she placed a hand on his shoulder and her touch sent his muscles rippling as sensations roared through him, made him clench his teeth.

After removing her shoes and socks, he stood, straightened his body to his full height and without saying a single word he reached for the waistband of her jeans. Somehow he managed to hold it together until she stood before him in nothing more than sexy, black, lacy, high-cut panties. They were panties he would be taking off her and he was fighting the urge to just rip them off her instead.

Getting back on his knees he began lowering her panties down her long, gorgeous legs, and sucked in a deep breath when her scent surrounded him. He shot a glance upward and saw the heated look of desire in her eyes.

It took all his strength to stand, and without wasting any more time, he reached out and swept her into his arms. Holding her gently he moved to the bed and together they tumbled back onto the covers.

Seven

Pam felt her stomach stir when she gazed up into Dillon's eyes. She had ended up on her back between his firm thighs, with him towering over her. At that very moment she felt several things. Captured. Ensnarled. His.

She forced the last from her mind immediately. How could a woman be engaged to one man and possessed by another? She didn't want to be confused by anything now, and she certainly didn't want to think about Fletcher. This was her time, this sensual interlude, her moment to seize something she might never have again.

You give. I take. No regrets.

And from the eyes bearing down on her and the arms locked on both sides of her, she had a feeling Dillon

Westmoreland was more than ready to take everything she had to give. And there would be no time for regrets.

He began lowering his head and she lifted hers upward to meet his mouth. The moment they touched, he began devouring her with a hunger and need that she felt all the way to her toes. He had kissed her greedily before, but this was a different kind of ravenousness, one that bordered on insatiability. As if, no matter how many times he kissed her or how deep and thorough the kisses, he would never be able to get enough. However, that didn't mean he wouldn't try. And in this case, trying meant using his tongue to pleasure her in a way she'd never been pleasured before. No man before had taken so much time, had concentrated on so much detail during a kiss. It was a practice that he'd perfected and she was the satisfied recipient.

He gave all and held back nothing. Provoking her, tempting her, almost demanding of her to give back. So she did, by boldly returning his kiss with his same voraciousness. She wrapped her arms around his neck as he sank his mouth even deeper onto hers. Her response was wanton, her desires keen and her senses at the moment were shot to hell.

He broke off the kiss at the same time his hands began to move all over her as he held her gaze. Starting at the center of her throat, he slowly inched a path downward toward her chest. When he reached her breasts and ran the pad of his thumb across the protruding tips, pleasure, as sharp as it could get, rammed through her and she almost forgot to breathe. And when he leaned closer to replace his fingers with his mouth, she felt heat circulate then settle between her legs.

When he brought his tongue into the mix she gasped. Suddenly she felt full as if she needed to scream out, but could not. The most she could do was summon up enough energy to moan. Then his mouth released her breasts and he began trailing a heated path down to her navel with his tongue. He seemed fascinated with her belly button and she felt his wet tongue all around it. She shuddered as her stomach tightened and then relaxed, over and over again.

And when she thought he would be returning to her mouth, he shifted his body, lifted her hips and dipped his head. The moment the scalding tip of his tongue went inside her womanly core, she emitted a loud moan. At the same time, she heard his growl of male satisfaction. It was evident from the way he was using his tongue inside of her, that he enjoyed this type of love-making. He went about it with such ardent dedication that she was nearly in tears. She was pinned between his mouth and the mattress. She realized that he didn't intend on letting her go anywhere until he got his fill.

And he didn't intend to be rushed.

He was meticulous in his lovemaking, pushing her just to the peak, driving her close to the edge again and again. She couldn't suppress her response and groaned shamelessly, holding firm to his shoulders while she was his enjoyment. And even moments later when she let out a scream as a tide of pleasure came crashing down on her, his mouth remained locked on her, as if determined to savor every last bit of her.

It was only later, when she felt weak as water and was panting for breath, that he lifted his mouth to withdraw from her. He leaned back on his haunches, licked his lips and gave her a smile that made her come all over again.

There was nothing more beautiful than seeing a woman clutched in the throes of ecstasy, Dillon thought, as he studied Pam's features. And just knowing he'd been the cause sent desire clamoring all through him and made his already hard body feel harder.

With her glazed eyes on him, he eased off the bed to reach for his pants. Going through the pockets he pulled out several condom packets and tossed all but one on the nightstand. He then proceeded to put the one on, knowing Pam watched his every move.

He was a man who'd never had a problem with his nakedness and the thought that he was on display, exposed and being checked out from head to toe, didn't bother him in the least. The only thing on his mind was making love to the woman in that bed. And what a picture she made. Sexy. Naked. Exposed. It seemed that she didn't have a problem with nudity, either, and he was glad of that.

He returned to the bed and drew her to him, needing to hold her, needing to touch her, needing to kiss her. His mouth found hers again and he moved his hand downward toward her parted thighs. Inserting a finger inside of her, he captured her gasp right in their kiss.

He even swallowed her moan when his finger began moving inside of her, slowly with determined and well-defined strokes, glorying in her wetness, breathing in her aroused scent. All the while their mouths and tongues were mating greedily, and with a need that he felt in every part of his body, especially his throbbing shaft.

Not sure he could last much longer, he pulled away slightly to ease her back deep into the mattress as he shifted into position, simultaneously spreading her thighs and locking her hands above her head in his.

He changed positions again to get the lower part of his body in perfect formation, with the head of his erection right at her entrance. And then, while she watched him, he began lowering his body, surging inside of her. The moment his head came in contact with her heat he wanted to thrust inside, but felt that this was something he had to savor, even if it killed him.

And with every inch he pushed inside of her, he felt as if he was literally dying. She was tight and her body muscles clamped down on him, clutched him for all it was worth, and in response he released her hands to grip her hips, determined to go as deep inside as he could go.

A world of absolute pleasure began closing in on him, engulfing him with an urge to move. He cupped her bottom closer, so he could delve deeper, and with slow, steady strokes, he began staking his claim on her. Every time he slid inside of her and every time he slid out, he felt a sharp pull on his sanity, an increased dose of pleasure and a fortitude to drive into her the same heated, silken force that was driving him.

It worked. She began moving with him, joined him, clenched him, milked him to the point he felt everything was getting pulled out of him. He locked his legs with hers and then, while buried deep inside of her, he began flexing his lower body in a way to get as close as he could get, sinking into her deep, mating with her hard, thrusting into her rapidly. And when she screamed his name, he threw his head back when the same infused pleasure that ripped through her, tore through him.

And the name that he moaned from his lips was hers. The body he was exploding inside of was hers. And the lips he knew he had to taste at that very moment were hers.

Everything was about her, as well as her ability to make him feel things no other woman could make him feel was artfully and enticingly being transmitted in a satisfying way. Emotions he couldn't define, and not just on a physical plane, energized his muscles and made his hunger for her that much more intense. Making love with her wasn't just good, it was brutally good. So good he actually felt whipped. His senses shattered in a thousand pieces and, as sensations continued to race through her and spread into him, he felt a sense of fulfillment he knew that he could only find with her.

Pam wondered if she would have the ability to ever move again, and wasn't sure if she even wanted to. Even now she was wrapped in Dillon's arms, their legs entangled, their arms entwined and their bodies still intimately connected. She felt drained, worn out, deliciously sated in a way that almost made her purr.

The way he was draped across her, she didn't have to move her head to look into his eyes, since he was there, staring at her with the same amazement and sexual fulfillment in his eyes that she felt in her body. This was what Iris had wanted her to experience at least once in her life and now she was glad that she had. This had been the ultimate in sexual satisfaction, the most gratifying, mind-blowing passion.

She had used muscles she hadn't ever used before, and she'd found every part of him, both working and nonworking, to have a definite purpose. She could only lie in awe, while her heart tried to slow down from beating so fast in her chest.

She felt cherished, protected and desired. Not only in the way he was looking at her, but at the gentle caress of his hand moving on her thigh, like he still had to touch her in some way, even in the aftermath of shared sexual bliss.

Pam moved her lips to say something but no words came out. It was just as well, because he leaned up and captured her mouth in his. She raised her hand to his cheek, needing to touch him, and to feel the movement of his mouth on hers beneath her palm.

When he finally broke the kiss she felt perfectly contented and when he finally released her, slowly pulled out of her to go to the bathroom, she felt a profound sense of loss. She watched for him to return and when he appeared, lounging naked in the doorway, his long, muscular legs braced apart, she thought his stance had a masculine sexiness that almost made her drool. Her gaze moved all over his body and the main thing she couldn't help but notice was that he was fully aroused again.

Seeing him in that state did something to her own body—made her feel alive, wanton, desired. His gaze scorched her, as he slowly scanned her entire body, lingering on her legs before moving upward to the juncture of her thighs. And there his gaze stayed, transfixed for a spell, and she felt the heat of it on her womanly core. She forced down a deep, shuddering breath when he began moving toward her and she couldn't help noticing the swell of muscles in his broad shoulders and the wide expanse of a strong, solid chest.

He paused by the bed, giving her a totally male smile while he proceeded to put on another condom. She watched the entire process, unable to force her gaze away. A heavy silence hung over the room.

And then she sat up in the bed and opened her arms to him. He moved, placed a knee on the bed, went into her arms and planted his mouth on hers. And as he adjusted their positions to ease her back deep onto the bed, the thought that continued to run through her mind was that tonight was their one and only time together. She desperately wished it could last.

A few hours later, they stood fully dressed together in the foyer of the academy. It was a little past midnight and time for them to part. Together they had stripped the bed and changed the linen. Then she had made them a cup of hot chocolate and they'd sat down at the kitchen table. Not much was said between them, as there was nothing left to be said. They were both deep in their own thoughts.

He had Jay Novak's journal back at the hotel, so he

couldn't use the excuse of visiting her place to read it. But he wanted to see her again. Be with her again. In fact, he intended to be a part of her life.

He mentally scrambled to make sense of that decision and released a deep breath when he finally did. She had touched a part of him in a way he could not walk away from. She might have assumed this was a one-night stand, but as far as he was concerned that was not the case.

He didn't harbor any guilt that he was no better than Raphel in cutting in on another man's territory. If nothing else he had discovered, before even kissing her that first time, that she really didn't belong to Fletcher; at least not the way a woman should belong to the man she was about to marry—heart, body and soul. Totally and completely.

Now was still not a good time to bring up that fact and ask why she would even consider marrying a man she didn't love, a man who hadn't introduced her to passion. At first he'd thought he could get beyond that curiosity, deciding it was strictly her business. But that was no longer the case. Now it was his business, as well, mainly because as far as he was concerned Fletcher Mallard was not the man she needed.

He was.

Some may consider him thinking such a thing as arrogant, possibly even a little egotistical, and they probably would be right in their assumption, he thought. But something had happened tonight in that bed, something he couldn't dismiss. Every time he went inside of her, he'd felt more than just sexual pleasure. He'd felt a sense of belonging. He'd felt a connection he could not explain and a deep, abiding need to claim her.

As far as he was concerned he wasn't taking anything away from Mallard, because it was quite obvious that the man didn't have a claim on her anyway. The only stamp Mallard had on her was the ring she had placed back on her finger. And, although he didn't particularly like the sight of it there, he would tolerate it for now.

His gaze moved from her hand to her face. She was staring out into the night. It was time to leave but neither was making an effort to do so. He knew he couldn't mention to her what he was thinking. For whatever reason she had decided to marry Mallard. He had news for her, but it wouldn't be delivered tonight. He would give her time to make her own decision about things— namely in his favor. And if she didn't, then he would intervene. He was the one who had introduced her to passion and he would be the one who would continue on with her lessons.

In the meantime, he would learn what kind of hold Mallard had on her to make her agree to a loveless and passionless marriage.

At that moment she looked up and met his gaze and he knew, whether she realized it or not, she was now his. That conclusion sent an immediate jolt to his nervous system, stimulated his brain and made every muscle in his body feel a strength of resolve he hadn't felt in a long time. He needed time to think, but for now, he'd just accept things the way they were.

Silently, he reached out and began buttoning up her

coat. Surprised, she blinked, then smiled up at him while studying his face. "Thank you. You take such good care of me."

He smiled back, deciding not to tell her the reason he did so was because she belonged to him. Instead, he said, "You've been too hot to suddenly have to get cold."

She laughed and then reached out and placed her arms around his neck. "Yes, I have been hot tonight and all because of you. You're special, Dillon. I've known you for only a short time, but it seems like I've known you my entire life."

He understood what she was saying, because he felt the same way about her. He'd never been a man who would lay claim to a woman after sleeping with her just one time. But with Pam, things were different. He didn't know how, he just accepted that they were.

He felt his lips curve into a smile as he asked, "I never believed in that paranormal stuff, but do you think we could have been together in another life?"

He watched her brow furrow and then moments later the answer was in her eyes. "No," she said. "Nothing would have obliterated from my mind the kind of passion I felt tonight had I shared it once before with you," she said and smiled.

"What I shared with you tonight is something I've never shared before with any man. So there has to be another reason why I feel so free and uncontrolled with you."

He felt the same way. There had to be a reason why he felt free and uncontrolled around her as well. But whereas she might accept what they had shared tonight as a casual affair, he could not. If she figured he would just walk away, leave Gamble and head back to Denver without a second glance, then she was wrong. Dead wrong.

And to show her how wrong she was, he raised a hand to her face and caressed her cheek. "Tonight was very special to me, Pam. I've never met a woman quite like you."

He could tell by the look in her eyes that she didn't know what to make of his words. That was fine because soon enough she would. He lowered his head and captured her lips in a slow yet greedy fashion. He felt her shudder beneath his mouth and when she tightened her arms around his neck, he deepened the kiss.

He wanted her. And he would have her. As far as he was concerned, she was already his. That was the Westmorelands' way. The ability to recognize his or her true mate when he encountered her or him, although they might initially try to deny it. He would be the first to admit some Westmorelands were stubborn, and he had discovered that trait wasn't confined to just the Denver clan. He'd been told that the Atlanta Westmorelands were just as bad.

He could now admit that he had made a mistake with Tammi in thinking she was the one. He felt certain there was no mistake with Pam. And for him to be so sure of that so soon might be a mystery to some, but not to him.

He slowly and reluctantly withdrew from her mouth, but for the moment he refused to release her from his arms. "I'm walking you out to the car and then I'm following you home to make sure you get there safely," he whispered against her ear.

She pulled back and a cautious look appeared on her face. "You don't have to do that."

"Yes, I do." For *reasons you can't possibly imagine,* he thought. But he simply asked, "Ready to go?"

"Yes, but..." She studied his face. "Tonight..."

She didn't continue, but nervously moistened her top lip with her tongue, an action that had him forcing back a rush of desire.

"What about tonight?"

"Tonight was tonight. Tomorrow remains the same. I'm engaged to Fletcher."

He looked down at her. A shaft of light from the fixtures in the parking lot came through the glass door and slanted across her face, making her look so beautiful he felt his heartbeat increase. He silenced the response he really wanted to make—one that clearly stated her engagement was evidently in name only and regardless, she was his, signed, sealed and so deliciously delivered. His stomach clenched just thinking about their lovemaking.

Her expression indicated she expected him to understand and to accept her words. There was no use telling her he wasn't about to do either. Instead, he knew he would do what he had to do. The first thing was to find out why she had gotten engaged to a man like Mallard in the first place.

So to bide his time, he pushed a strand of hair back from her face. "I know," he said.

Those two words were all he was capable of saying to her right now. "Let me walk you to the car."

She held back, refusing to move an inch as she studied his face for a moment. "You don't need to come to the house tomorrow, do you?"

He swallowed deeply. She was trying to cut ties now. She didn't have any regrets about tonight but she knew she couldn't continue. "No, I'll take the next couple of days and stay at the hotel and relax and read the journal. If you need me for anything, you know where to reach me."

She nodded and then moved toward the door. He walked by her side. He would give her two days and if she didn't come to him, engaged or not engaged, he would be going after her.

Eight

"We don't understand, Pammie. Why did Dillon stop coming for dinner?"

Pam glanced across the dinner table at Nadia, knowing how her baby sister operated. Nadia would ply her with the same question until she got what she considered a satisfactory answer. Pam wasn't sure that her response would be satisfactory, but judging by the three pairs of eyes staring at her, Nadia wasn't the only one waiting to hear what she had to say.

Pam could make it easy on herself and place the blame on the three of them by claiming they were the ones who'd scared him off, and that Dillon had been fully aware of their little matchmaking schemes at dinner and preferred to have no part of it. But telling her sisters that would not be the truth. Dillon had said on more than one occasion that he enjoyed her sisters' company and that they reminded him of his female cousins back in Denver. He had taken their shenanigans in stride and hadn't seemed bothered in the least.

"Pammie?"

Nadia's soft voice pulled her back to the moment and she glanced across the table. Before Pam could open her mouth to answer, Paige spoke up in a disheartened tone. "He doesn't like us any more than Fletcher does, does he?"

Pam was taken aback by her sister's assumption. "That's not true. Dillon really likes the three of you and enjoys dining with us, but he has our great-grandfather's journal and has been doing a lot of reading over the past couple of days. You must not forget the reason he came to town in the first place."

She took in a deep breath before continuing. "And as for Fletcher, you girls are wrong about him. He does like you."

"Then why is he planning to send us away after the two of you get married?" Nadia asked with a belligerent look on her face.

Pam was surprised by her sister's question. "Where on earth did you get such an utterly absurd idea? Fletcher is not planning to send you away after we get married."

Nadia's frown deepened and a worried look lit her eyes. "He is, too. He told Gwyneth Robards's father that he is, and her father told her mother, and Gwyneth overheard them talking and she told me."

Pam frowned. Gwyneth Robards was Nadia's best friend. Her father, Warren Robards, owned a slew of sporting goods stores across the state. He and Fletcher were good friends. Pam was not one to believe in gossip. She wished Nadia wouldn't do so, either. "Nadia, there's no way Fletcher would have said something like that."

"So, are you saying Gwyneth's father lied?"

Pam frowned. "What I'm saying is that Gwyneth apparently misunderstood what she heard from her parents' conversation. Again, there's no way Fletcher could have said that."

What she didn't add was that he knew why she was marrying him—to save her family home, to secure a future for her sisters and to keep the family together. Even if they were to lose their home, her sisters would return to California with her or they all would remain in Gamble and make do.

"Getting back to Dillon, Pam," Jill said. "I don't care how much reading he has to do, he has to stop and eat sometime. Did you invite him to dinner the last three nights?"

Pam nervously bit down on her bottom lip. She hadn't invited Dillon to dinner the first night because they had planned their secret meeting that night at the academy. And she hadn't invited him the past two nights because she had needed time to get herself together after their night of passion.

"No," she finally said. "Like I said, Dillon has a lot to read. He said as much the last time he was here."

"So you will invite him back?"

Pam's stomach knotted. Again, three pairs of eyes focused on her. "Yes, I'd invite him back but it's up to him whether he would come. Like I said, there's a reason why he came to Gamble and it's not to keep us entertained."

As if satisfied with her answer, her sisters resumed eating their dinner and the conversations then revolved around what had happened at school that day. She was glad their interests had shifted to other things, although hers remained on Dillon. Every time she thought about that night and all the things they'd done and shared, she would get all flushed inside, her body aching for a repeat. There was no doubt in her mind that if she were to see Dillon now, her body would weaken. If he were to make an attempt to kiss her, or even remotely suggest he wanted to take her to bed again, she would not be able to resist him.

She hadn't talked to him or seen him since that night. He had left a message for her on the answering machine yesterday indicating he'd decided to change hotels and had checked into one in Rosebud. Unlike Gamble, the neighboring city of Rosebud had a number of cell towers in close proximity so there was always a signal. She understood that he would want to stay connected to the outside world since he was a businessman.

He had provided the name of the hotel, which was only a ten-mile drive from Gamble. She had thought about calling him back to let him know she'd gotten the message, but had eventually talked herself out of it. She knew she would see him again, because eventually he had to return the journal. She was hoping that by then she wouldn't be thinking so much about how his kisses had felt on her lips, or just how good he'd felt going into her body. And then, how she'd felt when he was inside of her. She tightened her thighs together at the memory.

She licked her lips and then picked up her glass to take a sip of her cold tea, needing to relieve her suddenly hot throat. She forced her thoughts to shift to what Gwyneth thought she'd overheard about Fletcher's plan to send her sisters away. She'd ask Fletcher about the rumor when he called later that evening. She figured that he would be calling before she left for her evening class at the academy.

Halfway through dinner the phone rang and she pushed her chair from the table and crossed the room to answer it. "Yes?"

"How are things going, Pamela?"

A part of her wished she could feel some excitement, some fluttering of sensations anywhere in her body at the sound of Fletcher's voice, but that wasn't happening. Her heart slammed painfully in her chest at that realization. "Everything is fine, Fletcher. How are things with you? Is that problem in Bozeman getting corrected?"

"Yes, in fact, I have good news. I might be back in Gamble this weekend instead of next Tuesday."

She swallowed deeply and tried to put a smile in her voice. "That is good news."

"And do you know what would make me extremely happy, Pamela?"

She dared not try to guess. "No, what?"

"If you've decided on our wedding date by the time I return. I know you prefer waiting until February, but I want to marry this year, so a Christmas wedding is what I prefer."

All of a sudden she felt her stomach drop. Christmas was next month. "I can't possibly get things together by then."

"What do you need to do other than show up at the church? Besides, I hate to bring this up, but I'd like to satisfy that mortgage on your home as soon as possible. That's one of my wedding gifts to you."

Pam's eyes narrowed. In his own passive-aggressive way, Fletcher was reminding her of the reason she had agreed to marry him. "I'm sure you want that matter resolved and done with as soon as possible, right?" he added.

"Yes, of course."

"So will you have a date for me when I get back to Gamble?" he asked.

She stole a glance at the dining room table where her sisters were chatting away. They had happy looks on their faces and she was determined to keep it that way. They were smart, all three of them, and she'd made a promise to herself at her father's funeral to do whatever it would take to make sure they got the best life had to offer.

"Pamela?"

She breathed in deeply. "Yes. I'll have a date for you but I won't promise it will be this year."

He didn't say anything for a moment and then she

heard the frustration in his tone. "Let's start with the date and I hope it's one we will both agree to."

Knowing he was probably about to ask her about Dillon, she quickly jumped in to say, "Nadia is bothered about something, Fletcher, and I'm sure it's all a misunderstanding, but I thought I'd mention it anyway."

"What?"

"She thinks you're sending her away when we get married. I assured her that wasn't the case and—"

"That has crossed my mind."

Pamela stopped talking in midsentence. Her hand tightened on the phone. "Excuse me?"

He must have heard the cutting anger in her tone. "Calm down, Pamela. It's not what you think. You have smart sisters and I think they're getting a wasted education going to that public school in Gamble. As you know, I went to a private school and I received a top-notch education. The best. And I know you want Nadia and Paige to get accepted into a good college. Going to a private high school will not only assure them a good education, but also entrance into the best colleges. That's what you want, right?"

"Yes, but—"

"And just think, they would be associating with people who will benefit them in the long run."

"Yes, but I'm not for sending them away from home," she whispered, so her voice would not carry to the dining room. She had just assured Nadia that she wouldn't.

"I know, which is why I'm looking into schools in Cheyenne. That's not too far away," he said, as if she would be glad to hear the news.

She moved away from the kitchen and into the living room, which would afford her more privacy. "As far as I'm concerned, if it's not here in Gamble then it's too far away."

"But we'll be looking out for their futures. There's a wonderful private school there that has excellent living facilities and great security."

Pam tried to keep a ripple of anger from consuming her. "You should have talked to me about this first, Fletcher."

"It was going to be another one of my wedding gifts. I know how much your sisters' futures mean to you."

Pam closed her eyes. "We can discuss this more when you return."

"I don't understand why you're upset. I'd think it would be what you wanted. At least I believe it's what you told me you wanted that day you accepted my marriage proposal."

Pam couldn't say anything. Was it really fair to get upset with him when she *had* said those things?

"If that's not what you want, Pamela, then no sweat. I want to do whatever makes you happy," he said in a throaty, low voice that did nothing but frustrate her even more.

"I know, Fletcher, and I appreciate everything you're doing, but we'll need to talk about this when you get back."

"Okay, baby. Have a good evening. And by the way, is Dillon Westmoreland still in town?"

She could actually hear the coldness in his voice. "No, in fact Dillon has left town," she said. What she'd just said really wasn't a lie because Dillon was no longer in Gamble. Fletcher didn't have to know he had merely moved to a hotel in neighboring Rosebud.

"I guess he got what he came for and decided to move on. That's good. Maybe we won't be seeing the likes of him again anytime soon," Fletcher said cockily.

She frowned, not liking Fletcher's attitude. "I suspect he will be returning at some point since he still has my great-grandfather's journal." She figured she might as well prepare him now so he wouldn't go into cardiac arrest when he did see Dillon again.

"He can keep the damn journal for all I care. I just don't like the man."

Pam inwardly fumed. The journal was not his to decide whether Dillon could keep it or not. "Goodbye, Fletcher."

"Goodbye, Pamela, and I hope to see you Sunday."

Dillon smiled at all the voices he heard in the background of his phone conversation with his brother Micah. Micah, a graduate of Harvard Medical School who was only a couple of years younger than Dillon, was an epidemiologist with the federal government. Everyone often joked about Micah being the mad scientist in the family.

"So how long will you be home, or did you just drop in long enough to attend this weekend's charity ball?" Dillon asked Micah. His brother was known to travel all over the world doing work for the government. He had lived in China for an entire year during the bird-flu epidemic.

The charity ball he was referring to was the one the

Westmoreland family hosted every year to raise money for the Westmoreland Foundation they had established to aid various community causes.

"I'm here for the ball and I'll be home at least through New Year's. Then I'm off to Australia for a few months."

"Good to hear. I plan on flying in for the ball this weekend," Dillon said. A part of him really wasn't ready to put distance between him and Pam, even for a short while.

"I heard Sheriff Harper talked you into taking his sister Belinda as your date," Micah said in a teasing tone.

Dillon rolled his eyes. "It was either that or have Bane spend a night in jail for trespassing on the Newsomes' property in the middle of the night." He wasn't sure he appreciated his brother finding his pre-dicament with Belinda so amusing. His brothers and cousins knew Belinda had had her eye on him as husband number three for about a year.

"So how is the investigation into Raphel's past coming along?"

"I'm finding out more and more information about our great-grandfather every day," Dillon replied.

Micah chuckled. "Just as long as it's nothing that can come back to haunt me with the State Department. I can barely handle the fact that he ran off with those other men's wives."

Dillon smiled. "I told you the real deal about Raphel and Lila. He did it to protect her."

"Yes, but we still don't know what was up with him and the second one, Portia Novak. It should be a rather lively discussion at Thanksgiving dinner this year and will be the first time in a long time everyone will be home."

After a few more minutes of conversation with Micah, the phone was passed around to the rest of his brothers and cousins. Everyone wanted to know what information about their great-grandfather he'd been able to uncover so far. He didn't tell them everything he'd found out, but he felt he'd told them enough for now.

It was close to six in the evening when he finally said goodbye to everyone and hung up the phone. He glanced over at the journal he'd been reading over the past two days. He was surprised no one in the Novak family had taken the time to ever read the journal. If they had they would have learned just why Raphel had taken Portia away, and why Jay had given him his blessings to do so.

He glanced around the hotel room. It was totally different from the one he'd had in Gamble. It was a lot more spacious and the furnishings were early American instead of Victorian. Although CNN was alive and well on the big-screen television and the reception for his cell phone was perfect, he would be the first to admit that he missed the huge bathtub at the Gamble hotel. But he needed to be in a hotel that had fax and Internet service. His firm was working on a huge multimillion-dollar deal and he needed to be available if a last-minute snag developed.

And he needed to be someplace where if Pam wanted to pay him a visit, it wouldn't make the six o'clock news.

He walked over to the window and looked out. It was cold outside but nothing like it had been the night he'd met Pam at her drama school. He sucked in a deep breath when he remembered that night and how it had changed his life. He hoped she'd gotten his message about changing hotels. The one in Gamble was closer to her place, but this one was only ten miles away.

She hadn't returned his call so a lot of things were going through his mind right now. Had she broken their rule about not having any regrets? Had Fletcher made it back to town? He didn't have answers to those questions, but the one thing he did know for sure was that if he didn't hear from her tonight, he would be making a trip into Gamble to see her. He still had her journal and tomorrow would be a good time to return it.

On the drive from Dream Makers back home later that night, Pam was trying, really trying, not to recall her conversation with Fletcher earlier that day. She was even trying, as hard as she could, to give him some slack and believe he had her sisters' best interest at heart when he'd made the decision they should continue their education in Cheyenne and not in Gamble. But for him not to have discussed it with her was totally unacceptable.

He of all people knew how close she and her sisters were. Did he honestly think she would let them go off and live at some private school, leaving their family and friends behind? And as far as she was concerned, there was nothing wrong with public schools. She'd gone to one and had done pretty damn well.

She reached out to turn up the dial for the heat a little. It was cold, although it wasn't as cold as it had been the last night she'd driven home from the academy. That was the night she had spent almost three hours in Dillon's arms. She couldn't help but smile just thinking about it.

She had talked to Iris but hadn't told her best friend a single thing. She hadn't needed to. According to Iris, there was something in the tone of her voice. She sounded relaxed. It sounded like she'd taken a chill pill. Pam chuckled as she remembered the conversation.

She passed a road sign that indicated the exit to Rosebud was coming up. She immediately felt a pull in the lower part of her body and it wasn't a gentle pull. It was a voracious tug. She tried to keep staring through her windshield, determined to keep her eyes on the road and to drive straight home. She then began experiencing flutters in her belly and her nipples pressing against her shirt felt sensitive.

The physical reactions her body was going through just knowing she was an exit away from Rosebud made her release a quiet moan. The hotel where Dillon was now staying was less than five miles from the interstate.

Dillon had given her his hotel room number when he'd left the message, but had made it seem as if he'd provided the number for informational purposes only. As if he'd wanted to assure her the journal was still safe and in good hands. Now she couldn't help wondering if perhaps he'd had an ulterior motive. Was he hoping to see her again, although she'd made it clear that what they'd shared that night was a one-night stand?

But the biggest question of all was why she was contemplating getting off at the next exit. And she knew the answer without thinking really hard about it. She was thinking of doing so because she needed to see him.

She needed to be with him.

She sighed deeply and as she took the exit to Rosebud she refused to question her sanity any longer. She was merely enjoying an indulgence that would be denied to her forever once she married Fletcher.

Dillon lay in his hotel room in the dark. He had dozed off, after eating a meal that room service had delivered and taking a bath. The television was on but he wasn't watching it. Instead his thoughts were on the woman he wanted.

He wondered what she was doing. Did she think about their night together as often as he did, or had she put it out of her mind? He had just shifted positions in the bed when he heard a knock at the door. Assuming it was housekeeping coming to turn down the bedcovers and to make sure he didn't need anything else before they retired for the night, he slid out of bed and into the jeans he'd placed on the back of the chair.

He opened the door slightly, just enough to make out his visitor and, when he did, sensations tore into him and forced air through his lungs. He quickly opened the door wide.

He refused to ask Pam what she was doing there. For a second he seriously doubted he had the ability to utter a single sound, so they stood there for a long moment and stared at each other, speechless. He did glance down at her finger. She had taken the ring off again. He looked back up into her eyes and felt his pulse rate increase.

Then she broke through the silence and smiled. "Are you going to invite me in?"

"Baby, I plan to do a whole lot more than that," he muttered thickly, his gaze not leaving hers.

He took a step back and she entered his hotel room. He closed the door behind her.

"I guess you're wondering why I'm here," she said in a quiet tone.

He shook his head. "We'll talk about the *why*'s later. Right now I just want to hold you. Make love to you. I've missed you."

"And I've missed you, too," she said honestly, wondering how she could miss him so much after two days, when she hadn't missed Fletcher at all and he'd been gone nearly twice that long.

Knowing they didn't have a lot of time on their side tonight, she took in his solidly muscular, naked chest and the way his jeans rode low on his hips. They were unsnapped and the zipper was barely up, which meant he had slid into them rather quickly. She hoped he was ready to slide out of them just as fast.

Feeling her heartbeat almost out of control, she shifted her gaze from him to glance around the room. Her great-grandfather's journal sat in the middle of a wingback chair.

She returned her gaze to him, knowing he'd been watching her intently and was probably waiting for her to make a move. She decided to do so. Moving away from the door she crossed the room to him and, the minute she stood in front of him, his arms easily slid around her.

"I hope I'm not interrupting anything," she said, reaching up and placing her arms around his neck.

He gave her a dimpled smile that was so sexy she felt her knees weaken. "Nothing at all. In fact I was just thinking about you."

"You were?"

"Yes."

And if to prove that point, he pulled her closer against him and she felt the erection he wasn't trying to hide. The magnitude of it resting snugly against the juncture of her thighs felt hard and hot. "And just what were you thinking about?"

"This." And then he swept her into his arms and kissed a startled gasp from her lips.

He took her mouth with a greed that made her moan in his arms as he placed her on the huge bed. And he continued to kiss her as she felt the heat of his body over hers. Whenever he kissed her like this, he had the ability to make her forget everything but him and how he was making her feel. Her thighs were nested between his and, although they were fully dressed, she could feel every hard and solid inch of him.

Slowly he withdrew from her lips, and as she stared deep into his eyes she caught the light from the lamp that brightened the eyes looking at her. And she knew at that moment that she could see a mirror of herself in his eyes. What she saw was a woman fiercely attracted to the man she was with and thinking she didn't want to be anywhere else.

"I want to show you how much I've missed you," he said huskily, kneeling before her while running a fingertip along the side of her face.

She met the intensity of his gaze, recalled every single thing he had done to her the previous time and felt her inner muscles clench at the thought he would be doing so again. That in itself made her lean up and whisper the challenge. "Then show me."

"With pleasure," he whispered close to her lips before taking those lips to begin a slow, sensuous mating that she felt as a gentle throb between her thighs. This kiss had all the high intensity, provoked the stirring sensations of the kisses they'd shared that night, but she could feel something different this time. It was there in the way he wielded his tongue in her mouth. He kissed her with a possessiveness that made every cell in her body become hypersensitive. And by the time he freed her mouth from his, she could only stare up at him, totally and fully at a loss for anything except the man gazing back at her. The look in his eyes clearly said he was claiming her. Here and now.

Warning bells sounded in her head. She knew what the outcome of her future had to be. He did not. She had to marry Fletcher—she didn't have a choice in the matter. It was something he would not understand and something she could not let him or anyone else prevent. It didn't matter what sacrifices she knew she was making. What mattered most to her were her sisters.

She hoped the vibes she was beginning to intercept from him were wrong and that he was not considering anything beyond what they had shared this week. Maybe she'd made a mistake in coming here tonight. Had removing her engagement ring made him think that she was willing to put aside her future with Fletcher? She had to make sure he understood that was not the case.

"Dillon?"

He reached out and placed a finger to her lips and, as if he comprehended what was going through her mind, said softly in a husky tone, "Although I don't have all the facts, I do understand, sweetheart, more than you know, and I think it's time for you to understand something, as well. Regardless of who you might be engaged to marry, you *are* mine."

Before she could comprehend his words, he lowered his mouth to hers in a kiss that was as potent and powerful as any intoxicating drug. And it was just as effective. Her mind and body became meshed in a mirage of sensations so forceful she gave up any desire to convince him to think differently.

She only recalled bits and pieces of him removing her clothes. But she did vividly remember the kisses he placed all over her naked body once he had completed the task. And she had committed to memory the sight of him removing all of his clothes, every single stitch, and then putting on a condom—almost a difficult task due to the size of his arousal—before returning to her.

Concentrated desire consumed her the moment he rose above her as he took her mouth again the way a hunter would go after his prey. Moments later he pulled away to use that same mouth to trace downward, to latch on to her nipples, sucking gently and causing flutters to stir within, to the point of being breathless.

And then he was there, close to her face, raising her hips, widening her thighs, lifting her legs to hug his shoulders, and then entering her in one smooth thrust that made her moan his name. But he didn't stop there. He continued to stroke her, inside and out, bearing down on her mind each time like he was bearing down on her body. And with each stroke it seemed to relay words he had not yet spoken, words she felt each time his dark eyes met hers, each time they breathed in and out together as one.

Sudden tears sprung to her eyes when she realized the depth, the intensity and then also the uselessness of the love she felt for him, all the way in her bones, in the air she was breathing. Yes, she had fallen in love with him. She'd once heard that a woman's body could and would recognize its mate, and the thought that this man was hers almost overwhelmed her, and touched her very soul.

He saw the tears flow down her cheek and leaned in to kiss them away, as if he had the ability to make whatever was wrong in her life right. She wished it was that simple, but knew it was not.

She looped her arms around his neck when his mouth moved from her cheeks to her mouth, and then she kissed him in all the ways she had dreamed of kissing him the past two nights.

He gave in, allowing her to lead, to take the kiss wherever she wanted it to go and to whatever degree of passion she wanted it to be. And when she felt the explosion that ripped through her body to ricochet to his, she couldn't hold back her scream of pleasure. And when she felt him sink deeper into her, tail-spinning into his own massive release, she clutched him tighter to her, locked her legs around his back, knowing that, regardless of what he thought and no matter that she now knew she loved him, this was all they would have together.

Nine

"I want to know why you are marrying a man you don't love," Dillon said raspily, close to her ear.

They lay locked in each other's arms, their bodies entwined, drenched in sweat from the intensity of their lovemaking. The aftermath of pleasure was so profound they were still fighting to get their heart rates back to normal while they savored what had to have been passion of the most explosive kind.

Dillon watched as her gaze widened at such a deliberate and bold question, and then his heart began pounding in his throat while he waited for her to respond. When she nervously licked her lips, he was tempted to lick right along with her but knew he had to hold back and listen to what she had to say. Tonight he wanted answers and wouldn't be satisfied until he got them.

And then, not surprisingly, fire crept into her eyes and she tilted her chin slightly. "You have no right to ask me that," she said.

A smile touched his lips. His woman was feisty when she needed to be and he liked that. He liked even more the thought of her as *his* woman. "I have every right, Pam. I'm a Westmoreland, remember. Raphel's great-grandson. I take what I think is mine regardless of whom it might belong to at the time. And you are mine. I told you that. And if you have any doubt of that take a look at the position you're in. I'm still inside you because it's where I want to be, where I know you want me to be."

She frowned. "Doesn't my engagement ring mean anything?"

He was tempted to laugh at that question. "No, not even when you're wearing it. And I notice that you don't hesitate to take it off when it suits you to do so," he said, knowing his words would stir her fiery anger even more.

At the moment he didn't care. He had fallen in love with her. If he hadn't been sure of it before, he'd known it as fact the moment she had taken the initiative and had plied him with her kiss. It seemed while she'd been ravishing his mouth with her tongue, emotions he had never felt before, deeper than he'd ever thought they could go, had consumed him, broken him down and reeled in his heart.

"Remember what I said? I give, you take and no regrets? I may have forgotten to mention that in rare situations, I claim. This is one of those situations."

She shifted to ease up but he had her leg pinned beneath his. Her frown deepened and then she said, "It's complicated, so it won't do any good to tell you anything."

"Humor me. Tell me anyway."

She looked away from him but he heard her words nevertheless. "What makes you think there is something to tell?" she asked.

"Because you're here in this bed with me, and by your own confession a few nights ago, you've admitted you've never slept with Mallard, the man you're engaged to marry. And," he said, reaching out and tilting her chin upward, bringing her face back in focus to his so their gazes could meet, "you're not a woman who could be in love with one man and sleep with another."

"You don't know that," she all but snapped.

He continued to hold her gaze as he took her hand, led it to his lips and then placed a kiss on her knuckles. "Yes, I do."

For some reason deep down she actually felt that he did. No, she wasn't a woman who could love one man and sleep with another. In all actuality, he was the man she loved, but it would take more than love to help her now.

"Pam?"

She breathed in deeply and said, "I *have* to marry Fletcher."

He lifted a bemused brow. "Why?"

She hesitated for a moment before saying, "My father died and left a second mortgage on our home. Although I've worked out a monthly payment arrangement for now, which is being handled through my father's attorney, the bank in Laramie wants the loan paid in full within ninety days. I tried applying for a loan with a bank here in town but that didn't work out. Fletcher had offered to marry me to take care of it. And he's promised to make sure money is there when my sisters need it for college."

Dillon just stared at her. At first he wasn't sure he'd heard her correctly. Then to make sure he had, he asked in an incredulous tone, "You're entering into a marriage of convenience?"

She nervously licked her bottom lip. "No, not quite. He does want children one day, so it will not be a marriage in name only."

"If Mallard wants to impress you with kindness why didn't he just pay off the balance of the loan for you?" he asked, biting out the words through clenched teeth.

She looked surprised he would suggest such a thing. "I couldn't ask him to do that. I'm talking about a balance that's over a million dollars. Dad purchased adjoining land with the intention of reopening the dairy."

"Even if Mallard couldn't loan you the money, he could have cosigned for you to get it," he said, not accepting any excuses for the man. He could recall the number of times his signature had been on such a document for his family members. "And most banks require that loans of that amount be insured in case the borrower dies," he added. "Which bank holds the mortgage?"

"Gloversville Bank of Laramie. I guess somehow Dad got around it, which I still find rather strange. But

I've checked with his attorney and he's gone over Dad's papers more than once. Dad didn't have the kind of insurance that would satisfy the loan. Mr. Gadling has been most helpful, working with the bank on my behalf, setting up the monthly payment arrangements where he receives the money from me to pay them."

Dillon heard what she was saying but it didn't make sense. In his profession he didn't know of any bank that would loan that much money without requiring that some kind of life insurance be purchased with it.

"So there," Pam pronounced.

She'd said it like that settled it, but he had news for her. It didn't. His gaze traced over her features. A part of him saw beyond what she was saying. It saw beyond what she thought she needed. She assumed she needed Fletcher Mallard. As far as he was concerned, she needed him. And unlike Mallard, he would deliver without any strings attached. It could only be then, after the matter with Mallard was dispensed with, that he would ask her to marry him, for all the right reasons two people should marry.

But still, something about the way her father's loan had been handled bothered him and he intended to check a few things out for himself on Monday. Deciding it would be best not to tell her what he planned to do, he lowered his head and tasted her lips instead, stirring the embers between lovers back to a roaring blaze.

And moments later, when he eased back inside her body, he knew he was where he belonged.

* * *

"Where do you get so much energy?" Pam asked in a whisper, while watching Dillon ease from the bed and head toward the bathroom. He glanced over his shoulder and smiled at her. "You, Pamela Novak, give me strength."

He moved on toward his destination giving her a good view of strong, long legs and a nice, tight tush. He gave her strength, as well, she thought, closing her eyes and snuggling under the covers. She inhaled the masculine scent he'd left behind and knew at that moment, as crazy as it seemed, and unlikely as it could be, each time they made love she fell deeper and deeper in love with him.

Now he knew the whole story regarding her relationship with Fletcher, and although she had a feeling he didn't like it, at least she hoped he understood why she *had* to marry Fletcher. Shifting up in bed she glanced at the journal on the chair, just as she heard Dillon returning from the bathroom.

"Did you find out any more about why your great-grandfather ran off with my great-grandfather's wife?" she asked, trying to keep her focus on her question and not on his naked body.

"Yes, I found out," he said, walking over to the chair to pick up the journal and returning to the bed to hand it to her. "I marked the spot with a sticky note. Some members of your family had to have known the whole story, but I guess it was a family secret."

Pam lifted a brow before opening the journal to begin reading. A few minutes later she was lifting astonished eyes to his. "Portia was caught in bed? With another woman?"

Dillon nodded slowly. "Yes. And to protect her from the scandal it would have caused, the husband of the other woman and your great-grandfather decided it would be best to keep the matter between them. But it was decided both men would eventually divorce their wives, which during that time would have been a scandal in itself."

Pam nodded. "So since Raphel was about to leave Gamble anyway to head out to California, he and Jay came up with this plan to take Portia away so she could start a new life elsewhere. Do you think the other woman joined her later?"

Dillon shrugged. "Who knows? We're talking about the nineteen thirties. There's no telling how things turned out with Portia. But your great-grandfather did legally divorce her for desertion before marrying your great-grandmother. I'm glad to finally know why Raphel ran off with another man's wife for the second time."

Pam closed the journal. With the mystery solved, Dillon would be leaving Gamble. He had no reason to stay. "Both times Raphel came to the rescue of women who needed his help. Sounds like a high-caliber man, a real protector of women," she said.

His lips curved into a smile. "Yes, but so was Jay. He could have made things hard on Portia, but he was willing to step back and give her a chance to live her life the way she wanted to live it. Leaving with Raphel was still a scandal within itself, but it would have been far worse had the truth been revealed."

He took the book out of her hands and placed it on the nightstand before easing back into the bed with her. "I'm flying out in the morning to return home to take care of a few family matters, but will return by the end of the week," he said.

Confusion touched her face. "But why are you returning? You've gotten what you came for. You now know the reason Raphel ran off with Portia. He and Jay set the entire thing up to look that way to protect Portia's reputation."

"Yes," he said huskily, easing up on his knees in front of her and slowly advancing on her like a hunter stalking its prey. "That was the reason I came initially, but you're the reason I'll be coming back."

"B-but nothing has changed. I still need to marry Fletcher."

A dimpled smile touched his lips. "No, you don't. I'm a man known to make things happen instead of taking advantage of a situation like I think Mallard is doing, so I plan to offer you an alternative."

She lifted a brow. "An alternative?"

"Yes. I can't let you marry another man when I know that I'm the man for you."

She shook her head and gave a resigned sigh. She'd thought he understood, but he really hadn't understood at all. "Dillon, please listen to me, I—"

"No, I'm asking you to trust me," he said, gazing into her eyes with a plea that she felt all the way to the lower part of her belly. "I know that is a lot to ask when we've only known each other for a short period of time, but I believe there has to be another way out of this situation. A way in which you don't feel forced or obligated to marry Mallard or anyone else. I want you to trust me and give me time to find another way. Do for me what Jay did for Raphel. Trust me to make your situation better."

She stared deep into his eyes and then she said softly, "Fletcher expects me to have a date set for our wedding when he returns."

Dillon nodded. "When does he get back?"

"Sometime this weekend, probably Sunday."

"Then stall him. I need time to check out a few things," he said huskily. "Say you will trust me."

She continued to look into his eyes, searched his face for a sign of why she shouldn't trust him and knew she would not see one. "I will trust you."

A satisfied smile touched his lips. Raising his hands, he cupped the lower part of her face and leaned forward for their mouths, as well as their bodies, to mate once more.

Ten

"Pamela, I thought we agreed that you'd set a date for our wedding by the time I got back," Fletcher said, sitting down to the dinner table with her and her sisters.

He had called Sunday morning to say he would be arriving back in Gamble around noon and was eager to see her. She had invited him to dinner and the first thing he'd done, after giving her a hug and telling her how much he had missed her, had been to ask what day she had picked for their wedding.

"Maybe she's decided not to marry you after all, Fletch," Jill said, smiling sweetly over at him with a deliberate glare in her eyes.

"That's enough, Jillian," Pam said to her sister. Jill

didn't know how true her words were. "I've been busy, Fletcher."

He frowned. "Too busy to plan a wedding that we both know needs to take place?"

She frowned back, wishing he wouldn't discuss such matters in front of her sisters. "We can talk about this later, Fletcher." She knew he didn't like putting off the discussion. In truth, she didn't, either.

Thanks to her sisters dinner hadn't been pleasant. They had practically ignored Fletcher. Having been gone for almost a week, he had wanted to be the center of attention and hadn't liked being ignored. Although she had tried rallying conversation around him, Nadia, Paige and Jill had not bought into her ploy. He hadn't been any better, often times mocking things they'd said. By the end of dinner her nerves were strained and she was ready for her sisters to retire to bed and for Fletcher to leave.

"Oh, I almost forgot," Fletcher said, breaking into her thoughts as she walked him to the door.

"My private plane made a pit stop at the Denver airport and I went inside to grab a copy of a magazine and noticed today's *Denver Post.* Your friend made the front cover with a very beautiful woman plastered by his side when they attended a charity function together this weekend. According to the paper, wedding bells might be in order for the couple," he said, smiling brightly. "I figured you'd want to see a copy so I saved the article for you."

She lifted a brow, confused. "What are you talking about?"

"This." He pulled the folded article from an inside pocket of his jacket and handed it to her.

She unfolded the article that had been neatly clipped from a newspaper, and it took all she had to hold back a gasp from her lips. Before her eyes was the man she had fallen in love with, dressed handsomely in a tux with a very beautiful woman by his side. The two were smiling for the camera. Although there wasn't an article associated with the photo the caption read, "Is Romance Brewing for These Two?"

She swallowed and glanced back up at Fletcher who was watching her intently. "You seemed bothered by that photograph, Pamela. Is there a reason why?"

She lifted her chin and met his gaze. "You're wrong," she lied. "I am not bothered by it." In truth she was. She and Dillon had just spent time together a few nights ago. He had said he had to return to Denver. Now she knew why.

Fletcher smiled. "Now I think it's time I put my foot down regarding our wedding plans," he said, reaching out and catching her by the waist and pulling her closer to him. His move surprised her because he had never been so forward with her before. Being close to him did nothing for her or to her. It didn't have the same effect on her that Dillon had. Because she loved Dillon, and the thought that she meant nothing to him, that his words had all been lies, was too much.

"Put your foot down how?" she somehow managed to ask.

"I've been trying to be patient but more than anything

I want you as my wife, Pamela. I'm aware you're not in love with me, but I believe over time that you will come to love me. I offered you marriage to help you out of a bad situation, but evidently you don't see it as such anymore. And maybe the thought of losing your home and securing your sisters' futures aren't the big deal they once were."

"That's not true."

"Then prove it. I no longer want a wedding date. Now I want an actual wedding. This week. A very private affair. Here on Friday. Make it happen or come Saturday our engagement is off."

Her eyes narrowed. "Are you forcing me into marriage?"

His smile widened. "No, sweetheart, it's your choice. Good night, Pamela." He then opened the door and left.

Pam stood in the same spot and stared down at the photograph in her hand. She angled her head to study the picture. Dillon was smiling. The woman was smiling. Had they been merely smiling for the camera or for each other, she wondered.

And come to think of it, the issue of whether or not there was a special woman in Dillon's life had never come up. She had never asked and he'd never offered any information. All she knew was that he was divorced, nothing more.

But he had asked her to trust him while he checked out a few things. Came up with an alternative.

She closed her eyes for a moment and leaned against the closed door. Had she read more than she should have into that request? Deciding the only person who could answer that question was Dillon himself, she crossed the room to use the phone, but then realized she didn't have his phone number. He'd never given her his number. Had there been a reason for him not doing so?

She glanced down at her watch. It wasn't quite nine o'clock and Roy Davis at the River's Edge Hotel would probably have information about Dillon on file. She would have to think of a good reason why she would need him to give it to her.

She released a long sigh when Mr. Davis picked up the phone. "The River's Edge Hotel."

"Mr. Davis, this is Pamela Novak. How are you?"

"I'm doing fine, Pamela, how about you?"

"I'm fine, but I was wondering if you could help me."

"Sure thing. What do you need?"

"Dillon Westmoreland's home number. I know he stayed at the hotel for a few days last week and I need to reach him. He left something here when he visited," she said.

"Hold on. Let me check my records."

It didn't take Mr. Davis but a few moments and he was back on the phone reading off a phone number to her.

"Thanks, Mr. Davis."

"You're welcome, Pamela."

As soon as she disconnected the call she quickly dialed Dillon's number. The phone was picked up on the third ring. "Hello?"

Pam's breath caught in her throat and her hands trembled as she hung up the phone. A woman had answered.

* * *

"So now, when are you going home?" Dillon asked the woman who was sprawled on the floor in front of his television set watching a movie.

He had come out of the shower a few moments before to find her there. Ramsey had warned him that he would regret the day he'd given Megan a key to his house. His twenty-six-year-old cousin Megan was an anesthesiologist at one of the local hospitals. She was okay to have around until she got underfoot. Like now.

"And why aren't you at your house watching your own television?" He walked through his living room on his way to the kitchen.

"It's a scary movie and I don't like watching these types alone."

He rolled his eyes. "Did I hear the phone ring a few moments ago?"

"Yes, a wrong number I think," she said, not taking her eyes off the television. "Do you mind if I crash here tonight?"

"Nope. I'll probably be gone when you wake up anyway," he said, opening the refrigerator.

That got her attention and she turned away from the television and glanced across the breakfast bar at him. "But you just got back."

"And I'm gone again. This time to Laramie. I have business to take care of there."

Dillon took a drink of orange juice right out the carton while thinking about his business in Laramie. He couldn't help but think about Pam. He missed her like hell. He had been tempted to call her but because Fletcher was probably back he had decided against it. He didn't want to make waves just yet. He hoped she trusted him enough so she could tell Mallard that she wasn't going to marry him at all. Dillon had promised to give her an alternative. An option in which she wouldn't feel compelled to marry for anything less than love. In a way he wished he'd never left Gamble or, better yet, had asked her to come home with him and be his date at the ball. But he had promised the sheriff that he would escort his sister. He'd felt obligated to keep his promise. He had pretended he had been having a good time, but had been missing Pam the entire time, which hadn't been fair to Belinda.

Then he'd really gotten ticked off to find his picture plastered on the front page of this morning's paper with a caption suggesting there was something between them. The last thing he needed was for Belinda to get any ideas, especially since he was in love with Pam. That's why he was determined to be able to offer an alternative solution to Mallard's marriage proposal, so that he could go to work to capture her heart the same way she had captured his.

Pam woke up early the next morning and, before she could talk herself out of doing so, she dialed Dillon's number again. Just like the night before, a woman answered. This time in a sleepy voice.

And again Pam quickly hung up the phone.

She felt a tug at her heart and knew she could not

depend on Dillon to come through with an alternative solution any longer. He was back home and back into the arms of a woman who undoubtedly meant something to him. She had to remember that he had not promised her anything. *He gave. She took. No regrets.* But that still didn't stop every bone in her body from aching with the strain of heartbreak.

At least she had gotten a taste of passion that was so rich and delicious, she would savor it in her memories for years to come and they would be there to help her through the years ahead.

She drew in a deep breath. Her decision was made. She picked up the phone to make another call. This one to Fletcher. His voice, also sleepy, greeted her on the second ring. "Hello."

"Fletcher, this is Pamela. I'll make sure everything's set for our wedding on Friday evening."

Dillon had caught a plane early Monday morning to Laramie and went straight to Gloversville Bank from the airport. There he met with the bank president.

"Mr. Westmoreland, I recognized your name immediately," the man said, smiling from ear to ear. "Are you looking to do business in Gloversville?" he asked, offering Dillon a chair the moment he'd walked into the man's office.

Dillon was glad he had recognized Roland Byers as someone he'd once done business with a few years ago when the man had worked at a bank in Denver. "No, but I would like some information on one of your customers."

Byers raised a brow as he took the seat behind his desk. "Who?"

"Sam Novak. He passed last year and I'm helping his daughter close out his affairs. We were wondering why his loan wasn't paid off when he died. The balance was over a million dollars."

Confusion touched the man's face. "Umm, I don't see how that's possible. We require life insurance on all loans for that amount. Hold on a moment while I check. I can't give you any specifics of the loan due to privacy laws, but I can tell you whether it's still active."

Dillon watched as Byers called his secretary on the intercom and provided her with the information needed to look up the file. In less than five minutes the woman walked into the office carrying a folder, which she handed to Byers.

It took Byers less than a minute to glance through the papers, look over at Dillon and say, "There must be some mistake because our records are showing the loan is paid in full. That information, along with the appropriate papers, were given to Mr. Novak's attorney, Lester Gadling, almost a year ago."

"I can't believe you're actually going to go ahead and marry the guy," Iris said in a disappointed voice. "What about Dillon?"

Just hearing his name nearly brought tears to Pam's eyes. "There's nothing about Dillon. It was a fling, nothing more."

"But I thought he said he would—"

"I don't want to talk about it, Iris. Now, can you make it here by Friday?"

"Of course I can make it, although I prefer not to. But if you're determined to make a huge mistake, the least I can do is to be there and watch you make it."

The moment Dillon walked out of the bank and was seated in his rental car, his cell phone went off. He answered it immediately. "Hello?"

"Bane's in trouble. We need you home."

Dillon drew in a deep breath, released it as he shook his head and snapped in his seat belt. "Okay, Ramsey. What has Bane done now?"

"Eloped."

"What the hell!" Dillon nearly exploded. "And please, whatever you do, don't tell me it's with Crystal Newsome."

"Okay, I won't. But I will tell you that Carl Newsome is going to make sure he goes to jail this time for sure."

Nothing like a death threat to get the Westmorelands together under one roof for something other than to eat or to party. Dillon glanced across the room and stared at his baby brother and wondered if Bane would ever outgrow his bad-boy mentality. You couldn't help but love him even when you wanted to smash his head in for not having a lick of sense.

Luckily, they had found him before Carl had, although it had taken nearly two full days to do so, and had included traveling to five different states. It had been obvious that he and Crystal hadn't wanted to be found. It had also been quite obvious they'd been having so much fun that they hadn't taken the time to swing by Vegas for a quick wedding after all.

That had made Carl Newsome somewhat happier. He hadn't needed to put out the expense for a quick divorce. Something had happened years before to make the Newsomes and Westmorelands modern-day Hatfields and McCoys. Something about a dispute over land ownership. As a result, Newsome would never allow his daughter to marry a Westmoreland.

Now they were all at the police station where Bane had been charged with kidnapping, although Carl knew good and well that Crystal had gone willingly. Crystal had even said as much. She'd even gone so far as to admit to being the one who had planned the entire thing. She thought she was in love with Bane, but at seventeen her parents thought she didn't know the meaning of love. Bane thought he was in love with Crystal, as well.

"The judge has made a decision," Sheriff Harper said as he came back into the conference room and got everyone's attention. "Carl Newsome is willing to drop the charges as long as Bane agrees never to see Crystal again."

Bane, who had been leaning against the wall, straightened and angrily yelled, "I won't agree to a damn thing!"

Dillon rolled his eyes, shook his head and asked the sheriff, "And what if he doesn't agree?"

"Then I will have to lock him up and, since he violated the last restraining order with the judge wherein he promised not to set foot on Carl's property, we will transfer him to the farm for a year."

Dillon nodded as he looked across the room at his baby brother, held Bane's gaze a moment and then said to the sheriff, "He *will* agree."

"Dil!"

"No, Bane, now listen to me," Dillon said in a firm voice that got everyone's attention in the room. He had lost time in returning to Gamble and he wasn't too happy about it, especially now that he knew the attorney for Pam's father had lied to her.

"Crystal is young. You are young. Both of you need to grow up. Carl mentioned he plans to send Crystal away to live with an aunt anyway. Use that time to finish college, get a job at Blue Ridge. Then in three to four years she will be old enough and mature enough to make her own decisions. Hopefully, by then the two of you will have college out of the way and can then decide what you want to do."

He saw the misery in his brother's features. "But I love her, Dil."

Dillon felt Bane's pain because he knew, thanks to Pamela Novak, the intensity of love. "I know you do, Bane. We all know you do. Hell, even the sheriff knows, which is why we've overlooked a lot of you and Crystal's shenanigans over the years."

It didn't take a rocket scientist to know that Crystal and Bane were sexually active. Hell, Dillon didn't want to recall the number of times he'd come home from work unexpectedly to find the two had cut school, or how he would get a call in the middle of the night from the sheriff after finding Bane and Crystal parked somewhere when neither Dillon nor Carl had been aware they were out of their houses.

"But it's time for you to finally grow up and accept responsibility for your actions. Go to college, make something of yourself and then be ready to reclaim your girl."

Bane didn't say anything for a moment as he switched his gaze from Dillon to stare down at the floor. Everyone in the room was quiet. And then he looked back at the sheriff. "Can I see her first?"

Sheriff Harper shook his head sadly. "Afraid not. Carl and Crystal and her mother left a short while ago. It's my understanding they are taking her to the airport to put her on the next plane to an aunt living somewhere in the South."

Bane, with shoulders slouched in defeat, didn't say anything for the longest time and then he turned and walked out of the room.

Ramsey leaned against the door with a cup of hot coffee in his hand and watched Dillon pack. "You're leaving again?"

Dillon nodded as he continued to throw items into his suitcase. "Yes, I should have been in Gamble long before now, and I haven't been able to reach Pamela to explain my delay."

That had bothered him. He had tried more than once to phone her but either she was out or was not taking his calls and he couldn't understand why. He couldn't wait to meet with her father's attorney to find out just why he had lied to Pam, making her think that there was still an outstanding loan balance in her name. For some reason Dillon couldn't dismiss, he had a feeling Mallard was behind Pam's fictitious financial problems.

"Well, good luck. I hope your flight leaves on time. A snowstorm is headed this way."

"I heard," Dillon said, zipping up his suitcase. "That's why I'm heading out now. I'm hoping my plane can take off before it hits."

Ramsey took a sip of coffee. "I take it you're serious about Pam Novak."

Dillon smiled as he grabbed his coat off the rack. "Yes, and I intend to marry her."

Dillon did get stuck at the Denver airport due to the snowstorm, and it was noon the next day before he arrived in Gamble. He was upset that he still hadn't been able to reach Pam. He hadn't spoken to her since last Friday and here it was Friday again.

Once he arrived in Gamble he went straight to Lester Gadling's office, deciding to let the man explain things before going to see Pam to let her know what he'd learned. He got to Gadling's office only to discover he was out to lunch, so Dillon waited.

It was close to three o'clock before Gadling returned and, when the secretary told him Dillon had been waiting for him, he looked at him nervously before asking if he had an appointment.

"No, I don't, but I need to talk to you about Sam Novak."

"What about Sam Novak?"

Dillon didn't like the fact the secretary was sitting there all ears. "I prefer talking to you about this privately," he said.

Gadling seemed to hesitate for a moment, then he asked, "And what relation are you to the Novak family?"

"A friend."

Moments later Dillon followed Gadling into his office and as soon as the door closed behind them, the lawyer asked nervously, "And what is it you want to know?"

Dillon didn't hesitate. "I want to know why you've led Pam to believe she owes a balance on her mortgage. I know she doesn't, so you better have a good answer for me, Mr. Gadling. And I want to know what happened to those payments she's been making to you every month."

"I don't have to tell you anything," the man said.

Dillon gave him the smile that all his family members knew meant business. "No, you don't have to tell me anything. I can always call the state attorney's office to let them know about attorney fraud."

That got Gadling's attention. He went around his desk and to Dillon's surprise pulled out a bottle of scotch, filled a shot glass and gulped the liquid down. "I didn't want to lie. It was Fletcher Mallard's idea. I am being blackmailed."

Dillon stared at the man for a long time and then sat in the chair in front of Gadling's desk. "I think you need to start at the beginning."

The man began talking and Dillon listened. Every so often Dillon's hands would clench into fists at how Mallard had manipulated both Gadling and Pam to get what he wanted. Pam actually thought Fletcher Mallard had come to her rescue, not knowing he had orchestrated the entire situation.

"So, there you have it. Mallard was so obsessed with marrying Pamela Novak he would have done anything to have her at his mercy."

Dillon's jaw twitched. "I'm going over to the Novaks' and bringing Pam back here. I want you to tell her everything that you've told me."

The man seemed surprised at his request. "That might be hard to do."

Dillon leaned forward. He refused to accept any excuse from the man. "And just why might that be hard, Gadling?"

"Because she and Mallard are getting married today. In fact, the wedding is probably taking place as we speak."

Eleven

"Please, Pammie, you don't have to marry him," Paige said with tears in her eyes.

"And why didn't you want to talk to Dillon when he called this week?" Nadia asked. "Why couldn't we pick up the phone when caller ID said it was him?"

Pam closed her eyes and looked across the room at Jill who hadn't said anything but whose eyes were narrowed. She then looked at Iris who looked just as upset. "Listen you guys, this is *my* wedding day."

She then turned her attention to Paige. "And I do have to marry him. You don't understand now but one day you will.

"The reason I didn't want to talk to Dillon this

week is rather complicated, but I had my reasons," she said to Nadia.

She ignored Jill's undignified snort. "Come on, Reverend Atwater just arrived and we need to get this over with."

Pam glanced over at Iris, glad her friend had kept her mouth shut for once. Iris had been giving Pam an earful all morning. "Well, how do I look?" Pam twirled around the middle of the room in the new dress she had bought earlier in the week.

"Too damn good for that asshole," Iris said under her breath; however, Pam's sisters heard the comment. Pam frowned when her sisters fought to hold back their giggles.

"Okay, ladies, let's go," she said to everyone. "The minister is waiting."

Dillon didn't give a damn if he was going over the speed limit as he raced his rented car to the Novaks' place. Gadling's news that a wedding was going on and that Pam was the bride had sent him running to his car and tearing out of town at breakneck speed. It was a wonder the sheriff was not on his tail.

He had tried calling Pam before leaving Gadling's office but evidently someone had taken the damn phone off the hook.

He let out a deep breath when he finally pulled into her driveway and saw three cars parked in front of the house. He recognized the one belonging to Mallard but not the other two.

He had barely switched off the ignition before he

was opening the car door and leaping out. At this point he cared less if he was late and she had already married Mallard. If that was the case then she would become a kidnapped bride, a feat a Westmoreland was gifted in crafting.

The minister's words floated over Pam, but her thoughts were on Paige. That morning, Pam had found her baby sister sitting on the side of the house crying. Paige was unhappy because today Pam would be marrying Fetcher Mallard. And Pam knew her other two sisters felt the same way.

Her father's death had left all three of her sisters in her care and at that very minute Pam realized their happiness meant more to her than anything else. And if marrying Fletcher was causing them this much distress then there was no way she could go through with it.

Reverend Atwater's words then rang out. "If any man can show just cause why these two people shouldn't lawfully wed, let him speak now or forever hold his peace."

She opened her mouth to put an end to the ceremony, knowing she couldn't let it continue, when a male voice boomed from the doorway of her home, loud and clear. "I can show just cause!"

Pam swung around and her heart literally jumped in her chest when she saw Dillon standing there with a fierce frown on his face. He was moving quickly toward her.

"What is he doing here?" Fletcher asked loudly through clenched teeth.

"Looks like he's coming for Pammie," Paige said

smartly with a huge smile on her face, clapping her hands with glee.

Pam could only stare at Dillon, too shocked to move or say anything.

"What the hell do you think you're doing here?" Fletcher said, coming to stand in front of Pam, blocking Dillon's way.

A smile curved Dillon lips when he looked down at Fletcher. "What does it look like? I'm stopping the wedding. So move aside, I need to talk to Pam."

"I'm not moving," Fletcher snapped.

The curve in Dillon's lips widened. "I have no problem in moving you, trust me."

"Gentlemen, please," the minister was saying.

It was then that Pam found her voice. She moved around Fletcher to stand in front of Dillon. She met his gaze. "Dillon, what are you doing here?"

She saw the intense look in his eyes. "I asked you to trust me to come up with an alternative."

Pam's eyes narrowed. "I did until I called Sunday night and *she* answered the phone."

He raised a confused brow. "She who?"

"You tell me."

"Look, Westmoreland, I don't know why you're here but you're interrupting our wedding," Fletcher said in an irritated tone.

Dillon shifted his gaze from Pam to Fletcher and glared at the man. "There *won't* be a wedding." He then glanced back over at Pam and said, "We need to talk privately."

Pam stared at him for a moment and then took a step back. "No, we don't."

"If she doesn't want to talk to you, I do," Iris said. When Dillon glanced over at her, Iris smiled. "I'm Iris, Pam's best friend."

When Pam shot her best friend a glare, Iris shrugged her shoulders. "Hey, what can I say? He's a cutie."

Dillon shifted his gaze back to Pam. "We do need to talk, Pam," he said, crossing his arms over his chest. "If you don't want to talk in private then I can very well say what I want right here. Fletcher and Lester Gadling lied to you. There is no balance owed on this house or land. Your father did have the necessary insurance to pay it off. Fletcher was blackmailing Gadling to claim otherwise. And those monthly payments you made on the loan were going to Mallard."

"That's a lie!" Fletcher said loudly. "How dare you come here spouting lies!"

"It is not a lie. Pam can verify everything I've said with Gadling. You weren't counting on her finding out the truth until after the two of you were already married, and by then you were hoping she would be so beholden to you that it wouldn't matter."

Pam turned to Fletcher, shocked at Dillon's allegations. "Is that true, Fletcher?"

Fletcher reached out and grabbed her hand. "Pamela, sweetheart. Please understand. I did it to give you all the things you deserve. I had to get you to marry me some way."

She angrily shook his hand off her and took a step back.

The expression on her face was one of total rage. "You deliberately lied to me. Just to get me to marry you?"

"Yes, but—"

"Please leave, Fletcher, and don't come back."

He looked at her and then shifted his gaze to Dillon before moving it back to Pam. "Don't hold out for Westmoreland to marry you, if that's what you're thinking about doing," he snarled. "Remember that article I showed you? The one from the *Denver Post*. He already has a woman back in Denver, so I'm the best catch around these parts. When you want to renew our relationship, call me." He then turned and angrily stalked out of the house.

"Pam, we need to talk," Dillon said once the door had closed behind Fletcher.

She glanced up at him and narrowed her gaze. Placing her arms across her own chest, she said, "No."

His lips curved into a dimpled yet predatory smile and Pam had the good sense to step back. But she wasn't quick enough. Dillon reached out and swept her off her feet and into his arms.

"Put me down, Dillon!"

He gazed down into her angry face. "No. You are going to listen to what I have to say."

He then glanced at the minister's shocked expression before smiling at Pam's sisters and Iris. "Excuse us for a moment. We need to discuss something in private."

Ignoring Pam's struggles, he headed toward the kitchen and closed the door behind them.

"Put me down, Dillon!"

"Certainly," he said, sitting down in a chair and keeping her pinned to his lap. He looked down at her. "It seems I need to get a few things straight. First, that picture Fletcher was referring to that was in the *Denver Post* was about a date I had agreed to months ago. The woman, Belinda Harper, is the sheriff's sister. I owed him a favor for all the times he's helped me keep Bane out of jail."

When she didn't say anything, just continued to glare at him, he continued. "And the woman who answered my phone Sunday night was my cousin Megan. She stayed over at my place until Monday. In fact, I left her there to catch my flight into Laramie to check on things at Gloversville Bank."

Now, that got her attention. He watched as she lifted a brow. "She's your cousin?"

"Yes, I told you I have three female younger cousins. Megan, Gemma and Bailey."

He paused and added, "I would have gotten back to Gamble sooner, but we had trouble with Bane again, which I had to return to Denver to take care of. And then there was that blasted snowstorm that hit Denver. I got stuck at the airport."

Pam held his gaze. "You were trying to get back?" she asked as if still uncertain.

"Just as soon as I could. I made you a promise that I intended to keep. And then once I discovered the loan was actually paid off, I tried to call several times."

She glanced away, to look out of her secret window, before returning her gaze to his. "I didn't have anything to say to you. I wouldn't let my sisters answer your call."

"Because you thought I was involved with someone else." He'd made a statement rather than asked a question.

"Yes."

"And why did the thought of another woman bother you, Pam?"

She shrugged the feminine shoulders he loved so much. "It just did."

He leaned in closer. "Do you know what I think?" Before she could respond, he said, "I think it bothered you because you realized something. Those times that we made love, I made you mine. And you know something else you might as well go ahead and accept?"

"What?" she asked tersely.

"That I love you."

She blinked. "You love me?"

"Very much. I fell in love with you the moment I set eyes on you. And I want to marry you for all the *right* reasons. I want us, the Westmorelands and the Novaks, to be a family."

She hesitated, searched his gaze for the truth in his words. He could tell from her expression the moment she found them. A smile touched her lips. "I think Jay and Raphel would have liked that."

"So will you marry me? And I might as well warn you, marrying me means getting fourteen others."

She grinned. "I don't mind because marrying me means you'll get four. Oh, and there's Iris. She's like my sister."

A deep smile touched his lips. "The more the merrier. And I might as well warn you about my fifteen Atlanta Westmoreland cousins."

"Like you said, the more the merrier," she said, shifting in his embrace to wrap her arms around his neck. "I love you, too."

He leaned in closer as his gaze zeroed in on her lips. He kissed her there, slowly at first, then a little more hungrily. And when his tongue began dueling with hers, he almost forgot where the two of them were. He pulled away from her mouth and stood with her in his arms. He then placed her on her feet.

"I think we need to let everyone know there will be a wedding after all, but not today. We will set a date when we can get all the Westmorelands in one place."

He then leaned in closer to whisper, "I'm staying at the hotel in Rosebud tonight. Do you want to come spend some time with me later?"

A satisfied smile touched her lips. "Umm, I would love to. You give. I take. No regrets."

He chuckled as he pulled her into his arms. "Yes. No regrets."

Epilogue

Pam glanced down at her wedding ring. It looked perfect on her hand. She then glanced up at her husband of ten minutes and smiled before looking around the huge, beautifully decorated ballroom at the Denver hotel. She and Dillon had decided to have a Christmas wedding and everything had turned out perfectly.

Her sisters were talking to some of Dillon's brothers and cousins and seemed to be in a very happy and festive mood. She couldn't yet distinguish which were Dillon's brothers and which ones were his cousins, since they all looked a lot alike. Even those who had traveled all the way from Atlanta. He had introduced everyone, but she was still a little fuzzy on names and faces.

And yet she had become immediate friends with

Megan, Gemma and Bailey. They simply adored their
oldest cousin and let her know they were more than
pleased with the woman he had chosen as his wife. And
then there were the wives of the Atlanta Westmorelands,
with whom she was forming lasting friendships. Last
night during the rehearsal dinner she had held in her
arms the newest member of the Westmoreland clan,
four-month-old Jaren.

There was no doubt in anyone's mind that Dillon's
cousin Jared Westmoreland and his wife, Dana, were
proud of their beautiful baby girl. While holding the
baby Pam had glanced up and met Dillon's gaze, and
from the look he'd given her, she had a feeling that he
wasn't planning on wasting any time giving her a child
of her own to hold.

"Ready for our first dance, Mrs. Westmoreland?"
Dillon asked, whirling her around to face him, and
bringing her thoughts back to the present.

She laughed. "As ready as I'll ever be, Mr. Westmoreland."

And then he pulled her into his arms as they glided
around the dance floor. Her sisters were beaming
happily and that made her feel good. They had been
overjoyed to hear about her wedding plans. She and
Dillon had wanted a small affair but with all those Westmorelands that was impossible.

They would live in Gamble until the end of the school
year, and then once Jill left for college, Pam and her
sisters would move into Dillon's home in Denver. Paige
and Nadia didn't have any problems with moving and

looked forward to making new friends. The house in Gamble would be a second home for them. Pam would be turning the day-to-day operations of the drama academy over to the very capable hands of Cindy Ruffin.

After a few moments a deep male voice said, "May I cut in?"

Pam glanced up into the face of the one cousin she remembered well, because he was a nationally known motorcycle-racing star, Thorn Westmoreland.

"Just for now," Dillon said jokingly, handing her over to his cousin. After Thorn, she remained on the dance floor through several more songs as each of Dillon's male cousins got a chance to twirl her around.

Finally, she found herself back in her husband's arms for a slow number. They would be catching a plane later that day to Miami, where they would set sail on a cruise to the Bahamas.

He pulled her tight into his arms and whispered, "At last," before lowering his head and latching on to her mouth, not caring that they had a ballroom filled with guests. When he finally released her mouth, she couldn't help but chuckle throatily. "That was naughty."

"No, sweetheart," he said, brushing his knuckles gently against her cheek. "That was this Westmoreland's way. Get used to it."

"I will." She went on tiptoe and captured his mouth with hers, deciding to show him that Novaks had a way of their own, as well.

* * * * *

MILLS & BOON®

are proud to present our...

Book of the Month ★

★ The Accidental Princess
by Michelle Willingham
from Mills & Boon® Historical

Etiquette demands Lady Hannah Chesterfield ignore
the shivers of desire Lieutenant Michael Thorpe's
wicked gaze provokes, but her unawakened body
clamours for his touch... So she joins Michael on
an adventure to uncover the secret of his birth—
is this common soldier really a prince?

Available 5th November

*Something to say about our
Book of the Month?
Tell us what you think!*

millsandboon.co.uk/community
facebook.com/romancehq
twitter.com/millsandboonuk

All the magic you'll need this Christmas…

When **Daniel** is left with his brother's kids, only one person can help. But it'll take more than mistletoe before **Stella** helps him…

Patrick hadn't advertised for a housekeeper. But when **Hayley** appears, she's the gift he didn't even realise he needed.

Alfie and his little sister know a lot about the magic of Christmas – and they're about to teach the grown-ups a much-needed lesson!

Available 1st October 2010

www.millsandboon.co.uk

Meet Nora Robert's
The MacGregors family

1st October 2010

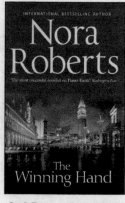

3rd December 2010

7th January 2011

4th February 2011

2 FREE BOOKS
AND A SURPRISE GIFT

We would like to take this opportunity to thank you for reading thi
Mills & Boon® book by offering you the chance to take TWO mor
specially selected books from the Desire™ 2-in-1 series absolutely
FREE! We're also making this offer to introduce you to the benefits o
the Mills & Boon® Book Club™—

- **FREE home delivery**
- **FREE gifts and competitions**
- **FREE monthly Newsletter**
- **Exclusive Mills & Boon Book Club offers**
- **Books available before they're in the shops**

Accepting these FREE books and gift places you under no obligation to buy, you may cancel at any time, even after receiving your fre
books. Simply complete your details below and return the entire page
to the address below. You don't even need a stamp!

YES Please send me 2 free Desire stories in a 2-in-1 volume and a
surprise gift. I understand that unless you hear from me, I will receive 2
superb new 2-in-1 books every month for just £5.30 each, postage
and packing free. I am under no obligation to purchase any books and
may cancel my subscription at any time. The free books and gift will
be mine to keep in any case.

Ms/Mrs/Miss/Mr _____ Initials _____

Surname _____

Address _____

_____

_____ Postcode _____

E-mail _____

Send this whole page to: Mills & Boon Book Club, Free Book Offer,
FREEPOST NAT 10298, Richmond, TW9 1BR